F.U.

F.U.

MAJORING
IN
CARNAL KNOWLEDGE

By Mickey Skee

alyson books
los angeles | new york

ALL CHARACTERS IN THIS BOOK ARE FICTITIOUS. ANY RESEMBLANCE TO
REAL INDIVIDUALS—EITHER LIVING OR DEAD—IS STRICTLY COINCIDENTAL.

MANUFACTURED IN THE UNITED STATES OF AMERICA.

THIS TRADE PAPERBACK ORIGINAL IS PUBLISHED BY
ALYSON PUBLICATIONS,
P.O. BOX 4371, LOS ANGELES, CA 90078-4371.
DISTRIBUTION IN THE UNITED KINGDOM BY
TURNAROUND PUBLISHER SERVICES LTD.,
UNIT 3, OLYMPIA TRADING ESTATE, COBURG ROAD, WOOD GREEN,
LONDON N22 6TZ ENGLAND.

FIRST EDITION: JULY 2002

02 03 04 05 06 [a] 10 9 8 7 6 5 4 3 2 1

ISBN 1-55583-649-6

COVER PHOTOGRAPHY BY MUNYON/STUDIO 1435.

TABLE OF COCKTENTS

I want to dedicate this to all the guys I fooled around with in school. You know who you are: Mike, the tennis jock, now with two kids and the manager of a Kmart; Victor, the closeted multimillionaire Fortune 500 exec; Tim, the blond political science major; David, my intellectual Jewish lover; J.R., the only out gay friend I knew and someone who really did know more about me than I knew about myself; and Erin, my supposed best friend who dated my sister and then declared me dead to him when I suggested he might be gay. And, of course, all the rest of you who may only be thinly disguised within these pages...

PREFACE

Nothing's hornier than a college campus. All you have to do is take a stroll through the hallowed halls of higher education to feel the testosterone pulsating through the red bricks of sturdy, strong, phallic-tall buildings.

It doesn't matter if the dudes within those walls are gay or straight; they've all got an urge to get off. Some guys walk through four years of upper-division schooling with a perpetual hard-on. It's hard not to when, on warm days, young lads in frayed shorts allow sneak peeks at their loose-hanging balls as they lie on grassy hills with opened textbooks and even wider-opened legs. And when, on cooler days, those same young men pack their penile packages into sweats that still allow careful crotch-watchers to see how they're hanging—and how horny the guy in question is at any given moment.

Every corner of a college campus simply seethes with sexuality. The urge to get laid permeates every dorm room, classroom, shower room, and toilet stall. It oozes from every wayward glance, every clump of brush, every hidden walkway—where the foliage is always lush and green with the excess special fertilizer spilled there.

Yes, sex is everywhere on a college campus. And most of the time, sadly, the guys are out there doing it alone.

C'est dommage.

Every time you walk down Fraternity Row, passing the guys lounging around together in their brotherly pack, know that some of their tribe are stroking themselves back in their private quarters. Know that in dorms where guys are packed four to a room, somewhere in between studying, some of them are pulling their puds in private.

Walking in the lonely stacks of the library, try to spot a guy alone in a corner with one hand resting on a bulge that's keeping him awake. Passing the gymnasium, catch a whiff of ammonia and chlorine and know it is there because someone had to wash away the come spots of guys who spilled their seed after a sweaty workout.

On a college campus, sex is omnipresent. Especially masturbation. I know, because I masturbated more in college than anywhere else. If I could have majored in it, I would have. If I could have saved my spooge, it would have filled an Olympic-sized swimming pool. I couldn't keep my hands off myself during college.

Not surprisingly, I still can't.

When I first entered college, I wore tight white cotton jockey shorts. I felt those cotton briefs rubbing ever so slightly against my firm round balls wherever I walked, and I'd always have a hard-on, or at least a hint of one. Whenever I could, I touched my stiffness, through my jeans and through my Jockeys. Sometimes in class I knew guys nearby saw me pushing my fist down between my thighs or stroking my pencil eraser along the shaft that stretched down my pant leg. Between classes I'd run to the bathroom and dive into a stall and jerk myself off during the 10 minutes we had to walk from building to building. Sometimes my crotch dripped a telltale stain. Invariably someone noticed, and smiled.

I kept a record of how many times I jerked off, marking in my diary how much I spewed and sometimes how far I shot. I also wrote about the liaisons I had. My collegiate diaries chart the self-discovery of my body, my sex, and my freedom.

Some of those stories are excerpted in these pages, with dates and times, names and places. It's nice that I've saved these memories. I'd forgotten some of them and they'd have been lost forever had I not kept good records of everything— and everyone—I did. Flipping through my diary gives me a peek at all the pleasure I had in school and chronicles my most intimate moments. The remainder of this book is composed of excerpts from my current diary—now that I've returned to school as a professor.

INTRODICKTION: BACK TO SCHOOL

I always knew, deep down, that some day I would return to my college campus. Today is that day. I'm returning as a teacher, an expert in sexual studies—my undergraduate major.

I'm a *come lotsly* graduate of the Fraternal University of Camaraderie and Kinship (FUCK, better and more affectionately known as F.U.). The Board of Trustees and Terms of Management (BOTTOMs) recently contacted me about an open position teaching sexology at the school's College of Carnal Knowledge (COCK). Apparently, some of them were familiar with my books about the gay sex industry.

They told me they were impressed with how I had gone out into the world after graduation to spread my knowledge and seed, becoming one of F.U.'s best-known alumni. So the BOTTOMs asked me to come back and teach sexuality to a new crop of horny young men.

What I don't know is how I'll relate to this younger-than-Gen-X group of guys. Earlier, as I strolled through the campus for the first time in nearly a decade, I wondered what we would dub this young generation growing into adulthood in the early part of the New Millennium. I'm hoping they'll develop into "Generation Sex."

As I pondered this, I was on my way to Dean Richard Richie's office, the same office I often visited when I was in trouble as a student. I strolled by the familiar 20-foot naked statue of the university's first president that stands outside the main administration building. That statue always stirred my loins; the guy was a Michelangelo's *David* look-alike, or so it seemed to me. The statue sports a foot-long cock, and legend has it the smaller, life-size version of the university president wasn't much different.

The aloof boys of today, however, hardly paid any notice to this fine specimen of a statue standing erect before them. (Nearly all of the students here are male. It's not that girls aren't allowed; they just aren't as interested as guys are in studying the Penile Arts.) Most of the kids wore baggy pants—a shame, I thought. Most had close-cropped hair or were altogether bald. Many had tattoos and piercings—the choicest decorations, I assumed, not easily visible.

As I walked in, I couldn't believe that Dean Richie's office looked almost exactly like it had a decade before when I was in school.

"We're still about 60 percent heterosexual. At least that's what the surveys say," Dean Richie told me as I shook hands with him. "Of course, more and more students are identifying as homosexual now, about 20 percent, and about another 20 percent claim they're bisexual. But we still lean toward the hetero side in our enrollment stats, so I'm warning you: No recruiting."

I stifled a giggle. From what I remembered, most of the 60% who claimed they were heterosexual were dipping into the remaining 40% for a helping hand. And the alleged 20% bisexual population leaned heavily to the gay side—at least for the four years they were in school.

Even Dean Richie, who's married and has kids, is a bit suspect in my mind. But of course I believe anyone is conquerable.

"We want you to teach some of the basic manual stimulation classes, and some of the more advanced penile studies courses," Richie said. Then he grew stern. "You gave me some trouble when you were a student here, and I want to let you know that we have standards and rules. I expect you to abide by them."

"Oh, come on, now. I've grown up," I said. "A little bit,

anyway." I smiled. "But the fact is, some of my classes I can only teach a certain way. That's the only way the guys will learn." Then I pointed out that my curriculum had been fully approved by the BOTTOMs.

The Dean was not deterred. "I hope you know it wasn't my idea to bring you back here. I warned the board you'd be trouble."

I nodded and beat a hasty retreat, feeling considerably less welcome than I had before visiting his office.

As I departed, the dean yelled, "As soon as you cross the line with me, you're out of here faster than a come-shot!"

I headed directly to the Administration building men's room. I looked at myself in the mirror. Despite my blond hair flowing down past my shoulders, I could have passed for one of the students outside. I still looked good, I thought. I could hold my own. And I still got stiff too.

I had originally come to this campus a nerdy, nervous, self-conscious kid who didn't like his body and was afraid to show it. Four years later that had changed completely. Now I was back as a professor, ready to give everything I'd learned to a new generation of needful young men.

I went into one of the doorless stalls, pulled out my raging hard-on, and jacked myself off till I shot across the stall and a big white spooge hit the floor several feet away.

"Whoa!" said a breathless voice in the stall next to me.

I hadn't realized I wasn't alone. I glanced in the mirror and saw a kid with jet-black hair and a nose pierce working on his erection with both hands while sitting on the toilet.

I stepped over the sticky white glob in front of me, letting my twitching shaft hang from my zipper, and turned to watch.

The kid yanked himself harder, looking me straight in the eyes and giving me a wicked stare. He stuck out his tongue, which had a huge metal stud.

I smiled. I guess I could have had him if I wanted. But it was too early to start breaking the rules.

As my shoes clicked on the marble steps, I could hear him trying to stifle a massive orgasm. I peeked back and saw his come-shot plop just outside the doorway, not far from my own sticky puddle.

I was glad to be back.

MY BURGEONING EXHIBITIONISM
AUGUST 28, 1988

Now that I'm back at F.U., teaching, I thought it would be good to revisit some of my early memories of campus. So I pulled out my college diary and flipped to this early entry.

Everywhere I look I get horny. Every step I take makes me hard. Every corner I turn puts me smack into a stunningly gorgeous guy, often a well-built jock. I bump into him, apologize, scurry off somewhere private, and jack off thinking about him.

How will I possibly make it through school? The first semester only just started, and already I'm distracted constantly—by dick.

It's not just my own dick, although that's a distraction too. It's everyone else's dick. OK, maybe I'm looking for it more, but jeez, the guys around here seem to be waving their cocks around everywhere they go.

I knew going off to school would allow me to be a bit more free and open, but I could never have guessed it would be like this. It's a perfect place to be a writer, because this is a place that inspires fantasy.

But not all of it is fantasy. Some of it is real. And some of those fantasies-turned-realities occur at the Library of Information on Carnal Knowledge (the LICK building), which also houses the Male Museum. Between the floors are sort of half-floors called stacks. I've perused most of the stacks already—for important reading information of course—and have seen a lot going on there.

One particular hunk fascinates me. He's blond with a muscular body and perfect red lips that form a welcoming smile. He always sits near the exit on Floor 3½. He's shy.

I watch him sit and read and sometimes his hand slips down to his cutoff shorts and he slowly rubs his bulge. I pretend I'm reading, but it's unmistakable that he's jacking off at his seat and that I'm watching him. Then he quietly slips away through the exit door.

I've followed him a few times to see if he's cleaning off in the bathroom, but no, he heads out of the building and back to his dorm, leaving me to fantasize about him.

Once while I walked through the stacks, I leaned over to look for a book called *Descriptions of the Phallus in the 17th Century* when I saw a big, long, dark cock poking through the shelf at my face.

"Suck it, man," the guy said from the other side.

I stood up and saw two hungry brown eyes staring at me through the stacks. The disembodied cock head stuck out between the rows of shelves. This had to be a big man to make his rod poke through a row of books. I looked around, but the only other person I could see was my blond dream man sitting at the end of the aisle.

I got down on my knees and quietly put my lips on the cock head. It tasted rubbery and smelled oily. I felt him thrust his hips between the stacks, which sent a book or two tumbling to the floor.

I looked over and saw the blond guy watching. Our eyes locked for a moment as he saw me chew lightly on the big black cock. I saw his hand reach for his crotch as I tickled the underside of the chocolate staff with my tongue, causing a few more books to go clanging to the floor.

The blond caught me staring at his bulge, then slapped his book closed and scooted out the exit door. I bit hard, a bit too hard, causing the black guy to pull out and scatter out of the stacks with a curse. Then I was left alone on my knees with a bunch of books on the floor around me and a stiff cock.

I went to the bathroom and into a stall, but none of the stalls on campus have doors. I am very pee-shy and can never stand at a urinal here because they are these long porcelain troughs where everyone pees in front of one another, and it's very uncomfortable for me to be checked out while standing there whizzing. I usually get a hard-on, making it even more difficult to squeeze out any pee.

This time, though, it wasn't pee I was trying to squeeze out. But as soon as my pants were around my legs, two guys came in.

One of them, with sandy hair, had a sharp, sloping nose and perfect cheekbones. He stood at the trough and pulled out a long, pencil-thin cock.

The other one, a brown-haired curly-headed guy with bushy eyebrows and a stocky well-built body, sidled up alongside the pencil-cocked guy and, midstream through the guy's piss, reached over and grabbed his skinny prick.

"Hey man, what the fuck?" said the sandy-haired guy.

But the brunet didn't let go, and the pisser didn't complain any further. He let the stranger's hand feel his shaft expel the urine, then he let the hand shake him off. Next, without a word, the brunet sat the sandy-haired guy's ass on the edge of the trough and popped the long cock into his mouth to give it a nice glistening spit bath.

I was too stunned to jack off or anything. This guy was getting the greatest blow job, just a few feet away from me. I was also too shocked to notice that others had gathered in the bathroom until suddenly the toilet paper roll popped off in my stall and a big white cock popped through the hole.

I had heard of glory holes, but now I was seeing one first-hand. Being the second cock-without-a-body I'd seen that day, it was less surprising, and I didn't need to be told what to do.

I chowed down, all the time watching the guys at the urinal.

The cock I commandeered was thick and veiny. The tiny mushroom head almost seemed too small for its knobby, wide shaft, but it made a nice little puckering sound as it popped in and out of my mouth. I slid my tongue along the veins underneath and around the shaft, tracing them down to as much of its hairy root as I could get at through the hole.

The cock pulled away. I wanted to see who was attached to this veiny monstrosity, but all I could see was a dark hole.

"Fuck it, man, he wants you to fuck it," said the curly-headed brunet. He had traded places, and was now being sucked by the sandy-haired guy. And he was getting off, watching me in the stall. From his vantage point he could see both me and the guy offering me his handsome ass through the glory hole. "He doesn't want your phone number, guy, he just wants your dick up his ass," he added rather forcefully. He obviously could tell I was new to this.

From underneath the stall, a thick, muscular hand reached out and offered a blue condom unsheathed from the packet. I fumbled a bit as I unrolled it on my ever-throbbing pud. Then I leaned down and shoved myself into the hole.

I didn't have to move; the ass at the other end knew how to work my pole, squeezing it up and down, wriggling out until just my cock head was inside and then backing all the way onto my stiffy.

"Beautiful, guys," said the throaty brunet, who looked like he was close to coming. He pulled his shirt up, showing his rippling stomach muscles, and he pinched his well-developed tits. "Great fucking going on there."

"Hey guys, you know who's outside in the stacks almost every day?" asked the sandy-haired stud, taking a break from appendage-sucking. "That swimmer guy who broke all the records. That dreamy stud Shane Coley...every single day he sits in the same chair out there stroking his beautiful meat. Right there in the next room."

Hey, that's my dream guy! I continued pounding, but fiercely now. I was mad, not only because someone else knew about my secret blond stud's wanking place, but also because they knew more about him than I did. They knew his name! Shane Coley. I cringed at the thought that one of those gorgeous guys, maybe even the guy I was fucking, had been with my dream swimmer.

"Shut up and suck me, Johnny, you know that guy's notoriously hetero. Guys have tried to bed him for two years." The brunet shoved his cock all the way into Johnny's throat, making him gag.

My rhythm got more violent too, thinking of Shane Coley.

"I think we should all go out there and do this stuff in front of him, then bend his pretty round ass over and fuck his cute cocky smile right off his face," said the angry brunet. Johnny pulled his head back and knocked it on the side of the urinal with a clang, as the brunet spewed jism all over the side of his face.

"Ow, Jason, that really hurt. I can't take all 9 inches like that."

These guys weren't strangers after all. This must've been a planned liaison. I looked forward to meeting my well-trained bottom boy on the other side of the stall. I could feel him orgasm as his butt cheeks squeezed around my cock in tight spasms. It made me shoot.

I leaned back and felt the blue sticky sheath pulled off my still-spazzing cock, and then I heard the door close. I sat on the toilet seat and looked around. The guys at the urinal were gone.

"Gosh, they left in a hurry," I said to my stall fuck.

I looked under the stall. No feet.

Without pulling up my pants, my dick still recuperating, I leaned out and looked into the other stall. I saw no one. My guy had left, taking my come-filled condom with him. I sat down again and caught my breath. Oh, well.

This campus has too many distractions. In the gym, everyone

works out in the nude. I went there today after my visit to the LICK building and watched the guys tackling, running, heaving, and pumping together. The wrestling was particularly erotic because the guys grabbed at each other's loose testicles and squeezed until someone yelled "Uncle."

After my trip to the gym, I stopped to watch the nude track team running around the track. Suddenly I saw a bunch of them head over to the chain-link fence around the pool.

"It's Shane!" said one guy, whizzing past me.

"Shit, he's swimming naked!" said another.

A girl from campus sped by, squealing, "Shane Coley in the flesh! It's the first time!"

I sauntered over as if I didn't care, becoming more and more aware that I wasn't the only one at F.U. lusting after this swimmer. But I felt a bit possessive, because I was sure I'd been the first to discover the sight of him groping himself off in the stacks.

I found an empty spot at the fence and almost fainted dead away. I swooned like a schoolgirl, as silly as the dozen or so others gaping through the fence.

Standing at the edge of the pool with his wet body glistening in the sun was the sunny-haired Shane Coley, totally bareass naked. No artist could draw a more perfect picture; Michelangelo couldn't have dreamed a better specimen. Shane stood erect, the line of bones beneath his neck stretched straight across his body, anchored by two thick but not overly muscular shoulders. His eyes were sparkling blue—almost turquoise— his eyebrows neat, and his eyelashes practically girlish in their length. His ears stuck out a bit big, but cute, and his square chin showed a faint peach fuzz.

His legs were thick, muscular, and covered with a fine layer of curly blond hair. His arms were long and hung past his hips. His abdomen rippled with waves of even-spaced muscles, and his pecs were firm and tight. His ass was white and moundy. Fleshy, yet powerful. His tan snaked around a small area, showing that he usually sunbathed with his Speedos on. He barely had any hair on his torso. His chest had only a few wisps of blond around the nipples. A few darker hairs around his belly button led to a light patch around his crotch.

But it was his cock that most of us came to see.

He stood with a half hard-on, seemingly ignoring the stares he was getting from all around.

His cock was long and even, as thick around at the base as at the head. It looked to me as if three hands could fit around that piece of meat, end over end, and still not cover the beautifully perfect mushroom that caps the dick so nicely.

"And he isn't even fully hard," commented the girl next to me.

"What a guy, look at those nice firm balls," said a guy next to her. "This'll give me jerk-off material for weeks."

Some laughter erupted around my area of the fence, and I looked down at Shane Coley looking up, directly at me.

I gulped. Then I waved.

He shot a smile at me, and I could swear his semihard cock twitched before he dove into the pool and swam off. I stayed and watched until the audience dispersed, but it was obviously going to be awhile before Shane finished his workout.

Rather than wait around, I wandered past the Sculpture, Portrait, and Religious Tableaus, Artifacts, and Crafts Undergraduate Studies building (the SPARTACUS building), where naked men pose for students to paint or sculpt. This is the building where all the nude Rodins, Reubens, Venuses, Cupids, and Prometheuses of the various classic artists are studied, where DaVinci's male sketches are housed, and where notes from Jules Verne's early theories of penis ejaculation are preserved. I always find a way to walk past this building, so I can take in the gorgeous men modeling their long floppy cocks. I am amazed at how free and simple it all seems.

I can't imagine being a student in those classes, though. How could you possibly avoid jacking off during class? Then again, maybe you don't. Maybe I should sign up for an art class and find out.

I'm getting really good at crotch-watching. Not near as good as Victor Nichols, a guy in my Penobiology class. For him it's an art form.

"I can guess a cock size, limp, to within an eighth of an inch without fail, ball size and full erections to within a centimeter," explained Victor. "Even guys with loose pants have telltale signs. Look at how he hangs left. Look how that guy has balls that bunch forward in his Jockeys. See that guy with the cock ring? He's a grower, not a shower."

At first I thought Victor was too full of himself, but then he told me my exact measurements—and we'd never even been naked together.

"You've got nice-hanging balls, too, Mickey. You shouldn't be afraid to show yourself off more," he said.

I was a bit embarrassed because I had hardly been naked at all on campus except for my quickie in the bathroom, but that made me determined to have Victor as a Lab partner and learn some more tips. His talents became more obvious to me as we had occasion to test his expertise.

In the Bio building, certain lab classes had a Speci-Men program where guys (mostly students on scholarship who needed a few extra bucks) would come in and essentially be our lab rats. We tested their hard-ons, observed their orgasms, measured their loads of semen, and performed other personal studies.

Inevitably, Victor could size up any of the Speci-Men lab rats long before they took their robes off. He would accurately predict their sizes soft and hard, and was even pretty good at estimating semen quantity.

One of the Speci-Men favorites was an olive-skinned Italian stallion named Vincent. His cock measured a perfect 7 inches along the top, from base to piss slit, and we got to touch it, ever so delicately, and measure it a few times.

It was the first time I touched a guy so clinically, and Vincent seemed to pay no attention as I moved his hard-on like it was a dead frog or something. My lab partner Victor grabbed it by the base and gave it a little squeeze before taking all the measurements for our project.

"If you need any money ever, being a Speci-men is a great way to earn a few extra bucks," Victor remarked to me.

"Are you crazy?" I said as I held a come-jar up to the handsome Vincent and squeezed some semen out of him for our Come Load vs. Ball Size report. "I'd be too embarrassed to have all these strange hands all over my body."

"Hey, it's easier than doing porn." Victor smiled. "And maybe you'd be lucky and get to be naked with swimmer Shane…if he ever signed up for the program."

For the first time, Vincent the Speci-Men paid attention to our conversation. Shane Coley even made a supposed straight guy like Vincent stand up and take notice.

A month or so later, while collaborating on a study comparing finger size to cock length, Victor worked on opening me up even more. He went out and helped me buy a vintage '65 red Mustang convertible and I got a license plate that said RED WRTR. The plate had multiple meanings: Not only was I a writer, and when I used red ink in my diary it was erotic nasty writing (which is what I wrote mostly), but Victor said the letters also stood for "Real Eager Dick With Radical Testicle Reach."

Victor couldn't get me to become a Speci-Men, but he was slowly convincing me to go to the Zyo-Sperm Cryolab off campus, where this dreamy Dr. Malin collected samples from horny guys. They advertised a lot in the school paper, but I knew I'd have a hard time not masturbating for a few days before I had to provide my sample, so I held off on doing that right away.

Victor also said I'd lose my inhibitions if I got on the waiting list to get into Naked Dorm on the north end of campus. That's a building where everyone walks around naked pretty much all the time. I've skulked past Naked Dorm and watched guys playing Frisbee out front without a stitch of clothing on, their nubile bodies sunning themselves freely without a care in the world.

I jacked off behind some trees near the Naked Dorm, imagining I was part of that select, open crowd. I could never do it, though. How embarrassing.

Despite all the cock that got flaunted around campus, there were plenty of shy, voyeuristic types like me who lingered around and went home alone to masturbate rather than show anything off. That prompted an idea in Victor for a Campus All-Nude Day in the Yard (or CANDY Day).

"Every Halloween it's a tradition for guys to walk around wearing their underwear in the yard, and guys go to class in just their skivvies, so let's just make it all naked!" proposed Victor.

Well, because I was working for the school newspaper, I secretly went in to run off CANDY Day flyers, which we spread all over campus the next day.

Somehow, pretty quickly, we got caught.

Dean Richie stood both Victor and I in front of his desk. He was a tall, stern guy with slicked-back hair. On his desk, a picture of his wife and young son screamed out his heterosexuality, while *over* his desk a big paddle mounted on the wall next to a photo of a handsome young stud in a leather jacket screamed out "bondage queen."

"You boys are bad, very bad. What do you think we're running here, a big old orgy?" the dean reprimanded. "If even one guy runs around the yard naked, you're both going to get booted right out of this school, so you better go out and warn your friends."

Victor spoke rather eloquently. "It's a way to let off all the pent-up steam your fine academic establishment builds up in us, sir," he said. I suddenly felt like I was in a scene from *Animal House.* "You, sir, have allowed a whole domestic situation here on campus where nudity is encouraged," Victor continued. "The Naked Dorm is a place not of eroticism but of freedom, and this is what our proposal is all about. Give it a try, sir, be a groundbreaker."

Victor continued snowing him, but the dean still threatened us with expulsion if Halloween meant no-costume for even a single person on campus. The problem was, Halloween was only two days away, and we certainly couldn't be responsible for the whole school.

The morning of Halloween, Victor knocked on my dorm door and I rolled out of bed in my stained cotton briefs. He stood there naked.

I had never seen Victor naked before and was surprised. He promptly pulled down my underwear.

"You're not wearing these anymore, and we're going out like this," Victor said. "If we're going to get expelled, we may as well go in style."

I protested. "I can't go out there like this!"

Well, after an hour of being convinced, I grabbed my notebook and two textbooks and went with Victor out into the yard at the center of campus without a stitch on. It was like my frightening recurring dream of going to class naked with an erection and no one noticing.

There we stood, exposed to the world, and hardly anyone paid any attention.

After a while, some guys came up to us and asked if they'd get into trouble if they too revealed all. We encouraged them, and they walked away, throwing their briefs to the wind.

Next, four girls walked by totally stripped down, as did Vincent—who is rarely without clothes unless he's getting paid to be at the Speci-Men labs. He gave us a thumbs-up as he strode past.

Then Dean Richie approached. He wagged his finger at us. Victor stretched out, his crotch exposed, on the stone bench we were seated upon.

"You two are out of here! I'll see to it myself and call the campus police right now," the dean fumed. "What kind of campus do you think we're running here?"

Just then the first period bell rang and out walked a few hundred students and teachers. All of them were stark-naked. Victor and I dropped our jaws, but not as far as Dean Richie's.

One of the professors said, "Great idea, Dean. Our whole class was clothes-free first period, and it prompted a great discussion."

"I never thought I could do it, Dean, but you're on the cutting edge," said a freshman.

"The Naked Dorm folks tried to get this approved for years, and so we thank you, Dean," added a grad student, patting him on the back. "And hey, take your clothes off!"

Before Dean Richie could protest, a group of eight students had their hands all over his suit. They depantsed him, leaving him in a T-shirt and socks. Someone neatly folded his clothes then handed them over to him. He grabbed the bundle and stormed off to the BOTTOMs building.

I high-fived Victor, picked up my books, and proudly walked across campus with my books swinging at my side and my penis waving in the wind. For the first time, I smiled at fellow students, looking them in the eye instead of the crotch, no longer afraid of seeming like a stalker or a voyeur. We were, after all, totally naked.

I reached my study spot in the stacks and looked over at an empty desk down the aisle of books. I figured Shane Coley would be mobbed if he dared to appear naked walking around campus. But then the exit door opened and my eyes widened as I saw the robust form of the sexy swimmer sit down at his favorite studying spot. He was buck-naked.

I gasped and looked around, realizing that we were alone. He shot me his perfect smile and didn't say a word as his hand went down to his cock. He stroked it under his desk, and I followed stroke for stroke on my own expanding dick.

Oh, my God, Victor would die if he saw me now. It was too good to be true. Here I was naked in public for the first time, and all alone with my dream man. He was jacking himself off about 20 feet away from me, looking into my eyes as if we were lovers.

I started grunting gently as pleasure filled my body, and I twitched knowing that if we came together, the next step might be my lips bathing every inch of his perfect skin, followed by my tongue diving into his pink, soft lips and down his throat. It wasn't just sex I wanted from Shane Coley. I wanted to kiss him too.

He put his other hand on his cock, and for the first time I saw him straddling his appendage with both hands. That showed me how huge and perfect he really was. Once his purplish-red rod was sticking straight up there'd be enough room for another hand—my hand—to finish him off.

But my dream was shattered. The exit door opened and banged shut as four guys dove into the aisles of the stacks, all naked.

"Holy shit, look what we're missing!" one of them said, standing a few feet from Shane, in front of me, and playing with himself in front of the swimmer.

Shane was out of there in a flash. He even left his notebook behind.

The masturbators turned toward me and began a circle jerk show, but I wasn't interested. I picked up Shane's notebook and headed out.

A few days later I left Shane's notebook by his locker over at the gym, where he practices with the swim team. I saw him every once in a while after that, but we never spoke, and we never even got close to the intimate moment we had in the stacks that day.

Shane never went back to his favorite spot. He must've found another place to study, and unfortunately I was never able to locate exactly where it was.

But I do know that he got his notebook back with all his class notes intact—and I hope he appreciated it.

I couldn't return it without a little present though, without finishing off what we started.

Two pages of his notes were stuck together.

TEACHING ADVANCED MASTURBATION 101
SEPTEMBER 11, 2000

I had a bad case of first-day-of-school jitters. How embarrassing: Here I was the teacher, and I was shaking in my shoes. First of all, I didn't know what to expect from the students, this Generation Sex of hot young men. *What will they think of me?* I wondered. *I mean, I'm 30. Jeez, that's over the hill!*

Then there was the note I'd found that morning in my faculty mailbox. It was from Dean Richie and simply said: "I'm keeping an eye on you! Consider this a warning."

But hey, a man's gotta do what a man's gotta do, right? I adjusted my cock ring through my loose jeans and headed to class with a handful of sticky notes.

It's a class I was born to teach, and something I know plenty about. In fact, I'm a world-leading expert. The college already had the Basic Masturbation courses well in hand, taught by some old wanker who lectured so much the guys fell asleep.

I was hoping my class would be different.

I walked into the room and saw 34 pairs of eyes look me over. For the most part they were handsome, some of them eager, most of them with an attitude of skepticism and aloofness, a few with a dead-eyed stare. It was a lab classroom with long tables and a big counter at the front. I started to adjust the overhead-projector screen, not saying a word.

Then I noticed a guy with jet-black hair sitting on the front counter, where I'd put my briefcase. He wore a black robe, and he let it fall open so I could see he was clearly naked and sporting a semisoft cock.

"I'm your lab Speci-Men for the quarter," he said dryly as he watched me take notice of his equipment. "Name's Lance."

"Oh, hey…Lance. I'm so glad we have our own lab rat. I wasn't…t-t-told, though," I stammered. It was as if I was back in school. Lance rubbed his crotch, then mercifully covered himself up a bit.

"I volunteered for this assignment especially to meet you," he said with forced sincerity.

I put my transparencies up on the screen, called the room to order as the bell rang, and took roll. I looked up occasionally as I read off the list of Benjamins, Jasons, and Lukes…but then I stopped.

"Richie, Connor," I said, looking up. "Connor? The dean's son?"

My eyes spotted a movement.

Raising his hand shyly was a clear-blue-eyed kid with short, spiky, greased-up hair. His blue, denim-style western shirt matched his eye color, and his lips shined like polished chrome. As his hand came down, it brushed his shirt open to reveal a defined chest.

"Yeah, we've met before, haven't we?"

I would have never believed that little punk kid I knew from 10 years ago—the same one who spied on me while I jerked off in my dorm room—would grow up to be such a looker. I could sense danger in him too: The same mischievous smirk he had as a kid was still plastered across his face.

"Good to see you again, kid. You've grown up."

"You have no idea how much," he shot back quickly. "It's good to see you, Professor Skee."

The class laughed, and I blushed.

I made my introduction, explaining how I'm cited as the world's leading authority on gay porn, having reviewed videos for more than a dozen years and written 10 books about the adult industry. I talked about *Adult Video News* magazine, the industry awards shows I created, and my first book.

"Professor Skee, how much of the first *Hollywood Hardcore Diaries* is true?" asked a rather serious, freckled redhead in the second row. "It's the first book I ever masturbated to."

"Um, thank you...let's see, you're Aaron Rymer, right? Yeah, well, a lot of it is based on truth, but for legal reasons we changed some names around. I think you could read between the lines, though, and figure a few of them out."

The class laughed a much-needed nervous laugh, but then Lance piped up. "I like the first chapter, where you talk about your cock in great detail, Professor." He then opened his robe to show his bobbing appendage. "Was that all true too?"

"For the record, we're calling it fiction." I smiled. "And this, class, for those who don't know, is Lance, our Speci-Men, who's going to demonstrate a few of the techniques we'll be explaining throughout the course."

I flipped on the overhead projector, which beamed forth a lame drawing of a cock with a few numbers next to it.

"I'm not going to ask how many of you masturbate, because I know you all do, and I don't need to identify the liars right off the bat. Now, statistics show that 64% of men say they masturbate once a day and 71% say they feel guilty about doing it."

A guy in the back shouted, "What's to feel guilty about?"

"Well, exactly, and I hope there won't be anything to feel guilty about after these 12 weeks of study. Now, the average number of erections per day for a guy is 11, while the average number of spontaneous nocturnal erections is 9. Most guys your age can regain their erections within an average of 12 minutes, with the record—which was set on this very college campus—being 2 minutes."

I went on spouting rote statistics as the guys wriggled their pens and pencils hurriedly across their notepads. I noticed Lance looking directly at Connor Richie and suspected there was some familiarity between them. How well did they know each other?

Then it hit me. I recognized Lance from jacking off in that bathroom stall the first day I came to campus. I was sure he recognized me too. But I didn't have much time to worry about that. I had to go on with my class.

"First, the most important thing you have to observe is how a guy approaches his penis. Is it the Underhand Grab or the Overhand Grab? OK, Lance, grasp your cock with your palm up and your fingers underneath the shaft with the thumb on top, facing you."

I looked at Lance, who stood up in front of the class and looked around stupidly. He threw his robe on the counter and stood naked, his cock waving stiffly in front of him, bobbing ever so slightly as it hardened. He grabbed himself awkwardly as I repeated the instructions.

"Just grab it like you normally would," I sighed, exasperated. "OK, well, Lance is doing the Overhand Grab, which is less common, and that is with the thumb down and toward the base while the fingers and palm are still underneath the shaft."

I gave Lance a slight scowl and continued.

"I want to cover the 12 most basic masturbation techniques in this first class so we can get into the more complex techniques quickly. Studies conducted throughout the world have revealed these to be the most common techniques used by men to achieve orgasm."

Lance stood erect now in front of the class, and I turned him sideways so they could all see. Some of the guys sat up in their seats and paid close attention. I could see a few hands move between their legs under their tables.

"The basic style is the Stroke, grasping the penis fully in your hand, either with an underhand or overhand grip, and, starting at the base, pulling the hand up and over the head, then going back down the shaft, back to the base. This is the basic procedure from which all other masturbation techniques derive. It is usually the most satisfying and all-encompassing, and it varies in grip and pressure."

Lance stopped stroking himself and smiled, flicking his tongue stud at me. I grumbled.

"Next there's the Squeeze. Starting at the base of the shaft near the balls, then working up the shaft to the head, you simply squeeze and release. Not stroking—just squeeze...and release. Usually, you want to squeeze a few times before moving up the shaft. This technique can also be used to keep ejaculation under control."

Lance squeezed his own cock hard. I continued. "Notice how the head of the penis swells and becomes blood-engorged. It quickly turns a purplish-red. If it hurts, let go."

"It don't hurt," Lance smiled. "Gets me harder."

"I thought silence was part of your job," I scolded.

I went through the Tickle, the Slap, the Pump, the Two-handed Roll, the Hole, and the Fist. Each time, Lance reluctantly cooperated, demonstrating the technique per my instructions and trying to catch my eyes (this I carefully avoided).

"Then there's the Wank, where you hold just the head and the top part of the shaft and twist like you're unscrewing a bottle top."

Lance looked dumbly, as if he didn't understand.

"Or, just tugging up and down on the head in short strokes."

Lance didn't seem to get it. I finally went up to his now fully erect penis, which was pointing to 2 o'clock high, and gave his blood-red cock head a big twist. He squealed.

The class laughed.

"Now then, there's the Jerk, often found in Asian cultures, where you're pulling the cock with a stroke that takes it in a direction it doesn't naturally want to go. If jerking off downward while sitting, the cock wants to go up."

Lance looked confused again as he looked down at his cock, which pointed to the left.

"If the cock bends naturally to the left, the Jerk is implemented while stroking it with a tug to the right. The Jerk is one full long stroke, and usually is from the base up and doesn't have a down stroke."

I walked over and pulled the stiff, smooth cock to the right. Lance squealed again, but this time he whined a bit too much and I knew he was teasing. Still, I liked the velvety feel of his young cock.

"It intensifies the stroke by forcing the penis to go in a different direction than normal, and thus causes the cock to harden even more." I smiled.

I noticed a few hands on or around their zippers, and knew some of the students could see my own bulge growing down the right side of my pant leg, straining my leather cock-ring. *I should have worn underwear,* I thought. *Just to keep myself down.*

"I'm going to need a soft cock for the next one," I said to Lance, but before I even asked for a volunteer, redheaded Aaron was up on the counter with his pants down around his ankles. I wasted no time as I saw his uncut, thick cock flop down limply.

"This is called The Grip and you grasp the entire cock and testicles and bend the head down into the balls, that's it. Now cup the whole package in one hand, squeeze gently..."

Aaron fumbled with his crotch. I waited. He didn't understand directions either. I walked over and put one hand over his long shaft and balls and pressed the shaft down against his balls.

"The balls are incorporated into this technique more than any other and the shaft may not get fully hard before ejaculation. The stimulus is more on the balls and head, because the underside of the shaft is bent in on itself."

"Oh, man, that feels great, Professor...keep doing it," Aaron groaned.

I immediately released my grip and sent him to his seat.

I looked out into the classroom and saw a few shiny cocks

F.U.

springing out through opened zippers as students tried out the techniques. A heavy-set Asian in the corner had left his zipper up, choosing to bury his hand down his pants instead. I looked over at Connor, who had a thick bulbous cock head poking out of his fly. He worked on his pink knob and watched Lance doing a Wank on himself.

"Now, Professor, it doesn't seem fair that we have to study these techniques without being able to try them out on ourselves," said the Asian guy. I looked at my notes; he was Eric Chun.

"You are all expected to try these techniques on your own at home. Now let me show you the One-Way Willy."

I got behind Lance, who was practically humping the counter at this point. A kid in the front row leaned over his desk as if to suck Lance's bobbing prick. I grabbed the cock myself and demonstrated.

"This is a constant hand-over-hand technique where the cock is stroked up from base to head in a constant one-way sensation."

Lance shivered and pressed his bare butt back into the hard-on straining in my jeans. I grabbed a large tube of lube and slicked up his heated shaft.

"With a lot of lube, this is a slick trick that creates an incredible sensation inside the tube of the shaft and produces one long squirt rather than a series of spurts. This is one to start off slow and as the come builds up, keep stroking faster and faster."

I lost all self-control as faster and faster, hand-over-hand, I kept stroking Lance.

"Oh, shit, man, I'm commmmming," he hollered as he shot a wad right into the face of the kid in the front row, who promptly wiped it off his chin, spit into his palm, and shoved his naturally slicked-up hand down his pants to fondle himself.

Lance spasmed some more, and the class applauded. Then up walked Connor Richie, a big smile on his face and a huge boner too. He had peeled off his pants and underwear and was unbuttoning his shirt as he came to the front of the class with a cock that stuck straight up, skyward.

The class marveled. So did I.

Connor dropped his last stitch of clothing on the desk of the kid who'd gotten the facial, then stood next to the still-writhing Lance and said, "I'm next."

I glanced down at the overhead projector and read: "The Twister begins as you grab the shaft with one hand and use the other hand to twist the head so it's facing you. Now keep twisting as tightly and as much as you can stand it."

Connor had a dreamy tanned body with perfect round nipples, and his rod stood well past his navel. It was a proud erection.

At this point, Lance had a renewed hard-on, and I pointed to him and said, "Now you'll demonstrate The Wag. Hold the base of the penis tightly between your forefinger and thumb, wagging the loose remainder of the shaft in the open air to get the sensation of movement, either around or up and down."

Lance muttered, "I'll be coming again in no time."

Eric Chun hurried up to the front of the class with his tummy bulging out of his T-shirt and no pants on. "Gimme one, gimme one," he begged.

"The O Grope. A circular O is made with the finger and forefinger, and the penis is lightly stroked through it; then the middle finger is sometimes switched with the forefinger, bringing the O a bit tighter."

He followed directions well, as I commented, "This masturbation is done ever so slightly, almost like the Tickle."

Eric's cock was as fat around as his own fist; it was a remarkable sight to watch him yank his thick pud with his fat, puffy fingers. By this time everyone in the class had their dicks out. Aaron and his freckled body joined the three masturbators at the front of the class.

"Mister Rymer will demonstrate the Ham and Eggs

technique, which involves squeezing and fondling the balls. Beat the meat by slapping the underside of the shaft while rolling and squeezing the balls with the other hand."

Aaron really beat his meat, even slapping it against the counter with a thwack that made me wince. He scrambled his eggs with rather amazing pleasure, despite the obvious harshness with which he was gripping his tender testicles.

The class was working itself into a frenzy.

"Don't let yourselves ejaculate just yet...everybody observe one another's technique and see if it is a basic or advanced method. Consider this a field experiment."

I gave in; I couldn't hold them back anymore. Then one of the students encouraged me a bit too much.

"Professor Skee, I've heard about a technique the O Boys named after you, and I wondered, could you demonstrate that one too?"

It's true, the renowned Orgy Boys made the Mickey famous, and it's a masturbation practice I taught the masses firsthand. It originated, as did the O Boys, on this very campus.

Well, that was my cue—I dropped my pants and the class stood to get a glimpse of my hard-on stretching out in front of me. With the leather clasp around the base of my shaft and my balls, my cock looked like it stretched out a full 7 inches.

I lightly tickled my whole crotch, letting the blond hairs excite my loins.

"This is the Mickey, class. Now everyone follow. Take one hand and pull your balls from the shaft up all the way to the head of your cock—or as close as you can stretch them."

I knew I had particularly stretchy balls, and a sac that let me bring my testicles up to the tip of my cock. I showed the class how I held my balls up to my piss slit so it looked like three giant cock heads together in my fist. A few of the guys could do it just as well, but some of the others strained themselves trying. Others just stroked themselves randomly as they watched in awe. A few were still taking notes.

"Now, lock a tight squeeze under the balls with one hand while you tickle the balls and underside of the head with the other hand. If you do this until you come, I guarantee an intense orgasm."

I walked around with my hand around my balls and shaft while tickling the hairs and skin with my other hand and coaching the guys who were trying to do the same. Most got it, and many appeared to be on the verge of an orgasm.

"No, hold it, guys—don't let yourselves blow. Keep it in control, and let's all do it together."

I could smell the maleness in the room as we approached a simultaneous orgasm. I felt the entire group build up, saw Aaron's face turn red, watched Eric blow his cheeks out, saw Lance's eyes roll back in his head, and as Connor looked me straight in the eye with a wicked gleam....

"Go! Let it go, class!"

In a grunt of 34 late-teen heaves—plus one 30-something heave—our ejaculation must have shaken the whole building. It was quite intense. The smell of spunk permeated the air. Jism slicked up the floors. I saw semen shoot across tables. Connor hit the same guy in the front row that Lance had hit. As Lance came again, he leaned over and planted a wet lip lock on Connor's shiny mouth. (Aha! I was right. There *was* a history there.)

Just then, the door opened. It was Dean Richie. He looked around and saw the class of half-naked youths standing around with cocks dripping in their final twitches of orgasm. He looked at me and beckoned me over with a crooked finger. Then suddenly, he looked to be on the verge of heart failure.

"Connor! What are you doing in here?"

He looked at his son's half-hard appendage, then at Lance.

"And you! What are you doing in this class? In this school for that matter!"

Still standing naked and wiping come on my shirt, I jumped to Lance's defense. "But sir, he's the assigned Speci-Men. We were doing a demonstration."

"My ass, you were! This kid is not part of the Speci-Men program. He's kicked out of school! I expelled him myself!"

I was knocked for a loop. Lance looked at me sheepishly and muttered, "I always wanted to meet you."

"Get off this campus, you piece of trash," said Dean Richie to Lance, and then he turned to me. "There is no demonstrator from the Speci-Men program because we were afraid of this very kind of depravity. Professor Skee, get into my office immediately. But put your damn prick in your pants first!"

Uh-oh, I thought, *this is it. My first day in class again, and I'm already expelled. Rats.*

The students dressed quickly and a few scampered out the door. The dean exited quickly too.

Connor lingered, waiting to hide his own massive piece of meat until he was sure I got another good look at it, and said, "Hey, I'm sorry this happened. I hope you continue teaching us. We all admire you, you know. A lot of us have been your fans since we could jack off."

It turns out that the dean had a closed-circuit TV camera videotaping the whole class, and he showed it to key members of the Board of Trustees in Terms of Management (BOTTOMs). Not only was he outvoted, but the BOTTOMs commended me for having a very educational class. I think a few of them probably got off on the tape too.

Even better, I got a real Speci-Men assigned to me, and I also had Lance back as a guest Speci-Men to demonstrate some of the more advanced techniques.

Before the semester was over, we had demonstrations of many advanced masturbation methods such as the Stretch, the Fiddle, the Pud Prod, the Bump and Grind, the Fold Over, the Reach-Around, the See-Saw, the Red-Hot Full Throttle, and more.

But that day the dean called me, it hadn't been as much to reprimand me as it was to talk about his son.

"That boy, Lance, have you seen him around campus a lot?" he asked. "He's trouble, and I think he's corrupting Connor. I want them to stay away from each other. But do me a favor, will you?"

He leaned in closer, as did I.

"Would you please check this Lance guy out and find out what he's up to with my son? Do this and I'll lay off you. Do whatever jacking off you want to with the students."

I didn't promise anything, but it did give me a chance to get to know Lance and Connor better, so I agreed to give him…uh…a hand.

ROUGH SEX IN THE 'HOOD

About a week after my successful class debut, I caught Lance
skulking in the bathroom at the main administration building
again—no doubt waiting for another unsuspecting professor
to seduce. I nodded to him as we both stood at the urinal, and
he dangled an unlit cigarette between his lips as he looked
down at my dangling half-hard pisser.

"So, what's up with you and Connor Richie?" I asked as
nonchalantly as anyone in such a vulnerable position can.
"What are you two guys up to?"

"That's our business." Without so much as wiping his
hands or even shaking his willy, Lance walked out. I followed
him. Stuffing himself back into his pants, he headed toward
the densest part of the park.

"Look, I've just noticed that he's coming in with bruises
on his arms, and he had a black eye earlier this week," I said,
keeping up with the bad boy.

He sat down at a bench and turned to tell me the story. He
held his hand in his lap, rubbing himself through his black
jeans as he spoke in his deep gurgling voice.

I clicked on the tape recorder I had in my jacket. I wasn't
sure I would actually give it over to the dean, but I did want
to record the story, which turned out to be great masturbation material (for my own personal use).

"You want to hear a story, Professor Skee, sit back..."

As he spoke I found my own hand falling between my legs.

Here's his story...

He's only a bit younger, but I'm much more experienced—
if you know what I mean.

The first time, I knocked him around a bit, grabbed the kid
by the ankles and dragged him into my pad, forced him into
my bedroom. When I heaved him onto the bed, his skull
knocked against the headboard. He tried to run, so I tackled
him then tied him up. He deserved it, the punk.

Hold on, before I get into details, let me tell you the history.
OK, maybe I'm known as the local hoodlum on campus. People
wonder what the fuck I'm doing here. I'm the high school
dropout who somehow finagled his way into this school, picking on young, unsuspecting freshmen and egging them on to do
all sorts of things. Things they like too, you know.

But Connor, man, he was the cool stud, part of the elite
crowd in high school. We didn't know each other much then.
But he and his ultra-rad friends would spend their time figur-
ing out ways to harass me. They'd smash my car windows, egg
my house, and chase me around the neighborhood calling me
"dick-breath Ricky Martin–lover" and "fag freak." Connor
was always the instigator too—the skinny, mop-haired sleaze.
I hated him. But then he came to F.U., without his clique.

I had been working late one night on a project in the
library when I saw him slumped over on a dorm doorstep,
drunk as a skunk after some frat party. He was slurring his
words, laughing to himself. I helped him up, and he seemed
a bit disoriented and couldn't find his keys. When he saw me
he giggled and said, "Help me, faggot. I'm a bit shit-faced.
Lemme crash with you for the night...got nowhere to go."

I held him up and plopped him on the back of my Harley
and he held on to me, his hands grabbing my leather pants as
we sped through town.

"Where we going man? Hey, this is Crankshaw. This is a
bad neighborhood," he protested.

"This is where I grew up, it's my 'hood," I laughed. "I could drop you off here and you could try getting a cab home."

No, no, he knew better, but he squinted and seemed a bit frightened as he followed me to the ragged apartment building with blaring music and couples fighting or fucking behind every door.

Once I dragged Connor into my place, I got my initial anger out with a punch to his gut. He buckled over and puked out a bit of vodka. I pushed his face down to the floor and made him lick it all back up. He gagged.

"That ain't the only thing you're going to gag on tonight," I warned as I stuck my boot under his nose and kicked him backwards. He wriggled and whined as I pulled out my chains and rope. He tried to get out of the room and yelled.

I tied his arms to the upper bedposts using various neckties I wear to work at the mall. Then I took a couple of belts and strapped both of his legs to the bottom posts. There he was, spread-eagled, face-up, with his jeans and vomit-covered shirt still on. I checked his restraints; he was bound securely. I then opened a bottle of bourbon and poured it over his face. Connor shook his head, wide-eyed and scared.

"You gonna hurt me?" he said sobering up pretty quick. "You gonna cut me up like Hannibal or something?"

"That's a good idea," I replied. I picked up a pair of garden shears—real big ones—and began cutting his T-shirt off. He shrieked like a madman so I shoved one of the sleeves of his shirt into his mouth. "Ah," I sighed. "Nice and quiet." He had a perfectly hairless chest, wonderfully developed. He mumbled and his face twisted. I assured him I wasn't going to hurt him unless he started screaming again, and I took out the gag.

"Oh, please let me go, man, don't hurt me."

He whimpered like a baby, and I loved it.

Then I began fumbling around with his pants, an expensive pair of Levi's. I ripped off the label, shoved it in his face, and spit on him. "Where'd you get these pants, punk?"

"I stole 'em, OK? Ripped 'em off from Chelsea's down the block. Walked right out with them," he said defiantly. "I can get you a pair if you want. Just let me go."

He was beginning to look very scared, which is just what I wanted. I began cutting his pants with the shears, cooing gently to him, "Connor boy, sweet Connor."

I called him like his Daddy calls him for dinner at night. I called him sweetly, kindly as I snipped through his jeans, slipping the cold shears down each pant leg. I made sure the sharp blades sliced right next to the rosy flesh of his erect penis. And I made sure that when I snipped those big shears together a few of his blond hairs went with them. I wanted him to know I owned that piece of meat—if I wanted it. Connor acted real scared as I licked my lips.

"You gonna cut off my wanker, you perv?"

"Sounds like you want me to cut you there, street boy," I teased. "You want me to make you bleed down there?"

"No, man, don't do it. Don't cut me, please. I'll do anything."

"That's what I want to hear," I said, unzipping my zipper. Connor's dick was standing stiff on end, poking out of its uncut sheath. This kid wasn't scared of nothing, really, I don't think he ever would be. I loved his defiance. I loved his young, untouched body. But I hated him too.

He smiled at me, the brat. I slapped him across the face, over and over again. I slapped him till his cheeks were red. He laughed, even after I slapped him so hard his upper lip bled.

That's when I shoved my stiff meat down his throat, gagging him so he could barely breathe.

"Deeper. Take it, you puss."

His eyes rolled back in his head as my large tool tickled his tonsils. His mouth pursed around my cock, and I stroked it in and out as he gagged violently, tears streaming down his face. I let him come up for air.

"I think my Pa is calling for me," he begged. "Lemme go."

"Fuck yeah, I think he is, you piece of shit, but you're not going anywhere until I plug you. You ain't ever going to be the same after me."

"Oh, no, Mr. Lance, don't do that, I've never ever had anything up there before."

I smacked his white lying ass as hard as I could. He was still tied face-up so it was hard to get in a nice fresh smack, but I still made those cheeks good and sore. His erection bobbed as if I was having no effect at all.

While he was still bound up, I lifted up his smooth red butt cheek and shoved an index finger into his tight little hole. He grunted, as much with fear as with pleasure. I dug deeper into that ass. Connor was pretty clean, but I shoved my hand into his face and made him sniff his own stinky butthole smell.

"Kiss my ass," said the brat.

"Gladly," I said, smacking that ass hard again, this time with his own belt. Then I alternately leaned over and licked his butt. I whacked a red stinging welt that rose on his left cheek, I could see the blood move under the skin as my tongue licked the red line I'd made on the poor boy's bottom. Another slap made it sting even more, and he started to cry like a baby.

"Oh, Lance, don't do it," he shouted as I started to mount him. "Don't make me a woman, don't turn me into a sissy."

He was new to this, and I was going to make him sorry for calling me names in high school. I was going to make him pay for every antihomo remark he'd ever even thought of.

I shoved one of his own stinky socks in his mouth as I opened up his butt muscles. I unsheathed a condom and slapped my dick on his balls, making him squeal even more. I shoved it in his dry ass in one fast powerful thrust, making him gasp and tremble. No lube, no slickness, just a hard dry fuck.

His dick stood on end and I grabbed it harshly as I shoved myself deeper inside his virgin hole. It didn't really feel virgin, and I figured he'd had his finger up there a few times before me. He didn't like this, though.

I gave him some hard pummeling, pushing deeper and harder inside. At first, he grabbed my arm and tried to push me away, but I easily conquered him. I developed a regular pounding, his arm flailed behind him, but then he grabbed me and pulled me close.

"You like it? You starting to like it?" I screamed at him.

He shook his head no, and I pushed harder, smacking him in the face.

"YOU LIKE IT? YOU LIKE IT?"

He still shook his head no and I smacked him again.

"YOU LIKE IT!"

He nodded. Tears streamed down his face, I removed the sock, he coughed and gagged, and I spurt a good load of jism after unsheathing my dick. I shot all over his chest and face. He began sobbing uncontrollably as I came and I couldn't help but notice how he was spurting his own creamy white jizz all over the place too. I didn't even touch his nice boner as it shot off.

"Nice," I said as I unbound him.

I grabbed his head of hair and shoved his face down on his own load that he'd spewed all over the floor. He lapped up every drop.

"Good job," I told him.

Still heaving his deep breaths, he tried to stand up. I knocked him down again. He grinned. Then I helped him up.

"That was pretty wild," said the brat. "Next time, be rougher when you cut my clothes off. That was hot!"

"Next time, don't pretend you're a virgin. You almost made me laugh," I smiled.

He threw four Ulysses S. Grants on the bed. The brat had called me after reading my ad in the personals.

"Hey, my Pa did call me. I felt my cell phone buzz…better go," said Connor. "You're good at what you do, Lance."

He gave me a big kiss as he changed into the Levi's and new shirt I had waiting for him.

"And you have too much time on your hands...and too much money, you little shit," I told him as he took off.

I knew he was the dean's son. I knew he had bucks. I knew he'd be back.

I checked my calendar for the next trick and began cleaning up.

"Spoiled rich kid," I smiled.

OH, THOSE HAPPY LAYS: AN INITIATION BY FRATZI

September 21, 2000

The next day I went into Dean Richie's office. By that time, I had jacked off three times to Lance's stories of sado-masochistic bondage games with the dean's young son, Connor. I wished I could watch sometime.

"What did you find out? I can tell you know something," the dean said desperately when I entered. "Do you have a tape or something? Any evidence?"

"Look, Dean," I said, putting my hand on his shoulder. "Look, Dean Richie, Richard, you've gotta face it. Your son likes what he does with Lance. They've been doing it for a while. Lance isn't even charging him anymore."

The dean turned to the wall and looked up at the paddle mounted above his desk. He walked over to the photo underneath it, of a guy in a leather jacket, a guy with slicked black hair who looked remarkably like Lance.

"That's Joey Frattazanni. I grew up with him and my friend Putz and Wolfie back east," the dean said. "I didn't want Connor to go through what I went through, but you know, the apple doesn't fall far from the tree. Just the smell of Lance makes me think of Joey again."

The dean and I went over to the campus pub and poured ourselves a couple of long ones. We sat in a dark corner and he told me his story. Because I still expected to be confronted, or fired, I had the tape recorder running. Unfortunately I taped over some of the Lance stuff, but you know what?

The dean's was a better story.

Instead of being canned, I captured a tender, delicate tale of true love.

Here's how he told it.

Sometimes it takes just a whiff, just a scent to bring all those memories spilling back. That's how it happened, the scent, the smell. The raw, rough scent of slick leather mixed with some motor oil, sprinkled with greasy hair goop, soaked with the unmistakably gamy smell of dried come. I smelled the same combination on my son's best friend, Lance, as he dropped by that night and headed for my son's room to crank up the new CDs. It time-warped me to nearly 40 years ago....

My best friend was Joey Frattazanni. We called him Fratzi. He was the coolest of the cool, and I wasn't cool at all, but somehow we connected. He was boss! At school, even though he was in the same grade as we were, our gang of guys all looked up to Fratzi because he was older. He was also smoother with the girls, so smooth. He had 'em, plenty of 'em. Although none of us would admit it, we were all virgins—and we knew the Fratz-man wasn't.

Putzy was the goof of the gang. He was very tall and lanky, with slicked-back brown hair and monkey arms that hung to his knees. Wolfie was the pal who wore a perfect ducktail on the back of his head and was so hairy his back and chest fur stuck out over the neckline of his T-shirt.

I was thinner then, with short-cropped hair in a sort of flattop that still allowed a few blond strands to fall down over my blue eyes. I was the intelligent one, but not necessarily rational.

No, that was Fratzi. He was always the levelheaded one among us. When we'd go bust heads with the 'Ricans, he'd be the one to figure out the odds and let us know when to back down. He was cool, the coolest. He wore his hair with a perfect curl, and his hair was slick, so slick. He had one of those pouty sets of lips that curls on command—James Dean lips—and he'd mastered the Brando hunch perfectly. He had high, sucked-in cheekbones and a sloping Italian nose. His eyes were like black marbles—strong, deep, probing.

I always got a strange tingle when Fratzi grabbed me from the back and gave me a hug, or put one of his arms on my shoulder and complimented me. I always got that sting of passion, that zing of electricity when he touched me, but I assumed it was simply my intense admiration for him. That is, until the day I went to his garage unannounced.

Usually the gang would call one another before getting together, or we just met at Annie's Diner. But for some reason, one afternoon I just popped over to the workroom in back of his house. He was working on a carburetor there, underneath the car with his back on a dolly. He had his leather jacket on, but nothing else. There was my best friend with the bottom half of his body sticking out from under a car and his cock stiff up against his belly. I was shocked. I didn't clear my throat or let him know I was there, but I did sit and stare at it awhile. I'd heard about his monster from the girls, and this was a chance to get a firsthand look.

The Fratz's dick was uncut; I'd never seen one before. Two thick layers of skin allowed the bright red point to poke through the loose folds. His stomach muscles were a lot more defined than I'd ever imagined. I watched him take one of his filthy, greasy hands and rub it against his stiffness. The thick rod squirmed stiffer.

I stayed and watched the action for what seemed like an eternity, then slowly backed out of the garage. His Elvis music was playing so loudly I was sure he didn't hear me, but as I neared the mouth of the garage he spoke.

"Could use a hand down here, ol' buddy boy," came his voice from underneath the car.

"Um. Hi, Fratzi. I didn't want to disturb you."

He poked his head out from under the car and looked me

square in the face. I looked into his eyes at first, but then found my gaze wandering down the length of his well-maintained, rippling body.

"Get one of those dollies and get under here and help me hold this thing up till I screw it in," he said to me. Then my breath was knocked out of me as he added, "And you'll get greasy, so take your clothes off."

It was a demand, not a request. I found myself slowly stripping. For a moment I hesitated, standing there with an aching protrusion in my skivvies, worrying that my pal would notice.

"Underwear too, wouldn't want to have to explain that to Momma, would you?" he said. I slipped off my underwear and folded them neatly, putting my clothes on the front seat of the car. Almost shyly, I lay down on the dolly cockside up and slid underneath the car next to him. He didn't even look down, just asked me to hold up this monster piece of machinery. I could see a large chrome piece of fender lying next to him, serving as a mirror to see everything going on above him in the garage. He'd seen me pretty clearly, probably the whole time I was there.

"You could see I was here," I said to him. "You knew."

I caught his smile. "Yep. Could see ya the whole time."

I smelled the wetness of his armpits as he held the screwdriver up close to me. I trembled as he got bolder.

"Saw how you lingered there for a while," he teased. "Guess you sort of caught me with my pants down. Can't abide getting my clothes filthy, so I work in the nude."

"But your jacket," I mustered.

"My jacket, I always keep *that* on, and besides, it smells so good when I'm sweating in it."

I could smell his soft cowhide jacket and his hair gel mixed in. My rod got stiffer between my legs. Suddenly, Fratzi unscrewed a nut beneath the car and a rush of warm black oil dripped onto my crotch. I yelped and slid out from under the car. He slid out too, and he got up and went over to shut the garage door.

Then he just stood there and looked at me. His jacket opened to his nakedness, his dick hanging limp just above a fine, deep bunch of hair. Even totally naked, he looked cool, so cool.

"Got a little greasy, huh, Rich?" His deep voice was as slick as the oil. He grabbed a rag and approached me, saying, "Let me help you with that."

But instead of wiping me with the rag, he reached over with one firm hand and grabbed my oily crotch. It twitched. Then, with the greasy rag, he reached behind me and gave me a sensation I'd never felt before. With his middle finger wrapped inside the rag, he fingered it up my butt. I was pushed, back first, against the car, and before I could protest he looked into my eyes and smiled, and I knew everything would be OK.

"Hey, bud, you'll like this," he said as he pressed his body against me, making his protrusion stiffer as he greased up mine. He rolled his hard one over me. His hand cupped my balls and squeezed roughly, momentarily making me forget the total violation I was feeling in the rear.

The rag went all the way up inside me, and I cried with pain as two, then three, then four fingers slipped inside and he wriggled them around in my butthole. Just as the pain was getting to be too much for me, and just as I was ready to stop this progression, he planted a greasy, slick, wet kiss on my mouth. His thick lips pressed up against my peach fuzz of an upper lip and I felt his thick, slick tongue reach down my throat. I stopped squirming.

Just when he knew he had me in his total control, he released the kiss and his finger-grip on my anus. He then put his hand on my naked shoulders and pushed my head down to his hot, musky crotch. I wasn't sure what he wanted, but my mouth involuntarily opened as if I had given it to him before. I couldn't imagine why I'd want that long thing in my mouth, but I did, and it was great.

It wasn't fully hard, so I chewed on the fleshy spongy part a bit, and he groaned. Then my tongue almost expertly sucked the rim of his loose flesh and he threw his head back in ecstasy. I was making him happy, and that's all I wanted to do. He gave me a few hip swivels and his dick thrust into my throat, and I almost convulsed until I found a position that would make an even deposit for his deep thrusts. Each time he dove his way in I had to catch a breath because my nose was smothered in the bushy mat above his dick. I looked up at him and his black eyes were smiling with approval. I smiled back as well as I could with his 9-incher in my face.

Then I caught his eyes darting disconcertedly at the doorway. There Wolfie was standing, mouth wide open, stunned. He didn't know what to say, but Fratzi spoke up.

"I'm just about to pop Richie's cherry, and I suggest you stay for the occasion," he said with ease. "Take your clothes off and stay awhile."

Wolfie was hypnotized, but very, very interested, as we could see from the growing length snaking down his tight pants. He kept his eyes on my sucking motion as he slipped off his boots and socks and pants and shirt and then underwear.

"Come 'ere," Fratzi said, rubbing one wet, gooey hand over Wolfie's very hairy body. "Touch this."

Wolfie hesitated, then with both hands grabbed the monstrous tool between Fratzi's legs.

"That's it, easy boy, easy," he groaned. "You know how to work it, Wolf."

While this yanking was going on, I was still on my knees, licking up Fratzi's balls and getting a good look at Wolfie's hairy underside as well.

"Now, I'm going to plug ol' Richie here, so I think you should make sure his face has something to work on," Fratzi said. So my nose was smothered in a thick bush as I felt Fratzi's long thick prod going up my prostate. I squeaked. Fratzi gripped my shoulders like only a man can and eased himself inside. Past a certain point, it slid a lot easier and my butt muscles relaxed.

"Oooh, ah," I groaned, more with pleasure than pain now. I was loud, but lost.

Suddenly the door flung open, and in rushed a sweaty, concerned Putzy.

"I heard the screaming, Richie, are...you...all...r...?" Putzy's face held an expression of sheer and utter horror. He watched his friends, naked, connected by various appendages, and he just couldn't believe it.

"C'mon in, there's plenty of room," said the easygoing Fratzi, and we kept doing our respective slurping and pounding as if nothing was happening. It was hypnotic. I felt like my erection would never go down.

"B-b-but I'm not...I can't..." he stammered.

"Don't mean nothing, buddy boy—it's just a way of hanging out with the guys." Fratzi could make just about anything seem normal. "And, we know you can, 'cause we've all seen your boner poking out when you're asleep on our camping trips."

He noticed! How funny! I'd always awakened early on our camp outings to spy the long, snaking protrusion of Putzy poking out his pajama crotch in the morning, but I'd never seen him fully naked. Putz was always shy about his pud, even during our beer-pissing sessions out in the woods together.

Now he seemed terrified but eager. Could he be even bigger than Fratzi? I wanted to know.

When Putzy wouldn't strip, we stopped what we were doing and backed him up against a motorcycle. Wolfie grabbed his shoes, I ripped his shirt and belt, and Fratzi planted a big hairy kiss on his face so he couldn't scream. After I slipped the belt off his pants and made for the zipper, I was knocked in the eye by a large one-eyed monster. I thought it was his fist at first, but it wasn't. Putzy had the largest, most glorious dick I'd ever seen.

"My, my, you've been holding out on us all this time?"

Fratzi gurgled. "This is big enough for three."

We all three got on our knees and sucked a nervous Putzy into submission. I tasted the musky, smooth dick and my tongue sometimes lapped some of Fratzi's spit as he worked the fat cock head. Sometimes we kissed as our lips brushed each other during the blow job. I locked lips with Wolfie and his eyes half-opened with drunken pleasure. We could feel our prodigious pal getting close.

Putz came in gushes, with loud exaggerated gasps. He shot all the way across the garage. And, most remarkably—after the puddle he left on the floor—he was still hard!

Then he got on his knees and started sucking off Fratzi's boner, and we all began worshiping our cool friend's body. This was our mentor, our hero, our teacher, so everything was OK. He was cool.

"I'm going to finish off ravaging Richie's tight ass, but Putz, I want you to slide it into me, OK?" Fratz said. He mounted me and then eased Putz's penis into his own butt, much to my surprise. I didn't think Fratzi would allow that to happen, but apparently he was into every possible kind of sex. Seeing that my greasy protrusion still poked straight up, Wolfie slapped a handful of grease between his legs and backed his butthole onto my pole.

There we were, the four of us, connected in a wild groping frenzy of a sexy and powerful train. We grinded and grunted for what seemed like hours until we were all on the verge, then pulled out and formed a circle.

"I'm coming again! I can't believe it!" Putzy said, shooting off.

"Me too, oooh, aaargh, oh, baby!" Wolfie shot across our circle and hit my belly button. I scooped up the rubbery come and smeared it under my balls as my load came out in oozy white gushes.

"Quite a load, my men! Now help me out," said Fratzi.

We all had a hand on him. Mine was on his red cock head and another underneath his balls just before his butt. I could feel the sperm building, the load swelling till it shot up through his dick. The other guys squeezed hard and Fratzi practically covered us with puddles of goop.

"Wowie-zowie, that was great," said Putz.

"Cowabunga, dude!" said Wolf.

We never really talked much about our liaisons, but after graduation we spent the whole summer in that garage—sometimes twice a day—exploring every inch of each other's bodies in every possible way.

We all ended up having girlfriends and marrying, except Fratzi. But even until recently he'd visit one or the other of us, still on his motorcycle, still cool as ever, and he'd stay a few days. He still drives up here to campus to see me too. I know the other guys wouldn't admit it, but we all get pangs of yearning for those times that summer in the garage. He's the only one I've ever cheated on my wife with, and I love both of them dearly.

Connor's met him, loves him. I think he's always known that Fratzi has a place in his Dad's heart.

Now, as my son heads into his early 20s, I can see his attraction to this dapper young stud named Lance, who's the spitting image of Fratzi.

I guess things have come full circle, eh? Short-cropped hair is back in. Slicked hair is back in—and so are those grungy leather jackets. Sometimes Lance stays the night and leaves early in the morning right under my own roof! One morning I spotted them, both guys looking sheepish, my son a bit bewildered—but smiling. And they had that smell, you know? That scent of sweat, and leather, and oil, and grease, and sex. It literally wafted through the air.

I think I'll have to sit down and have a talk with my son soon, don't you think? We'll talk about *my* good ol' lays.

GETTING INTO THE NAKED DORM
AUGUST 14, 1989

It was sweet to see how the relationship between Connor and his dad mellowed out after my true confession drinking session with Dean Richie. Obviously, he went ahead with that heart-to-heart—or perhaps hard-to-hard—with his son. I don't want to know.

The success of my first class in Advanced Masturbation and the dean's reminiscing about his younger days led me to flip through my old diaries and think back to a more innocent time.

I knew one of the scariest days in my life, and one of the most exciting, was when I finally got accepted into the Naked Dorm.

This was one day that pretty much changed my life forever. Here's the diary entry.

The entire time I was at college, I fantasized about getting into the Naked Dorm. It was kind of a campus experiment, and they rarely talked about it off campus, but a few magazines and newspapers caught wind of the unique concept and wrote their own in-depth analyses.

One whole dorm building on campus—two stories, with a pool and its own grassy park area—was a clothes-free zone. Tucked in the northern part of the campus, on the other side of the pond, away from most of the school buildings, the Naked Dorm looked like any other building until you walked closer and noticed the bare flesh.

Not surprisingly, not many of the girls on campus enrolled

in the Naked Dorm. Since most of the guys were het (or so they claimed), the girls worried about being the obvious prey at a place where people walked around in the nude all the time. I found out pretty quickly that the girls had little to worry about.

When I got my transfer notice, I was elated. I didn't have too much stuff, so I packed my two suitcases and backpack and headed out for my new room—room 212. There I'd meet my new roommate and neighbors in the dorm.

As I walked up the hill and hit the last rise in the path, for the first time I didn't feel like that creepy voyeur who sneaked up regularly to watch from behind the trees as the guys played naked volleyball or nude tag football. I remembered how I'd often watched the guys sunning themselves by the pool, then flung myself on my knees in the thick brush, stroking myself slowly to the sight of those basking bodies without tan lines. I'd watched their cocks bob up and down as they lunged for balls (footballs and volleyballs, that is), as the wind wafted through their free and wild clumps of pubic hair.

Now I was one of them.

Oh sure, anyone could come up to visit and strip and join in whatever activity was going on, but you didn't truly belong until you took the complete plunge and joined Naked Dorm.

Even though I was just discovering my own exhibitionist tendencies, a hint of nervousness gripped me as I walked up to the building and dove headlong into the biggest self-revelation I've ever experienced. More than coming out of the closet, more than having sex for the first time, this was a moment of major self-expression. And there was no turning back.

Three guys were playing Frisbee outside on the grass: a muscular black guy with a huge, bobbing cock, a curly-haired, red-headed white guy with freckles all over his body and an even huger cock, and a surfer dude with hair down to his butt who looked like a girl until he turned around and showed he was sporting a shiny white piece of meat dangling down joyously as if his serpent had a smile on it.

I whistled to myself, wondering how I could possibly "hang out" with these guys.

"Visitor or newbie?" shouted one of them. It was the black guy, whose cock actually hung halfway to his knees—soft. I'm not exaggerating.

"Uh, I'm m-moving in—" I stammered.

"Newbie!" shouted the curly-haired guy. "Joey, get the book!"

Suddenly, from out of nowhere, about a half-dozen naked guys ran toward me, joining the three well-hung Frisbee-players. They all lunged toward me. Jeez! I took off running. One of my suitcases broke open, my clothes spilling all over the place. I huffed and puffed with the remaining one, my backpack flopping up and down. I headed for the steps at the front doors of the building.

A huge, muscular wrestler guy with a big fat cock tackled me before I got to the steps. "He's not a LUMPWUG—at least we know that," the wrestler bellowed. The other guys pounced on me in a dog pile and then started ripping my clothes off. Not *pulling* them off, mind you, but literally ripping them off in shreds.

My school T-shirt was torn off my chest, leaving only a left shoulder sleeve. My pants were unbuckled and off of me in seconds.

"Look, dudes, he's wearing undies. Nice whities!" hooted the surfer guy. "You'll learn to break that bad habit."

My underwear was yanked off and pulled down over my head. I could smell my own crotch as my nose poked through the pee slit. I continued struggling, but the big arms of the wrestler kept me pinned. Through the pee slit, I watched a handsome brunet with green eyes and a dimpled chin saunter up with a half hard-on. He had with him a tape measure, an old leather-bound book, and a pen. I recognized him as Joey

Dillus, a notorious cocksucker on campus. He knew me too.

"Hope he's not a Normie or a Stiff, we got too many of them," Joey said. "Who's fucking him first?"

"It don't look like a Stubbie. Too bad, we need more of 'em. More like a Choker," said the black guy.

"Don't need no Chokers, got a lot of those too—especially with you around. This guy's an Eater, what do you think, Joey?" said the redhead.

Four guys held me down as I struggled helplessly. Joey stood over my naked body, spread-eagled on the grass in front of him. The wrestler handed him my office slip.

"Let's see...Skee, Mickey, Room 212, Transfer," Joey read. "Hey, wait a minute, pull those undies off his head. Hey, dude, it's you!"

Yeah, I recognized him. He was No. 94, a jack-off buddy from the Cryolab, not far from campus, where we'd earned a few bucks jacking off into plastic cups more than a year before. We met while we were in neighboring stalls and had given each other a hand occasionally to make sure we spilled big loads.

When I looked at the guys around me after the underwear was ripped off my head, I recognized a few others from the Cryolab.

"Yeah, Dr. Malin's Cryolab, where I donated sperm for a while. I know you were there," I said, pointing to the surfer dude, and then saw the wrestler. "And you were there too."

"And you were there, and you were there, well, darling, this ain't no Oz, and now we're all going to fuck the living shit out of you," said the black guy, stroking his cock, which easily stretched more than 9 inches. "Welcome to Naked Dorm. This is your initiation."

"Hey guys, I haven't...I can't...but I can't take you— you're all too big for me!" I pleaded.

My underwear was bunched up and shoved in my mouth. My eyes welled up with tears and I wondered if I had made a big mistake. How would I ever be able to transfer out of this living situation—especially after practically begging to be admitted?

I closed my eyes as I felt an amazing soft feeling on my crotch. I opened to see Joey working on my outstretched cock with his bulbous pink lips. The few licks of his tongue and perfect pressure of his lips took me to the brink instantaneously. He lived up to his reputation.

Joey held out the tape measure as the surfer dude held my cock upright, giving it a bit more of a squeeze.

"Six and a quarter? A Stiff just like me?"

The surfer guy squeezed my dick again, and the wrestler smiled and said, "Relax."

I felt something invade my butthole and looked up and saw the wrestler grinning as one of his fat stubby fingers wriggled its way up my bottom. It made me stiffen even more.

"Aha, it's not over yet. This is a juicy one too," Joey said, sliding the tape measure like a noose around my reddening cock. "It's six and a quarter around too. He's got a Box Cock, man—as big around as he his long. This is great!"

As the finger wriggled in my pulsating ass, I felt my cock grow harder. Joey slid the tape measure back along the top of my cock, from piss slit to hairy stalk, as the surfer held down my mat of pubic hair.

"Well, he's a bit bigger now," smiled Joey. "Final tally: This guy is 6⅞. He's a Score. A Thick Score!"

The guys let me go and I collapsed in a ball, hiding my invaded crotch area as I heard cheers. I looked up. Eyes were peering out the windows and heads were poking from the doorways as many of my new neighbors saw my boner and heard my very personal measurements being broadcast for the world.

"Mickey Skee, a Thick Score, welcome to Naked Dorm," said Joey, rather officially now. "By the way, I'm Joey Dillus. I'm a Stiff, and I'm also your new roommate."

My head was reeling as I was helped to my feet, with a bit of precome dribbling from my dick.

"So you're not going to rape me?" I asked.

The black guy, Jake, smiled and reached over to shake my dick. "Disappointed? No, man, we just did that because it gets some guys really hard if they think they're going to get raped, especially the straight guys."

The wrestler also grabbed my shaft, gave it two tugs, and said, "This is how we say Hi. You'll get used to it. I'm Kam Likikime, and I'll just have you know that my talented finger has helped every guy we've measured by at least half an inch."

"Um...thanks, I guess," I stammered. "I was afraid I wouldn't be able to live up to you guys, everyone seems so well-hung around here."

"They're just the show-offs," said the surfer dude. "See, we measure everyone in the dorm so we know where we all stand. It's the Dimensional Inch Count Knowledgeable Yardstick, your DICKY rating. It tells us where you stand among us. By the way, I'm Sandy."

"Good to meet you, Sandy."

Tapping the thick leather book, Joey added, "Everyone has been recorded in this book since the Naked Dorm was established nearly 50 years ago; that's when they came up with this rating system for cocks all over the world."

They took me inside the building, where, along the hallway entrance wall, the Naked Dorm's founders stood together in a black-and-white photo with their flattops and white bodies, along with some pretty nice hard-ons. Photos of all the officers of the dorm throughout the years were also along the wall, showing progressively larger hard-ons and more impressive-looking guys—especially in the color photos.

And at the very end of the hall was a bronze plaque with the rating system.

Dimensional Inch Count Knowledgeable Yardstick

Below 3½ inches	Winny	0.4% of all men
3½ to 4½ inches	Stubbie	3%
4 3/4 to 5½ inches	Butch	6%
5½ to 6¼ inches	Normie	50%
6¼ to 6¾ inches	Stiff	25%
6¾ to 7¾ inches	Score	5%
7¾ to 8½ inches	Eater	4%
8½ to 9¾ inches	Choker	3%
9¾ to 11 inches	Tenor	2%
11 to 12½ inches	Foot	1%
12½ to 14¾ inches	Phreak	0.6%

I looked over the list and marveled. Half of all the guys in the world were listed in a certain cock size: the Normie. One in four were Stiffies. It was a marvelous chart.

"It's calibrated and changed every decade or so, as measurements grow worldwide. You know, more guys are getting bigger cocks, generation to generation," explained Joey.

"And our stats show that this is pretty much reflected in the Naked Dorm ranks too."

I suddenly felt my semihard cock twitch as I saw that many of the guys in the hall were staring at it.

"And I'm a Score?" I asked.

"Yep, and only one out of 20 guys are Scores, dude. You're pretty lucky. Dude, you're a thick one too," Sandy said. "You're almost a Box. That would mean you were as big around as you are long, but hey, you got a pretty thick piece of meat there."

"Um, thanks, but you guys all seem to have great cocks yourself." I got a bit self-conscious as I spoke and realized I was looking at all the bobbing appendages around me. The guys all just seemed happy to show themselves off, and a few of them spanked and tugged at their cocks to get a bit harder for me.

"Well, darling, that's because I'm a fine, sublime 9—big black inches, that is. I'm a Choker," said Jake, flopping his limp meat in my hand and squeezing the juice of precome out of my cock.

"And I'm what you'd call a Phreak. My name's Big Red, just measuring in at the 12½ mark. Of course, there's more of me around than there are Winnies, but I guess I'm still a bit of an anomaly."

As his enormous hose was placed in my hand, I found myself putting my other hand to it, needing to use both hands to sufficiently handle the thing. It was like a huge red veiny vine, and it seemed to glisten in my hands. At the tip of his bushy red stalk, right on the end of his cock head, there were two marks that looked like freckles. I let go and Big Red laughed. "There's a story behind those. Later, though. Welcome, it'll be nice to have you."

And nice to have that, I thought to myself.

Waving his long blond hair away from his face, Sandy, still looking down at my cock as the others went about their business, said, "Hey man, sorry we scared you like that, but it's our kind of initiation, you know, dude. Don't take it too hard. Hey, you know, nice cock, man."

Sandy took my pulsating cock in his hands and lovingly cupped my balls as if they were precious gems. "Did you guys get a look at these balls, these are darn righteous testicles," he said to no one in particular. "I bet they pack some great loads."

Joey grabbed one of my bags and led me up the stairs and Sandy backed away with his cock twitching as he headed back out to toss the Frisbee. He gave himself a few stiffening tugs as he looked back at me again.

I liked Sandy, he was pretty sexy. I wondered if I'd ever have a chance to play around with this guy with the nice mane of hair. Joey edged up next to me as he escorted me up the stairs and whispered, "He's straight, guy. You won't have him."

"Oh, come on, the way he talked about my dick back there?" I whispered back.

"You'd be surprised," Joey winked. "And besides, he's just a Normie, anyway."

"And I'm not into cock size if they know how to use it," I shot back.

"Yeah, but it's nice to have a bigger one than most, isn't it? At least you're not a LUMPWUG. A Large Unwieldy Massive Penis on a Weird Ugly Guy."

"A LUMPWUG?"

We passed an opened door to a room, where a zit-faced, obese guy was sitting on a lounge chair with a penis pump, sucking a huge cock into it. The cock stretched up past his rolls of flesh.

"That's Charlie. He's a Big Foot. That's an 11⅞-inch cock there, Mickey, and he's trying to get it to a full foot. He's a LUMPWUG. Wave to the Score, Charlie."

Charlie waved his penis-pumping cock. We continued down the hall.

"The cafeteria's open at 8 and stays open until 7. The pool's open until 10. We have a daily wank-off at midnight and the lounge is open all night. The TV room is only open until 2 and—"

"A what? A daily wank-off?" I asked.

"Yeah, sure, how many times do you get off a day?" Joey eyed my crotch hungrily. "I mean, I'm doing a study that's proving that the more times a guy orgasms a day, the more his immune system is heightened and the more healthy he is. You need to have an orgasm at least three times a day, you know, just like eating, pissing, shitting. It's very important you ejaculate three times a day."

We passed an open door to a room in which two guys were sucking each other off in a slurpy 69. The long skinny guy was ravishing the stockier one on a yellow faux-leather couch. They both made incredible sucking sounds and seemed on the brink of shooting.

"This is Marlon and Stroker. They're roommates, and they live two doors down from us. Marlon's a frat boy—he's the straight one."

"Hey," said Marlon, the skinny one. Marlon had short brown hair and big brown eyes and was holding out a sticky come-covered hand. He licked it off first, then I shook it. "So, you're the lucky one who rooms with Joey this quarter."

The stocky one, Stroker, held Marlon's erect cock out toward me. "You want some?"

"Um, no, th-thanks," I stuttered. "I just ate."

"These guys are part of the Speci-Men program. Have you had those guys in your class yet? They're the ones who work in the labs—the naked lab rats. The students treat them like cadavers, study them, poke and prod them. I couldn't do it, but they say it's good money and sometimes fun."

Marlon gurgled with a mouthful of cock, "You should try it, it's a lot of fun. If you need some bucks, just let me know. Come in with us and sign up for the program."

"Um, no, thanks, I don't think I could...do it." I blushed as we continued walking. "Is everyone so horny and sexual all the time around here?"

"We get a lot of work done, we really do. It's just that we tend to be more open than most about what goes on behind closed doors." Joey kicked open a door with a poster of a penile-shaped rocket ship on it. "For example, meet Jason and Johnny."

Inside the room, large, phallic inflatable rocket ships dangled from the ceiling and constellations were painted on the walls. A dark, curly-haired guy with a square, beefy body stood with his cock in his hands as a sandy-haired younger guy with a long pencil-dick swung toward him on a trapeze. The younger guy was facing backwards so his butt cheeks landed on the standing guy's cock, and he groaned each time he swung back to get fucked.

"Jason's the top, Johnny's the bottom on the swing. They're studying for the astronaut cadet program."

"I want to be the first come-shot in space," smiled pencil-dicked Johnny as he grunted with another thrust from Jason.

"Nice to meet you, you're a lucky fuck," said Jason. "Hey, didn't we meet in the bathroom once?"

That's right. These were the two guys who put on a show for me when I sucked off that stranger through the bathroom glory hole.

These guys looked more like porn stars than cadets in training for space, and as it turned out they did both become famous porn stars many years later.

Joey slammed the door just as abruptly as he'd opened it and laughed. "Don't let that skinny dick of his fool you, he's an Eater—an even 8 inches. It goes down nicely. And this is our room."

He opened the door and I saw two beds across from each other, a desk with a computer on it, and a small sink. "Showers are down the hall. That's my bed, that's yours near the window."

"So, you've been with all the guys here?" I asked.

"Almost all of them, let me think…all the straight and bi ones, all the gay ones…well, yes, actually, all of them—except one." Joey flashed his green eyes. I knew this was going to happen, but I didn't think it would be so quick. He sauntered up to me, next to my bed, and whispered in my ear, "I've not yet been able to conquer him. HIM!"

He pointed out the window to a guy stretched out on a towel under a flowering magnolia tree. It looked like a painting. An olive-skinned Italian stud with a large, brown, uncut cock flopping hard against his stomach was laying out reading a thick, green book. His brown hair blew lightly in the breeze.

He was referring to this handsome man outside.

"Vincenzo Lamaz, dreamy Vincent," sighed Joey. "He's hetero, and as far as any of us knows the only sex he gets is by being one of the Speci-Men lab rats. Marlon and Stroker joined up just to see if they could get anywhere near him. They haven't yet."

"He's the only one you haven't been with in this whole building?" I asked.

"Whole campus, practically!" Joey came up close to me, his pink cock head bobbing in front of him, almost touching my thigh.

"How many times did you come today?" he barked.

"Um, well, I jacked off once this morning."

"Aha, then," he said, dropping to his knees and covering my cock with his mouth. I was immediately erect.

Joey had such suction in his round lips, and he knew exactly how to work a shaft. He tickled my piss slit with his tongue, then engulfed my cock in his throat. His velvety lips slurped me up. I couldn't even protest. And why would I?

He built up a quick rhythm, and I closed my eyes as he worked on me expertly. His lips were tight around my thickening cock as I felt him gently flick the tip of my cock with his soft tongue. Then, even as my shaft went down his throat, I swore I could still feel his tongue-tip playing with my slit. It was impossible, but hey, who knows? Joey was a pro. A tongue-fluttering pro.

But despite the cute face and great butt on Joey, it wasn't him I was thinking of during that blow job. It was the beautiful body and face of Vincent, just outside the window.

Joey kept working his lips around my hard-on, and in a few more strokes I was gushing hot come all over his chin.

"You were pretty close to gushing when we all pretended we were going to rape you," smiled Joey. "Nice dick. I figured you'd be pretty easy. I think I've got you pretty well-pegged. And now you know why everyone is saying you're a lucky dog. You've moved in with the best cocksucker in the building, maybe on the whole campus."

I picked up a towel and headed for the showers.

"I think I'm going to like it here," I smiled shyly.

"Well, this is only twice for you today. You've got another one coming before nightfall."

He snapped a towel, which gave me a red sting on my butt. I scurried for the showers.

MUSCLE-MEN MEAT

Reading about my days back at the Naked Dorm made me
want to go see what it was like now. I felt like I was sneaking
over to a part of campus where I didn't belong anymore. I
saw the naked guys out front playing volleyball with their
cocks prancing freely just like ours did in the old days. These
days, the cocks had a lot more jewelry on them.

Then, just like the old days, I was tackled from behind and
my pants were pulled off. As I scrambled to turn around, I
was shocked to see big, burly Kam Likikime, the guy who
brought me down in exactly the same spot so many years ago.

"Hey! It's so good to see you, Kam." I hugged him as we
got back on our feet. I'd had a twinge of regret that we'd lost
touch so soon after we graduated. "You old horndog. How
are you? How's the gang? What are you doing here?"

"I'm the maintenance man and official groundskeeper. I'm
living in Naked Dorm too and helping some of the kids out."

"I'll bet you are," I smirked.

"No, really—especially the scrawny ones who get picked
on. I tell 'em what it's like to be a 97-pound weakling and
how things can change," he said.

"I know you always said you were 97 pounds, but I can't
believe it. You're all muscle now."

Kam plopped down on the grass. "Well, sit down, Mickey,
and I'll tell you the whole story of when I lived in Waikiki. I'll
catch you up on some of the gang too."

F.U.

Here's Kam's story—from the horse's mouth.

It happened just like in those ads in the comic books. In fact, I was reading a comic book when it happened. There I was on the beach, weighing in at only 97 pounds, sharing a blanket with cute Connie Coutsarias, explaining to her the evil characters in *Dick Tracy* when the biggest dick on the beach walked up and kicked sand in my face. He was a bronze muscle man.

"You asshole" was all I could muster. My face turned redder than the sunburn on Connie's thighs.

"Kam the Scam, man," Nick said, flying some more sand onto our blanket.

"You're such a jerk, Nick Kanelos!" Connie said stupidly.

I liked Connie, but sometimes she was such a ditz. We'd been going out all summer, just before our last year of high school, but we hadn't done anything sexual yet, you know. I was being careful with her. But we were on the verge—it would happen as soon as we were both in the mood. Anyway, as Nick left she turned on me. "Why don't you stand up for yourself, Kam? Or are you really a wimp?"

She asked it jokingly, and I know she meant no harm. But it did hurt. It was a turning point for me. She really pissed me off. And the next time we *were* both in the mood, I just couldn't get it up. All I kept thinking of is how she called me a wimp and how much I despised Nick the Greek. So it seemed appropriate that only a week later Connie stood me up. Then a week after that I saw Nick necking with a girl at a party and sure enough, it was Connie.

I was furious and walked up to them on the dance floor.

"What are you going to do about it?" Nick said, shoving his chest out.

"Yeah, what *are* you going to do about it, Kammy?" Connie repeated.

I wanted to punch her out as much as I did him.

Nick had been my nemesis ever since grade school. He was always bigger than I was and always pushed me around. He called me "Gummy Kammy" in first grade when he poured Elmer's Glue down my pants. Then in junior high P.E. class he got all the guys to chant "Sissy Licky-Licky with the little dicky." Of course, that made me all the more embarrassed in the locker room, when they proudly paraded their muscular teen physiques and I was just a scrawny nothing.

But it was the latest nickname, just after high school, that really made me boil. "Kam the Scam, a Mockery of a Man!" he called me. A mockery of a man. That was bad.

So, after years of boiling, after years of shame at the hands of nasty Nick the Greek, I decided to fight back. I decided to answer one of those ads in my comic books. How could it go wrong?

"Are you a 97-pound weakling?" the ad screamed.

Yes, I was. Actually, 97½ pounds. I'd always been a bit lazy, but I ate a lot. People said I was a beanpole because my metabolism was too fast. Well, it wasn't just *that* ad, but *every* ad I could find that had anything to do with muscles, health, diet, and becoming bigger in any way. I did it all: the Build-a-Man Gym Set, the Incredible Hunk Health Kit, the Stiffen Your Stomach Book—everything. Being Hawaiian, you'd think I'd have it in my gene pool, but I didn't. I had to work for every inch of muscle on me. Every inch.

I spent my allowance on the gimmicks, the diets, the programs. I dove for seashells and sold them to tourists. I was driven.

I hibernated the whole summer. I joined the Coral Reef Gym around the corner and befriended Sandy, a surfer who worked as a personal trainer there. He gave me pointers from the beginning. In the locker room, I stood naked in front of him as he assessed me.

"Hmm, yeah, we've got plenty to work with. This is what you want to work on, dude," Sandy said, grabbing my tiny little nipples. He could touch both with one hand. "Your chest. And we'll also work on these." He reached over and grabbed my hunched shoulders. He straightened them and put my head up. He winced a little at my scrawny frame. I was red-faced.

"Look at your legs, I can put my hands around them," he said incredulously. I saw how he put his hands on his own thighs. They were tremendous, taut and strong.

I looked at his chest. His pecs protruded out like loaves of bread. I could count at least a half-dozen ripples between his tits and his belly button. And Sandy could make them ripple better than the waves on Surfrider Beach. For a young guy, he was perfectly fit. Sandy was ripped.

"I want a body like yours, Sandy," I said lustfully.

"You'll have to work for it, kid. Do you think you want it that bad?"

"Yeah, man, I'd do anything."

I suppose I didn't understand the true meaning of what I said at the time.

And work I did. All summer. I sweated and I learned. I rode the Life Cycle 40 miles a day. I pumped the Erectus Set until my chest felt like it was going to explode. I stroked for two hours a day on the Compu-Row. I worked myself up to 200 sit-ups a day.

By the end of summer, Sandy took me surfing. I didn't think I was coordinated enough, but he said I had finally developed the arm strength to propel myself onto a decent wave.

"You're looking good, dude. You're gaining weight in just the right areas," he said, slapping my ever-plumper butt, now tucked into shiny blue Speedos.

I put on my goggles, and as soon as I lugged my 10-footer out to the waves with Sandy we were cut off by a large, hot-pink board ridden by none other than the Greek Geek of the beach, Nick.

"Hey, man, this is the learning territory, get your ass out

of here," Sandy warned Nick. I turned my head so he wouldn't see me. I had my goggles on, and he didn't recognize me.

"Fuck off, you sun-fried moron," Nick snarled.

"Hey, I don't have to take that from you," Sandy replied.

I cringed. Once again, someone else was fighting my battles; I was the one who had been cut off.

Sandy caught a massive wave that was brewing up behind us. Nick stood up on his pink thing, and Sandy maneuvered his little green board around him as if it were a skateboard. He was a pro, there was no doubt about it. Nick was turning to slug Sandy, but the surfer cut back and was suddenly in front of him on the wave. It was great! Then, ever so delicately, Sandy reached over with his big toe and nudged Nick's board, sending him tumbling. Nick's board flew up in the air, and he swallowed some sea as he gargled on a scream. Sandy surfed out the wave as I and other spectators on the beach cheered him. Nick didn't look at me or anyone else as he flopped out of the water, seaweed in his hair. He flexed his superdeveloped body and slinked to shore.

I was always jealous of Nick. I can't imagine how he developed so well. He had a hairy chest in junior high. He had a slight moustache in high school. He could crush a full Budweiser between his elbows. And his arms were so strong that he punched holes in the sides of Toyotas. He had thighs that were smooth and big as trees. It wasn't fair. It just wasn't fair. I hated him so much. It's a kind of hate that builds inside you.

Summer turned to fall, we started school again and I kept working out. I jogged miles. I ate only healthy foods, even during the holidays: salads, protein, no fats, vitamin supplements, oat bran, lots of grain, seaweed tablets, some horrible green stuff mixed with water every morning, and a chocolate Nutri-Pump milkshake at night.

I entered the Honolulu Marathon in January, something my family thought was crazy. I trained with Sandy's help.

During the race, I felt my body really click into gear. I

could feel how much control I had as the sweat trickled down the ever-growing crease in the center of my chest. The droplets plunked off each developing ripple in my stomach. I reveled in the fact that my T-shirts were so tight they'd rip as I flexed my shoulders. My thighs were so wedged into my shorts, I had crease marks for days. I passed Nick at the marathon. He didn't even look at me. He was heaving. He was hurting. I sprinted by.

I finished 42nd. Not bad for a beginner, with more than 12,000 people in the running.

I could feel my testosterone pumping inside of me as winter turned to spring. My worked-up glands triggered something and I could feel that adrenaline just surge through my blood and ooze into my muscles. My arms were wide and wiry with veins poking the hot blood through them. My legs were thick and meaty. My buns protruded in a round, fleshy mass. All this time I wasn't thinking about sex, I wasn't thinking about girls. However, as I became increasingly aware of my body I also became increasingly horny.

Masturbation suddenly became enjoyable. Very enjoyable. I stared at myself in the mirror for hours, holding my super-erection as I flexed my new muscles. I bought a full-length mirror and sometimes I took it off the wall and laid it next to me on my bed. I'd rub my crotch up against that mirror image. I had a great body. I used to be ashamed of masturbating, especially when only a few dribbly drops of jism fizzled out of my cock. But now I was proud of my rugged, strong hands grasping the blood-red poker between my smooth, strong thighs. I learned how to squirt high enough to hit my own eye in the mirror. Masturbation became a reward for a day of tough working out with the guys at the Coral Reef Gym.

Learning about my body was such an experience: the *femoris,* the tibias, the rectus. As Sandy rattled off the names of the muscles, it sent a chill up my spine.

"OK, you need to develop your *vastus externus* here," he said, gripping my thighs. My palms twitched and my heart leapt. *Wow!* I thought to myself. *It's the same tingling sensation as when I masturbate.*

Sandy taught me about the deltoids, the biceps, the pecs. He worked on my gluteus maximus and showed me how to isolate my *latissimus dorsi*.

"Man, you're doing great! You've become a stud!" Sandy squeezed my bulging bicep.

I had to admit I was proud. It had almost been a year of working out, and I unbelievably and totally looked superb. Charles Atlas, Johnny Weismuller, Arnold Schwarzenneger, and Lou Ferrigno look out! Kam was back, and he was all man.

I was obsessed with my muscles, and it paid off. But now what? Sandy had the answer.

"Look, guy, there's this contest for Stud of the Summer at the beach next week, and I think you've got a great shot at it."

"That's ridiculous," I said seriously.

"C'mon, you've got to enter," Sandy insisted. "That muscle dude, Mario, the porno king's going to enter, and a few fat frat kids from the college, and then there's Nick. C'mon, Nick's got the odds beat with that kind of competition. You're the only one who could give him a run for the title."

"Nick's entering?" I said with a grin.

It took even more training. Although I was up to 197 pounds, that extra 100 didn't figure when I was still a 97-pound weakling on the inside. I worked on my walk.

"Hips out, legs apart, chest up, groin out, now strut your stuff," Sandy coached.

I tried. He groaned. I walked like a geek.

"Take your underwear off; do it naked."

I hesitated, then ripped them off.

"Now follow your cock," he insisted. "Stick it out as far as it will go and let the rest of your body just follow."

I followed his instructions as my bulbous head bobbed

under a subtle erection. The more I walked like Sandy said to, the harder my cock got. I looked in the mirror and saw the sexy effect. Yeah, I looked good. Real good.

"You got it, dude," Sandy said. "You got this contest wrapped up."

Twelve guys lined up in front of the screaming crowd at the beach that weekend. We posed and shined for them as girls squealed and cooed.

Nick was well-oiled and shiny. He looked great. He had a slightly hairier chest than me, and his ripples were still a bit more defined, but he'd developed a slight pudge. He never noticed me. He never noticed anyone but himself.

Suddenly, it was down to the final three. They named me, Nick, and Mario Puzzi, who's held the title for years. Mario claims he's a famous Italian porn star, but his real name is Fred. Anyway, we three finalists had 40 minutes to prepare for the last round.

Back in the showers, Sandy oiled me up all over.

"You're holding your poses great, dude, the girls are screaming for you, man." Sandy squeezed the lotion into my throbbing hips. "You're really going to score after this. They'll be all over you."

Score? I wasn't thinking about scoring. I just wanted to beat that fucking asshole Nick the Greek. I wanted to pulverize his face in the sand, and if I couldn't do it literally I'd humiliate him with all his friends watching. The guy was such a self-centered twit he still hadn't even recognized me.

Sandy left me to get myself psyched up. He joined the crowd outside, hitting on the best of the feminine litter out there. The other two contestants came in. Mario introduced himself to me. I shook hands as we all stood there naked, ready to put on our tight suits for the final round.

Nick stood in front of the mirrors and flexed his muscles as he watched himself. I saw his cock stiffen as he pleased

himself with the way he looked. Without even touching anything below his navel, his cock grew. Mario and I watched.

He looked over at me and smiled as he noticed I was
watching. Then he did a double take. His cock plummeted.

"You! YOU! Kam, what the FUCK are YOU doing here!
How—"

"Hey, calm down, man," Mario warned.

"I can't believe it!" Nick said, clenching his fists as hard as
he clenched his teeth. "How did you do it? What did you do
to yourself? You're a scrawny worm! How the fuck?"

"Hey, ease up, man, I'm getting the judges," Mario said as
he grabbed a towel and took off.

Nick grabbed me roughly. Then he shook me. His grip
loosened as he marveled at how strong my arms felt in his
grip. He could see how tight and stiff I was.

I grabbed him back and let all my rage rip into him. I
knocked him down, and the bench near us crashed into splin-
ters. I leapt on top of the hairy torso and we fumbled with
each other, rolling on the floor, knocking things off the sink
and counters above us.

"I hate you, Nick Kanelos! I've hated you most of my life!
There's no one in the world I hate more than you!"

"You runt, you're a fucking wimp," he snarled as he
heaved under the weight of my armlock.

"This is why I did it, you jerk! This is why I worked so
hard!" I cranked him into a vicious thumbhold and he just
crumbled. He was in my complete control. "I wanted to
shove your face into the ground."

With that I forced his nose into a shower drain and held it
there while he squirmed. Suddenly, a wave of ecstasy swam
over me. Revenge. The unbelievable aphrodisiac of revenge. I
had spent my youth dreaming of it, a year of intensive physi-
cal strain working toward it. In one moment every ounce of
teen angst I carried with me was released. Suddenly other
thoughts flooded into me: Sandy's flawless smooth body, the

pecs and delts I'd seen all these months on so many men; Dr. Frankenfurter's song from *The Rocky Horror Picture Show*— "In Just Seven Days I Can Make You a Man"; the half-naked physiques I studied laboriously in magazines and books as I picked out the man I wanted to be—or was it the man I wanted? It overwhelmed me. I turned Nick over and his green eyes faced me, looking scared.

I straddled him and grabbed both sides of his face and kissed him. It wasn't just any kiss—I shoved my tongue deep between his lips. I invaded him. It was wild! I'd never thought of doing something like that, at least not consciously. My dick was standing straight up as I sat on his chest. And Nick wasn't resisting me. In fact, his tongue was toying with my tongue.

He was welcoming it.

Without a word he let his head sink lower and lower until I felt his tongue lick the slit of my dick. For a second, I thought he was going to bite it—but no. Then he touched my balls and guided my stiff hard-on between his lips. "Ohh," he groaned.

What is he doing!? I wondered. *Doesn't he know how much I hate him? Doesn't he know I'll tell everyone he's a faggot! Doesn't he...* But I couldn't think anymore. I was in bliss. My body was being caressed and explored by his strong hands. One hand touched my chest, the other landed between my legs and probed my buttocks. I felt his lips reach all the way to the base of my dick and he breathed in the scent of my hairs. His tongue licked the twitching underside of my dick as I groaned with him.

"You're wonderful! You're my dream come true," Nick whispered to me.

I was shocked. I was mortified. Kam the Mockery of a Man was his dream? I melted.

"Fuck me, you man of steel. Pierce my ass," he begged. He spread his legs and hunched himself over the fallen bench. I could see the drool spilling from his lips to the floor. And at the other end of his body his throbbing, stiff cock had a long stream of ooze dribbling out that stretched down to the tile floor.

I tugged a few times at my dick. It didn't need to get any harder. I held the base and guided it into one of the hottest holes I would ever hit. I could feel him squeeze his buns together as he ached for my pole. He really wanted me. He desperately wanted me. He had such control of me as he milked my dick in his ass. I plunged into him harder and harder. He screamed and squirmed and writhed.

"I love you!" he screamed. "You're fantastic! You're a god!"

I came in explosions, splattering his insides, and as I pulled out I heaved even more come all over his balls. He swirled the cream around his own rod and in two quick jerks squirted so hard he hit me in the eye.

We laughed. We rolled down on the floor next to each other and just howled.

I went off to college, and Sandy got interested in the phallic arts and came to the same school. I left Nick behind, but when I graduated with all my sexual knowledge I was bigger, smarter, and even more of a catch. Nick had waited for me.

For five years, Nick and I were lovers. We lost the contest that day, by the way. Mario told the judges we were fighting and they disqualified us. While Nick and I were in our major throes of passion for the first time, Mario was collecting our Stud of the Beach honors. But that's OK. I finally won the title when I came back the year after I graduated, then I bowed out of the running and Nick won the year after that. Mario's a tired porn star, still getting it up in videos with Viagra, no doubt. His body fell apart.

Everyone knew about Nick and me. We lived together, we romanced together, and we surfed in tandem. We were not ashamed in the least. Our openness really pissed off Connie. It also somewhat surprised my very straight friend Sandy.

Poor Sandy. I suppose I was really very much in love with him, but I'm glad nothing ever happened between us. We were too much like brothers, and still are.

I dumped Nick eventually. He was just too infatuated with me. It was too one-sided. He let his body slip and got fat. I got bored with him pretty quick. He was devastated when I left to come back to work at the school.

A few months ago back home, I was walking the beach when I saw Connie with some scrawny dude. I walked over to her and she called me a shit. Teasingly, I kicked sand at her. The scrawny dude just smiled and gulped. She started screaming at him—not me.

After Sandy graduated, he became a lifeguard on the beach. So on that perfect sunny day, he was working and heard Connie screaming. He came over to see what all the commotion was and I introduced him to her. Somehow, it was love at first sight. After a few short months, they got married. I was their best man. How appropriate, since Sandy helped make me the best man I ever was. And Connie helped me realize I was a man's man.

As for that scrawny, wimpy dude who was with Connie...well, he's cute. I'm working with him to develop his body. I'm not picky. I like a challenge and am willing to train a man from the beginning.

Who better than me to break him in?

SHOW AND TELL

I was so primed when I heard Kam's story, it gave me extra enthusiasm for my class the next day.

I was rather pumped to find out about Kam's new boy toy he stole from Connie, who turned out to be Aaron Rymer, the skinny redheaded kid from my class.

Dean Richie had backed way off and was letting me do whatever I wanted with my class. The Board of Trustees and Terms of Management (BOTTOMs) seemed to approve anyway, and many of them watched the videotapes of classroom activities—only as a precaution, of course.

But I was also aware of the renewed connection between Connor and his father (thanks to me), and that made me equally aware that Lance and Connor were potential spies for Dean Richie if he were ever to start up a campaign against me again.

I felt safe for now. I enjoyed living on campus. My partner, John, was away in China for the first few months of the school year, so I was forced to find distractions on campus.

The students served that purpose well.

"All right, boys," I said, loving to call them "boys" and get away with it. "Let's hear it. Today I want to hear about the biggest cocks you've come across in the past week."

I walked over to my desk and saw that Scott, the B+ student who eagerly sat in the first row, had put a shiny red apple on my desk again. I looked over at the guy with the big brown eyes and the yellow cap he always wore backward, and I smiled. He flashed a smile back.

"I thought about you last night," he announced rather loudly in front of the entire class.

"That's nice, Scott, I thought about you too," I smiled back, not saying that I jerked off to this stud almost every night. "I thought about how poorly you did on your masturbation quiz last week."

The class laughed. It frustrated me, because I knew Scott was a far better student than his grades were showing. I knew there was more behind those doe-like eyes than he was revealing.

It was cute that he had a bit of a teacher's crush on me, but I was ignoring my own feelings. I didn't want to call on him first.

"All right, you know how important it is to understand cock size throughout history," I started out, sounding very professorial. "The measuring of European cocks over the past century has required that they increase condom sizes there. Also, recent statistics prove that men identifying as homosexual seem to have larger penises than their heterosexual counterparts. OK, who's going first?"

A shy kid in the back of the class raised his hand, and I pointed him out. He stammered but smiled as he spoke, saying, "I met this guy, very cute and skinny—well, I guess my Mom would say 'lanky'—and it was the other day, off campus. He had black hair and the bluest eyes you could ever imagine. His eyes totally got to me, and I invited him back to my place at the dorms. Well, after talking and drinking a beer, we started to make out. It was kind of like he was on top of me, and we were really getting into it. As we made out, we began to feel each other up, and I was in total shock when I got to his cock. I mean the tent this guy made had room enough for a family of six and the dog. I got him naked, and it was really fat and quite long. I wanted to measure it but I didn't want to break the mood or sound stupid."

"*Hands,* son, how many *hands* was it?" I said, putting my fist over fist. I taught them that last class, how to estimate without a ruler.

"Oh, that's easy, it was a 3-hander," he said, looking at his hands and then taking out his tape measure. "I suppose he was nearly a foot long!"

The class laughed as a cocky blond boy in the back piped up. "One cock I had the other day was a 12-incher for real, and easily 8 or 9 inches around. I sucked on him until my jaw ached. Later, he fucked me, and he went extremely slow until he got it in, then he plowed me hard and fast."

As the class grew a bit restless, I smiled at how wonderful it was for them to open up so freely about their gay experiences. Most of them, like Scott, considered themselves straight—and loved pussy—but they didn't mind assignments like this, where they were to find a large cock.

I saw Scott staring at my crotch as I walked through class. He allowed his zipper to slide open again, and I saw his blue underwear with white polka dots. I tried not to react and called on Don, the A-student in the front row.

"I have no idea how many inches it was, but at the hospital where I work I went to catheterize a patient and when I pulled the sheet down I found a fat, uncut black beauty that extended past his knees. Even while he was asleep he got hard! Men and women came from all over the med center to get a look at it. A 4¼-hander, and stiff for hours. I know this sounds like fiction, but I swear to God it is the truth."

Then Yuri, the Russian exchange student, said, "One of my new friends took me down into the city of L.A., where there was an underwear party. I joined in, as I was adventuring with another lad or two. Suddenly down come his shorts and out pops this...this Sputnik missile, or something. Huge. I estimate conservatively, at least 11 inches, and rock-hard. Needless to say, I forgot about our other playmates and set to applying my oral skills to him. I must have done well, aside from the evidence of an eventual splooge-soaked chest, because he was sending folks over my way the rest of the night by saying that *This Soviet guy over there gives the most incredible head job.* I did my best to live up to expectations, but after him my jaw was quite tired. I think the next day I could barely open my mouth."

The class applauded. Yuri stood up and took a bow while Don slipped a piece of paper over to him, obviously with his phone number on it.

Lance smiled. He was now enrolled as part of the class, and would give demonstrations when I asked. But he had a story this time, and Connor looked nervous.

"I've met someone who has quite the thickie too. Not superlong, but a fattie, and he was a short little guy so it looked even bigger. Probably explains why I stayed the top. Anything that made my mouth *that* happy wasn't about to get shoved anywhere else—ouch."

Connor had kicked him under the desk.

"He's 6⅛ inches," said Lance, rubbing his shin.

"6½!" said Connor proudly. "And 8 inches around."

In the back, a normally quiet lad said, "There's a guy in my dorm who is always called 'Tripod'—but we never call him that to his face. He is gay, by the way, and I did see him naked this past week. Tripod is a fair-skinned northern European type. His dick doesn't even look like it belongs to him. It has a very sinister look to it—with darker skin than his balls or his thighs. I saw him in the showers and I tried to get him to stroke it for me, but he didn't seem interested. It's over 10 inches soft, to be sure—and thick too. He is very proud of the thing. He never wears underwear, so his tripod is very visible hanging down his left leg."

Another guy in the back stood up, with an obvious boner in his pants.

"I was on the Net in a chat room while my roommate Zeke was asleep in the same room. He's 5-foot-9, about 135 pounds, a German Filipino with green eyes, very cute but very hetero."

"That's what they all say," piped up Lance, and I shushed him.

"So I'm talking to my regular Internet jack-off buddy, LuvJackN, and he's sending me a picture of his 8-incher and telling me how guys gag on it and can't deep-throat it well enough. So I have my dick out and it's hard and I'm writing him back that I'm taking a class in Deep Throat Techniques and I'm getting an A+ in it, and he's asking me why I don't try to seduce my straight roommate, who's snoring up a storm."

"Like that isn't every guy's fantasy in college," smiled Connor.

"So I'm insisting that I wouldn't gag on LuvJackN's 8 inches, even though he's telling me he's 6 inches around, and he's wishing I would be sucking on his cock, kissing it, and he's talking about loving to take cocks down *his* throat too. He says he's premed. My roommate is a Peni-Psych major."

I saw Scott squirming in his seat and turning beet-red. Hmm...I recalled from the class roster that Scott was premed. The 8 inches is what I wondered about. See, Scott was shy during classroom jerk-offs.

"So, I'm stroking my dick at the computer while this guy is telling me about his 8 inches, plus giving me advice about how I could make it with my roommate. I'm stroking away, stroking away, when suddenly I turn around and there's a big stiff boner in my face. My roommate's reading over my shoulder."

Scott piped up, "So what did he say?"

"Well, Zeke's standing there all hard and I'm telling him I have this class assignment to find a long cock and so I ask him if I can measure it and he says he's never measured his before. So I measured it, and it was 9 inches."

"And you wrote that back to LuvJackN?" Scott queried.

I got suspicious about Scott's questions.

"Yeah, and he says, 'OK, prove that you can take 9 inches,

right now.' So I asked Zeke if I could do that and he let me try and it was great."

"And you don't know who LuvJackN is?" I asked.

"No, but I'd like to thank him for opening up my world to Zeke!" laughed the shy guy.

The class was finally taking an interest. The discussion was having the effect I'd hoped. They were paying attention and taking notes. Scott kept his eyes on me as I felt my loins press against my pants.

A guy with longish blond hair—a bit like mine—wanted to take his turn telling a hot story. "I was down at the Venice Boardwalk early Sunday morning and I met these two guys who were obviously cruising me. They must have thought I was a surfer dude 'cause of my hair, and they asked if they could suck me off. I told 'em only if I could suck them both at the same time. They flashed me by pulling their pants down. They had these two big white cocks that I wanted coming in my blond hair. They said they liked my shorts and they could see my hairy balls hanging out."

This story had turned on some of the guys in class. I saw a few hands reaching for zippers as the long-haired student continued. "One of the guys said he had 8 inches, and I told him I wished mine were that big but I couldn't stretch it out that far. And when I saw both of their dicks, I realized how big they were and dropped down on my knees right there in this alley off the boardwalk and took both of them. They almost smothered me. I couldn't breathe with both of them stuffed in my mouth."

"Windpipe, don't clog the windpipe, just a tip of the neck and you could've handled them fine," I instructed. "Do you have a chance to try it again with them?"

"Yeah, maybe at the gym—we all go to the same one. That's when I like to go in the shower and let the straight guys watch me play with myself under the spray nozzle."

"I do that too," said Lance. "I let guys watch me at the

urinal, because I have a big dick and I guess guys like to see how my dick hangs big even when I'm pissing." Lance looked at me as if I knew, and I did.

"Dude, take advantage of that!" came a cry from the back.

"It's hard to hide," added Connor. "I love pissing, but I'm pee-shy. Still, having guys watch me is such a turn-on."

Next Aaron Rymer, the redhead who was slowly coming out of his shell, opened up with his own story.

"I was in the gym and this guy had on a wet jockstrap with a monster cock so big it could barely stay inside," said the kid who usually hated to talk in class. "He had big bollocks, and he asked me to suck it right there through the wet jockstrap, and it smelled so nice. I never thought I'd be into that kind of thing. Well, this guy was 5 inches across, with a large, fat head, and he had a big piece of leathery foreskin to chew on that slid out past the jock. But the guy wouldn't unleash his cock so I could wank it or suck it freely. He insisted I suck through the sweaty wet jockstrap, licking up the shaft through the elastic. I could still taste the juice through it, though. That jock was full of precome! And I swear to God, his head was the size of a lightbulb."

Eric Chun, the big Asian kid, whistled in the back. He wanted to go next, but Aaron wasn't done.

"I probably would have choked on it if it wasn't all wrapped up tight like that anyway," Aaron said, pushing his crotch against the table. "I just rubbed it with my face, my chin, and my tongue till I felt his spunk shoot all inside the jock. He said he wanted to meet with me again someday, and I said, 'Only if I can save your jockstrap.' I still have it in my room, under my pillow in a plastic baggie."

"Very good! Don't be afraid to describe these liaisons in detail," I urged. I wondered if Aaron was talking about my old friend Kam Likikime, because I knew Kam also had a jockstrap fetish, and his big balls and thick, uncut cock sounded exactly as I remembered.

"OK, I got one," said Eric Chun as if auditioning for a

play. "There's this guy on campus who acts like he's part of the wealthy elite, and he has this pair of stretch shorts that show off his perfect ass and rippling thighs when he jogs across campus every morning. He has a terrific torso that you can easily see when he's wearing his baby blue loose tank top, and I've masturbated to him a number of times. He's at least 6-foot-2 and hasn't an ounce of fat. When he runs the sweat glistens over his body, and he displays a nice bulge. I followed him to the bathroom in the center of the quad yesterday and saw him at the urinal. He had to totally peel off his tight pants, so I could see his beautiful butt cheeks with no tan lines. He had a growth of dark hair coming up out of his crack that spread up over his waist a bit."

The class became very horny as Eric Chun stood up on his chair and whipped out his cock as he talked. I didn't bother to stop any of the extracurricular activity that was taking place under the desks.

"His naked body was so handsome, so perfect, so virile, and so desirable that I nearly shot my wad just standing next to him," Eric continued. "I shivered, and he reached over to fondle my bulge then walked us over to the sinks and put each of our crotches under warm running water, where he fondled our dicks, his and mine, one in each hand, and we watched in the mirrors in front of us. The streaming water washed over our cocks, and then he bent over to slowly nuzzle his face in my genitals."

Size, Eric, size! I didn't want to break the rhythm, particularly because Scott had his hand down his jeans, and it was well past the waistband of his blue and white polka-dotted undies.

"He was an even 7. I could tell from oral calculations. Anyway, I moaned as he stood up, and I felt our naked skin sliding and slipping against each other in a bone-breaking surge of passion. He sent shivers of excitement all over my body as he worked on my engorged manhood."

The class giggled; it sounded like he was reading from really bad porn fiction.

"My whole body shivered as he taunted me with his talented tongue. I felt my head slide against the soft roof of his mouth while his tongue rubbed along the underside, causing me to shake all over with this explosive orgasm."

The class laughed and applauded. By now Lance and Connor were leading about six guys in a corner in a mutual circle jerk. Some of the other guys were more shy, still rubbing their hard-ons still inside their pants—like Scott.

"Then it was my turn to service him, and that's when I made my estimate of his hard-on, as we learned in class," Eric smiled and nodded proudly to himself. I checked off his name in my book.

"This past weekend," said a guy who had his hard-on out of his pants and stroked as he talked, "I was staying at my parents' and my sister's friend and her boyfriend stayed overnight, and I could hear them getting it on in the next room. I stood outside their door and jerked off while they were moaning, and then I heard him fumble and he walked out into the hall."

"Caught, dude. What did you do?" Lance asked.

"I tried to put my cock back in my pj's, but he noticed. He was only looking for a condom anyway, but then he pulled me into the bathroom and asked if I would relieve him. 'Sure,' I said. I figured it was the least I could do. Then he asked me if I'd ever seen anything like what he had. I sure hadn't. It was truly impressive—an 11-incher. He told me guys appreciate his cock more than girls. He let me stroke it and, I swear, we had all four of our hands on that cock and there was still room for more. After he came, he said she was probably asleep by then anyway and he wouldn't need a condom after all."

A jock in the back stood up and rubbed his flat hand over his bulge as he unbuckled his pants and joined in the open crotch-massage. "I love to stand naked and stroke off at night on the front porch of our frat house. There's enough illumination from a nearby streetlight so that someone on the footpath or in a car passing on the cul-de-sac can see me if they take a good look. I squirt my load of jism over into the plants while guys watch and jack off in their cars at the same time. This past weekend, one of the neighboring frat guys was standing over by a tree, and he looked like at least a niner. Used both his hands, easy. But my fellow frat brothers are a mystery. I don't know how big any of them are."

"None of them do it with you?" I asked.

"No, and it's too damn bad," said the jock, as his hard-on sat in his open hand.

"That's it, class. Everybody on your feet. Now get in a circle. We're going to reenact an old-fashioned tradition. There are 12 specific kinds of circle jerks traced throughout history. There are circles like the Helping Hand, where each guy reaches over to jerk the dick on his right, and the All the Way, which ends up in a round suck and anal penetration session."

As we stood in a circle with our cocks out of our pants—my cock out and hard too—we stroked ourselves, and some of the guys let other guys stroke them too. Scott was shy and stayed back, his hand still down his blue underwear.

"This is the classic Basic Circle Jerk, a right of passage, a tradition," I said. "Often guys egg each other on to come first. Some want simultaneous orgasms, some use it just to measure the biggest among them. This is not a strictly homosexual ritual."

"I'll say. I've never done this before," Lance said.

"How many of you guys have never done this before?" I asked.

About half of the guys raised their hands. I noticed most of the straight guys didn't raise their hands, proving that many heteros do have circle jerks amongst themselves in their early years.

"Well, well, first time for everything, now let's hold off

until we're all close. OK, let's go."

Fat cocks, long cocks, skinny weenies, 2-handers, 2-fingers, all were out and stroking. One guy tried to get on his knees and take my boner between his lips, but I yanked him up.

"No sucking, just stroking—at least this time," I ordered. "Another variation of this is the All Hands on Dick, where guys all put their hands on one guy's dick to get each off one at a time. There's also the Long Distance, where we see who can shoot the farthest."

After about 20 minutes of intense jacking off in relative groaning silence, I said, "All right, it looks like we can do it soon. Let's all get close. Feel that come build up in your balls, stroke deep. All right, come!"

I burst forth in a big explosion and my jizz shot across three rows of desks and hit poor Aaron Rymer. That set off a chain reaction of young come-shots all over the room—about 20 of the 34 guys came at the same moment, while the others soon followed.

Just then the bell rang, and the guys gathered up their books and their pants and rushed out, leaving puddles all over the room.

I stuffed my cock back into my pants and smiled, but then I turned to Scott, who was still lingering with his jeans down at his ankles.

"Scott, can you stay after class?" I asked.

"Don't have a class until fourth period, so yeah. What's up, Professor?" He smiled, knowing my crotch was already twitching with another hard-on.

"I want to talk to you. Do you have a problem jerking off in class?" I asked. "You're the only one, including the shy guys and the straight guys, who is afraid to whip it out. And you have one of the best bodies in class, as far as I can tell. You need to be proud of it."

Scott simply said, "Fuck you!"

That made me mad. "OK, Scotty, you clean up all this

come, and then write on the board, 'I will play with myself in class' until it's all filled up."

"You've got to be kidding!" Scott said. "That's so kindergarten."

"Better do it by the time I get back," I said. I walked down the hall and stayed away for about 15 minutes, then went back into class, where Scott had peeled off his shirt and stood in his underwear and yellow cap. He'd disobeyed and written: "I will NOT play with myself in class."

I smiled at the irony.

"Scotty, I don't know why you're so belligerent. I know you're premed. I know you're smarter than this, so why do you act this way?"

Scott smiled an innocent but wicked smile and said simply, "I think you should spank me, teach. Maybe that would help me out."

I walked over, yanked his underwear down, and smacked his beautiful round bottom until each cheek was bright red. Only then could I see that he was getting a slight erection.

I thought the youth liked what I was doing, but I saw tears stream down his face.

"I've been bringing you an apple a day so you wouldn't make me jack off in front of everyone," Scott sobbed.

I put my arms around his beefy shoulders and hugged him. "But Scotty, you've got a nice body, you've got a beautiful ass, and your cock is perfect. You could be a great porn star if you wanted. What's the problem?"

Through his sniffles he said, "I can only come if I sing or whistle 'I've Been Working on the Railroad' while I'm jacking off."

"What?!" This took me by surprise. I'd heard about this sound sexual stimulation syndrome in Peni-Psych but had never met anyone with such a problem.

"I can't masturbate in front of someone because I can't ejaculate unless I'm singing that stupid song. That's why I'm LuvJackN on the Internet because I can sing at home while

I'm getting guys off on the computer," Scott said, still crying. "It sounds stupid, but it really bothers me."

"Oh, so that's it!" I went to my desk and pulled out a dildo. "Start whistling," I ordered.

He put his hands on his cock and began whistling, and his cock grew to about 7 inches pretty quickly. By the time he got to the "Dinah, won't you blow" part he was singing, and I went behind him and gently shoved the dildo up his crack.

Then I shoved the bright red apple he'd given me into his mouth so he could neither sing nor whistle, and he looked like a wide-eyed stuffed pig as I made the motion of the dildo go a bit faster and deeper inside his butt.

He looked uncomfortable at first, but his cock was still hard in his hands, and I kept working his butt as he bit down on the apple.

"Come for me, Scotty boy, come for me."

Scott shot huge gobs all over my desk. He spit out the apple and came some more. I removed the dildo, washed it at the sink, and plopped it back into my drawer.

"Wow, thank you, Professor Skee! Thank you!"

He slipped on his pants and scampered out of the classroom with a big smile on his face.

The next day and every day after that, in place of an apple I got a dildo left on my desk. I'd started a new tradition, and that was nice.

FRATERNIZING WITH MY BROTHERS

SEPTEMBER 15, 1989

My session with Scotty actually led to the creation of a monster. With his newfound sexuality he launched a career in gay adult video (even though he still considered himself straight). It helped put him through med school. I certainly enjoyed watching him work. In addition to his awesome cock, his love of dildo play while masturbating in front of people made him a natural porn superstar.

Scotty's bright-eyed innocence brought me back to the days when I first came to this campus and was deciding between the Ejaculation Enhancement and Potency Potential classes. I had no idea whether Creative Crotch-Shaving 101 and Cooking with Come courses were really necessary or just part of my own horny interests.

I was just entering the Sexology Social Studies section of the College of Carnal Knowledge, or COCK College, and was finally settled and happy with my pals in the Naked Dorm. It was a time of friendship and fraternity. Yes, that's right, fraternity. When I made the decision to pledge, I never thought I'd be accepted. Let me tell you, it was quite a rush.

I didn't really want to join a fraternity. Part of me was simply attracted to the idea of brotherhood they kept espousing in their posters and literature: handsome guys arm-in-arm, laughing, smiling, having fun together.

I used to walk past their houses, all on a row in a tiny cul-de-sac on campus, with their statues and Greek letters and those large windows I loved to linger at. It seemed like no matter what time of day or night I strolled by Frat Row, I'd catch a glimpse of a guy getting out of the shower and toweling himself off. Inevitably he'd jack himself off in front of the window.

Could I possibly fit in with all that?

"We want you to join, Mick. You're the kind of guy that would make our frat proud." Marlon Brandeis leaned over his Phi Kumma Lotta table in the quad and I could see his strong pecs jiggle through the crack of his T-shirt.

I knew Marlon from when I first moved into the Naked Dorm. He moved out shortly after I saw him in a compromising position with Stroker Palmer. Once he got into the frat house, we didn't see much of him anymore.

Besides his great pecs, one of the first things I noticed on Marlon was his big, protruding ears. His ears looked even bigger because of his short-cropped haircut that he always parted just perfectly, with every hair slicked back to perfection. He probably used the same gel as his daddy.

Marlon had a strong handshake. I knew he was a good student and pretty popular on campus. I was with my roommate, Joey, and I asked if he could pledge along with me. Marlon nodded but kind of winced.

"Sure, he could try, but I think *you're* more the caliber we're looking for." Marlon grunted and then whispered, "Joey's a bit too light, if you know what I mean."

Sensing the homophobic attitude I knew prevailed at these frat houses, I encouraged Joey to come out and pledge with me, if only to laugh in their faces and expose them as the homophobes they all were. Besides, I didn't want to go alone. Joey reluctantly complied.

That cool, mid-September night, on our way over to the three-story house with the lion statue out front, I couldn't stop gushing over Marlon.

"I think he's dreamy, don't you? He's gotta be at least 6-foot-7, and you know he's got those beautiful, bushy, brown eyebrows and these tight little lips that barely ever break into a smile," I swooned. "I've been watching him for a few weeks now, and he's cute."

"Honey, listen to you. You act as if you have a chance scoring with this frat boy," Joey laughed. "So, he has big ears. So, that means he's got a big schlong. But so what? He's straight. He was only diddling his roommate because he gets an occasional hard-on, so please don't get all goo-goo over a straight frat boy. But I think he has a big dick, let's bet."

Maybe, maybe not, I thought, *but it really doesn't matter.* He did wear baggy pants, so it was hard to gauge the bulge.

As we walked up to the Phi Kumma house it looked like Tara from *Gone With the Wind,* except instead of hoop skirts everyone wore sheets. I saw a few drunken guys on the porch in bedsheets and slapped my forehead, remembering that it was a toga party.

"Come on, boys, you didn't come dressed," boomed Marlon from the doorway. He stood there in a toga that was held up by a gold tassel, and his bare, muscled chest revealed a bit of hair. He stooped over as Joey eyed him up and down, then he led us upstairs.

"We're weeding out the pledges we think we like, and frankly not many of them can hold their liquor very well," he laughed. "Here, strip down and tie this around you."

He threw us some sheets and stood there as we looked at the room full of clothes and shoes. He headed for the bathroom but left the door open in full view of the two of us as we stripped. I could see the stream of yellow piss arch up as he relieved himself, but I couldn't see much more.

I clumsily tied my toga around my waist. Joey kept floundering with his, so Marlon helped us tie it up right. Suddenly, Marlon reached down, grabbed my crotch through the sheet, and said, "No underwear, right? Good."

As we went out to join the others in the frat house, Joey

turned to me and whispered, "I thought you said they were all straight."

After an hour or so of touring the house and meeting the other guys—most of them very frat-boyish cute—they cut the music. I spotted my old lab partner Victor Nichols, the expert crotch-size estimator. Victor was pledging too, and he bragged that by the end of the night he'd know exactly how big Marlon was. Little did we know! Then the guys lined up the pledges, introducing us one by one.

Blond, handsome Paul Masters, the House Master, explained that tonight the pledges had to "give it their all." As each pledge was named, his toga was tugged off him and he stood there naked in front of everyone. Joey just let his hard-on poke right out at attention, while Victor covered his nakedness quickly, and the three Latinos who had come together stood in mortified embarrassment. When my toga was unleashed, I had a half-hard boner, and I noticed a slight curl in Marlon's lip, as if he approved.

Next, each of us was led to one of the many spacious window ledges of the Georgian-style frat house. There, on every ledge, sat a keg of beer and a big wooden bucket.

"This is our gargoyle game," Paul explained. "You gotta fill up the bucket while you perch out here all night."

"What the fuck?" asked Joey as he was led off to his window. I stood out on a ledge and looked down about 15 feet below, then at the bucket next to me. Marlon poked his head out the window and nodded at me.

"You can piss and come in it. Just keep drinking the beer and fill up the bucket!"

I was mortified and ready to jump back in the window and call it a night, but down below, guys from other parts of campus and Frat Row were cheering us on. I saw Victor unleash his pee into a bucket as the guys whooped and hollered.

Talk about pee-shyness! This seemed like a good opportunity for me to overcome my biggest fear. If I could do this, I'd never be shy at the urinals again. I drank till my whole gut was filled with bad beer, but my cock stayed almost fully hard anyway.

I stood in front of the bucket and strained. Nothing came out. How embarrassing.

Finally, I let it rip and gushed all over the bucket. I couldn't stop. Once I paused for a second, then another flood of piss came splashing out all over my hard-on. The guys below cheered and waved.

"Go, Mickey!"

I wagged my cock at them.

I was up there a few hours, bored and getting cold as the crowd below passed out either on the grass, the benches, or over the lion statue. Some retired to their warm beds. A few of the drunken pledges slipped off their window ledges, their falls broken by the bushes or by frat guys waiting to catch them down below. Joey, Victor, at least two of the Latinos, and a few other guys—including me—kept on at our perches, naked and drinking.

I saw Marlon and Paul standing at a window: two long-bodied, bleary-eyed masculine specimens. I could see the outline of their cocks under their drooping sheets. As Joey had predicted, Marlon was huge, even in his state of half-arousal. Paul was no less huge, though fully aroused. It was a sight to see.

"Let's see ya come, Mickey," Marlon shouted. "I wanna see ya come into that bucket."

Before the request was even finished, I had my hand over my cock, slicking it up with stale beer. Marlon and Paul watched from the window as I rubbed myself to orgasm and shot straight into my bucket. I looked over and watched Marlon and Paul step away from the window arm in arm, then I plopped down next to my keg and my bucketful of piss and jism. And I passed out.

The next morning I was warm and naked in my bed, not

really sure how I got there, when I heard Joey pounding at our door.

"They left us out there naked! We were in a cow pasture, naked, tipping over cows. I never heard of anything so stupid, but we were knocking over cows while they were asleep, and then those assholes drove off and left us there! I didn't have my keys."

I was a bit bleary-eyed and hungover, but I laughed.

"We had to hitchhike without a stitch of clothing on, and this trucker picked us up. There were six of us, and he wanted to suck us all off, but Victor distracted him by letting him do him, and I just got away from that scene fast. Ugh. Why couldn't they just spank us all and get it over with? Why'd they have to do this?"

I didn't have an answer but figured none of us filled our buckets enough to become a Phi Kumma Lotta. That night, still nursing a hangover, I heard Joey answer the door. It was about midnight, the lights were off, and I was just getting ready to conk out. Suddenly, I felt a bag go over my head and two pairs of strong arms pick me up and lift me out of bed.

"You go, Mickey. Looks like you got in!" Joey said as they kidnapped me out of the room.

When the sack was taken off my head, I found myself in the basement of the frat house with dramatically lit torches all around and seven other pledges on the floor with me in front of a naked line of frat boys. Their bodies gleamed with slick oils and the firelight from the torches made them seem even more imposing.

Paul spoke. "Welcome, pledges. You have made it past our first round and now you must pass our most important test. You will learn our greeting, and you will learn about each of us intimately."

The frat boys filed in front of us, grabbing us one by one by our cocks. They groped us gently from the underside, and told us their names as they did so. When Marlon got up to me, he winked, stroked my stiffening rod, and said, "Marlon Brandeis. You'll want to remember me."

A little dazed by the end of the line, I had a throbbing, dripping cock pointed upward to the sky. A naked Paul clanged a gong, then total frenzy ensued as all the guys in the room sprang to action.

Marlon and Paul reached for my rock-hard cock and spread my legs gently. Marlon leaned over and whispered, "Remember how this feels, remember me." He covered his fat cock with lube and Paul slipped a condom over his dick. Paul licked my stomach and sucked on my neck while Marlon shoved into me.

I looked around and saw a hunk with an uncut cock pumping another pledge next to me as the pledge spewed a creamy load all over himself. I saw Victor in a corner being entered by a rather large African-American frat boy. It was Jake, from my dorm. Jake was a dancer, so his thrusts were powerful and graceful. Victor seemed to be really enjoying himself.

Come was flying everywhere as I got my ass ravaged by Marlon's monster and Paul shoved his shaft down my throat. His cock had a distinct downward curve that helped with deep-throating—but I didn't really have a choice about the angle of entry.

Across the room, Victor groaned as Jake gripped his butt and shoved in his impressive meat, and on the other side of the room I watched frat lads splash their loads on the back of a young pledge's ass and thighs.

The orgasms continued. A beefy, long-haired brunet approached Marlon and played with his hairy butt from behind as he kept riding me. Even with Marlon's cock inside me, I felt this brunet's fingers working my ass as he leaned over and said, "I'm Marshall, man. How are you? I like your cock."

He leaned over and licked the slit of my cock, which was straining high over my belly button. Just then, Marlon ripped off his condom, leaned back, and convulsed in a volcanic spew, shooting his gusher over my shoulder and right into Marshall's bushy hair.

I looked around the room full of athletic chests, buttholes, and curves as each guy introduced himself to me in this hypnotic frenzy. Allan, with the smooth shaved crotch; Jay, who looked vaguely familiar and sported a beautiful red hard-on that curved to the left; Stroker, with the fist-sized mushroom head; Eddie, with the cock that hangs halfway to his knees; Toro, with the squat cock and round butt; John, with the long cock and blue eyes. We were becoming a fraternal link of cocks and orifices, connected by moans, come-shots, fingers, mouths, and buttholes.

About 30 guys were having an all-out silent ritualistic sex orgy. Without even a slight "yeah" or "suck that dick," they dropped to their knees, taking mouthfuls of uncut cock, trimmed dickhead, and lubed-up matted butthole.

My cock was dripping with saliva as my mouth hungrily tasted every dick in sight. At one point, I had two tasty treats in my kisser at once and looked up to see Marlon and Paul tonguing each other's mouths as I serviced them both. Marlon's pursed lips turned to a smile as he gently swaggered his hips deep into my throat. I tried smiling back, but my mouth was quite full.

Guys all over the stone-rock basement were jerking themselves off and offering encouragement and cheers. A small group of them shot huge gobs of come over Victor's face. The two Latino pledges got kind of dog-piled, with the frat boys on top, in the center of the room, crawling, writhing, wriggling, and coming all over the place. Hands were all over me, on my cock, my tits, my thighs, in my twitching hole. I felt smooth pubes, a pink, puckering butt in my face, a cock slapping my shoulder. I buried my face into this perfect ass as the throbbing, beating, and humping continued.

We were one large, grunting, groaning, orgasmic fraternal organism.

My tongue dove into a butthole as I loosened my jaw and

let it go deeper. Then a gong sounded and the sticky men stood up in silence, all of us breathing heavily.

"Now for the moment of truth, the test of your observation," Paul said, as each of the pledges had dark blindfolds put over our eyes and were forced down to our knees.

"Now that you shared in our ritual," Paul said, "you must identify each of us as best you can."

One by one, the pledges were led out for the blindfold test. Still reeling with orgasmic spasms, I was worried and not sure I could do it. Still, I had to try.

When my name was called, I was led forward into a room, and I could feel the guys around me with their spent and quivering cocks.

"Identify whoever you can!"

I felt their bodies shuffling around me and I reached out with my hand to touch a few dicks. They were not hard, so it was going to be tough. But then I let my lips take over—and my nose—driving them into familiar pubic areas. Jay, Spike, Allan, and Toro I identified immediately.

I could smell the familiar bouncy butthole of John. I could taste the mushroom head of Stroker and the long slender cock of Eddie. Big Red's cock, with its two indentations, was a cinch. I pointed out Marshall, and of course Marlon, whose 2-hander still twitched from pummeling my hole. Paul's fine cock was no problem to identify. And I was sure of about a dozen others in the group.

Dried-come smells, bush textures, and different bum tastes all helped me name the frat boys.

"You, Mickey, can now stand and be a part of us," Paul said as he pulled the blindfold off my head. "Stand here and let's see how the other remaining pledges do."

I smiled as I stood up and became a part of this select group. Marlon put an arm around me and whispered, "You know your cock, Mickey."

That I do. That I'm sure of.

BECOMING A SPECI-MEN

The Phi Kumma Lottas got into a lot of trouble for their nasty gargoyle game. Marshall and Allan took a select group from the frat and broke off into their own secret society called the O Boys.

All the most important Phi Kumma members—Jake, John, Spike, Toro, Marlon, Paul, Eddie, Stroker, Jay and many others—became regular members who got together for great sex.

Jake and Toro became dancers for Grammy-winning Baby M on her concert tours. Allan and Jay developed into fine actors. Marshall turned into a rock star. Eddie worked in movies. Paul and Spike became porn stars. John became a successful entrepreneur, and my boyfriend—but of course, we're not supposed to talk about that.

It was with this group that I developed the Mickey—a technique of masturbating with your balls stretched up to the head of your cock so you can stroke everything at the same time.

I was spending way too much time playing around with the guys and too much money on frivolous things like fraternity pledges. I remember when I ran out of money for necessities like condoms, lube, and dildos and was forced to consider the dreaded idea of becoming a Speci-Men lab rat.

Marlon needed extra cash and was doing it too, but the biggest incentive was that dreamy guy Vincent Lamaz.

I flipped to the middle of my diary, where my first semester as a sophomore at COCK College was recorded. Here's that diary entry....

I gulped as I walked up to the door reading "Speci-Men," but I knew this was a way I could get closer to Vincent. The thought of his straight brown hair, deep dark eyes, and olive skin helped me conquer my fear of exposing myself to the world. I took a deep breath and opened the door.

The same muscular, tattooed guy I used to see down at the Cryolab greeted me at the front desk. Steve was the guy who'd watched me masturbate into a cup, scrutinizing me with his dark eyes and perpetual sneer. After I filled out the financial aid forms in the sterile front office, Steve asked me some probing questions. I answered truthfully.

"We'll probably use you in some of the advanced courses. That way you won't be embarrassed about being worked on by some of your peers," Steve said rather stiffly. "You donated at the Cryolab, so we know your sperm count is adequate. You will have to remain unemotional and cooperative, never speaking to the guys in the lab unless they ask you something. As far as they're concerned, you're a lab rat, a cadaver, an experiment."

Steve put it rather coolly. It was more frightening than I'd even imagined. This was going to be much harder work than simple nude modeling. It paid better, though. Sure, some of the guys had to pose with hard-ons for a long time in the Erect Art classes, and a few were required to keep stiff for hours in the Phallic Sculpture courses, but this was Penile Biology. The real tough stuff.

"It separates the men from the boys," smiled Steve. "Now take your pants off."

I hesitated for a second, but he hurried me along. "Don't be shy. There's no time for that. If you're not sure about this, you better get out now."

Just then, the door opened and in walked Vincent. Standing absolutely naked with a raging hard-on, he used a small, yellow towel to wipe the perspiration on his bushy brows and the small beads of sweat gathering on his chiseled chest. He smiled at me as I stood with my white Jockey shorts on, and I immediately sprang to attention.

"Hard day at Coitus Interruptus, eh, Vincent?" Steve winked.

"Yeah, they had their hands all over me and measured the thickness of my veins and my heart rate. But they didn't finish me off today," Vincent winced. "They're going to give me blue balls."

Steve saw that I was still half-dressed and ordered me to hurry up.

"New recruit?" Vincent asked, as if I weren't there. "Looks like he's got the qualifications."

I flushed beet-red as I noticed my white cotton briefs poking out toward the bronze god in front of me. My red mushroom head was slipping through slightly.

"This is Skee, Mickey. Number 69," Steve said. "Off with those, you need to jack off for me and let me time you. This ain't the Cryolab. We need quality now, not quantity."

"How cute. Hi, I'm number 96. Lamas, Vincenzo."

Standing there in my nakedness, I couldn't even croak out a hello. Steve handed me a plastic cup, and I held it in front of my erection.

"Here? Now?" I gulped. It wasn't Steve who made me nervous.

Steve clicked on a stopwatch. I could see Vincent's cock twitch ever so slightly as he dropped his towel to the floor.

"Mind if I watch?"

"No, whatever," Steve answered, ignoring my concern.

My cock drooped to half-mast as my hand cupped my hairy balls.

"We'll have to shave those balls, but they're nice, eh?" Steve remarked, inspecting them.

Vincent rubbed his own smooth ball sac as he watched me.

He put his other hand to his lips and then let his slicked hand rub the underside of his shaft.

I reached down and squeezed both my hands around my shaft. Both guys smiled as they watched the precome ooze quickly out of my mushroom head.

"Juicy guy here," Steve said. "He'll work good in the Precome Studies as well as the Sperm Count class."

Vincent began stroking with me from across the room, and I matched him stroke for stroke. He rubbed his left tit. I did too. He grabbed both his balls in one hand. I did too.

He shot a huge load into his hands. I did too.

Well, mine went into the cup. Steve scooped it up and slapped on a label. He clicked off the stopwatch.

"We'll have to train you to withhold the come-shot, and you can't be grunting and groaning so much," Steve said. "Come quietly!"

Vincent smiled as he picked up his towel and headed for the showers. "Yeah, you can't look like you're enjoying it."

My first day on the job as a Speci-Men was two days later, but before I was allowed to report to a class Steve ordered me to strip and then took a razor to my balls. He had me dunk them in cold water. Then with his lubed, gloved hand, he squeezed my shaft until I got hard. His nimble fingers worked over me delicately as he said, "It's easier to shave if the balls are tight and the shaft is hard."

Steve shaved me ever so delicately, including all the hairs around the shaft of my penis. I got real hard as I watched my hairy crotch disappear, and as Steve squeezed my shaft harder.

"Come for me, 69. Give me some of that juice," he grunted as he thrust his muscular body against mine. His grip was so tight I didn't think anything could even squirt out of my pee slit, but within a few massive squeezes of his manly hands my semen was gushing all over him.

"Good, now that I've already made you come once, you

won't come so fast in the class," he said. "Now go take a shower. You'll report to B-48 with Stroker, Marlon, and Vincent."

I was terrified. My cock drooped. Out of the showers walked Vincent, who grabbed a towel from his locker. He smiled shyly.

"First-day jitters?" Vincent asked.

I gulped and nodded.

"Don't worry, I'll be there with you," he smiled.

We were each lying on a comfortable table with cushions, totally naked with our cocks to the front, as the bell rang and the class walked in to B-48.

Marlon, who is Number 55, is the long-bodied, straight frat boy, with a broad nose and short brown hair. Stroker, Number 27, is shorter and heftier and has a thick cock.

Four guys surrounded each table. The instructor called us each by number. Four fairly cute guys stood around me, but I didn't pay any attention to them. I looked across the room at Vincent, who was staring back at me.

"In the flaccid state, the three sets of erectile tissues are readily visible, as we've studied. The *corpora cavernosa* on Number 27 and *corpus spongiosum* on Number 55 are particularly pronounced, and on Number 69 you can see how the *spongiosum* connects to the urethra."

I felt a strange hand move my limp penis as I kept my hands at my sides and four pairs of eyes stayed on me. Five pairs, if you counted Vincent. One of the guys tickled the underside of my cock head near the pee slit.

"With stimulation, note that the first change occurs in the lengthening of the organ, usually at up to 300 percent of the flaccid state."

They measured us like cattle. One guy monitored blood pressure and heart rate, one had a ruler along our cocks, and one had a device around it measuring the average circumference and cock contractions. They measured us soft, then squeezed our dicks using some lube.

Three cold hands rubbed over my slick cock. I looked over at Vincent, who had five hands on his stiffened, glistening rod. He was, after all, slightly bigger.

"Erections are a two-part process—first lengthening, then thickening—with the glans sending blood to the *spongiosum* tissues, manifesting in a hard-on. The degree of firmness depends on the amount of blood flow."

Marlon measured 6¼ inches long and 4½ inches around, a Long Normie. Stroker measured 5.1 inches long (the mean standard for most white males) and 6¾ inches around, a Fat Butch. Vincent, who had the only uncut cock, was an even 7 inches long and 6 inches around, and I came in a close second with 6⅞ inches and 6¼ inches around—we were called Scores. Those were the nicknames of our cock sizes, and that's how we all knew who measured up around campus. I wondered about the guys who were working on me, but I couldn't tell by their crotches how big they were. No one was hard in his pants—yet.

"Now touch the Cowper's gland. This gland emits the pre-ejaculation fluid, whose alkaline base feeds the spermatozoa now building in the urethra. Feel the build-up, if you can, in the testes. Check out Number 69 in particular."

All these hands suddenly went for my balls, and I screeched an "Ouch" as they squeezed my large sacs—which, I didn't realize until this particular measuring session, were 2½ inches each and hung 3¾ inches. The monotone of the professor droned on as the four sets of hands touched parts of my penis I never knew existed.

"Notice the glands directly above the perineum. During the initial stage of sexual arousal, fluids are secreted from the Cowper's glands, even though a full ejaculation may not occur. Note the heart rate and contractions of the shaft as the sperm boils up toward the urethra. See if you can feel the build-up at the prostate."

As one pair of hands worked on my shaft near the head, another pair felt down at the base of my shaft where my balls connected. I looked over at Vincent, who was smiling at me. I felt weird.

"If you continue to stimulate the epididymis, you will note a swelling of the vas deferens. The prepuce of Number 69 will prove to you that the frenulum is particularly sensitive."

As fingers stroked the inside of Vincent's foreskin, he smiled over at me and mouthed out the words, "Wait for me." I felt fingers rub my precome, and one guy took a sample and inspected it under a microscope.

"Pay special attention to the stretch receptors and the sulcus between the glans and the shaft. Measure the ejaculate culminating at the urinary meatus as you maintain stimulation. Continue applying friction at a more rapid pace."

Within seconds, both Marlon and Stroker spurted big orgasms, with Stroker heaving and grunting and breaking the rules about loud orgasms. They both looked a bit sheepish afterward.

Vincent and I looked at each other as our cocks were massaged harder and harder. My rod was slick and red, and I saw his thick, olive cock stroked by disembodied hands high into the air above him. Our eyes locked as our blood pulsated through our cocks, and we both held off, tensing the muscles at the bases of our cocks to keep our precious fluids to ourselves. This went on for about 10 minutes, frustrating our respective groups as they tried to bring us to orgasm.

"We will allow numbers 69 and 96 to stimulate themselves, and then you can measure their sperm count for the next lab. Please note their methods of stimuli in order to re-create them for the next class."

That was our cue. Vincent rose to his knees and pointed his long cock my direction across the room as I began jacking off while looking his way. The whole room had their eyes on either his cock or mine as we matched each other again, stroke for stroke.

I could see a few hands in the class reach for their own cocks, straining in their pants, as Vincent and I put on a show for them. Vincent worked the base of his hard-on, and I pressed my shaft up against my abdomen so that the head was pushed high above my navel. I rubbed up and down along my tight hairless balls. The professor droned on, ignoring the class's heightened excitement.

"The average amount of ejaculate is one teaspoonful, and could go up to four. There is five calories per teaspoon, with five milligrams of protein. The average number of spurts in an orgasm is three to 10, with each spurt from one to as many as 45 seconds apart."

We both shot across the room as our lab teams tried to catch some of the fluid. I spasmed far more than 10 times...and so did Vincent.

"The average travel of ejaculate is 10 inches, but it can go farther. There are 50,000 spermatozoa generated a minute, about 72 million a day..."

The lesson continued, but for now Vincent and I were spent.

Back in Steve's office, he gave us good reviews.

"It's interesting that the heterosexual and the asexual came first, and the bisexual and fag came last. That's usually the other way around," Steve said, pointing to Marlon, Stroker, Vincent, and I.

I looked over at Marlon as he slipped his pants on in front of his locker and grumbled, "It'd be a lot more fun if there were a bunch of babes feeling us up and down. At least I could get off and then go home and dream about it."

It was hard for me to believe him, knowing how much he enjoyed having a guy suck his cock. Oh, but I guess that was only for hazing's sake and didn't count.

"It's going to be a lot more challenging for you as the course goes on," said the experienced Vincent. "Straight or gay, these guys know how to work a dick."

A few weeks later, our groups got our orgasms pretty well under control. One guy had the right technique and knew how to massage my shaft to get me off even without lube. Sometimes a dry come-shot is what they needed for the class.

We were getting into more advanced stimuli, and the boring prof kept droning on, but one thing he said made all of our ears perk up.

"Now, you've all read your homework, so I want one of you to decide who's going first. The lesson today begins by licking the testicles with the tip of your tongue. One of you stimulates the nipples, and the others measure the heart rate and penis spasms."

Two of the guys in my group were shoving each other about licking my balls as I spread out in front of them on the table. "I've never seen such a big ball sac. I want to go first," I heard one say as if I wasn't there.

"Notice if the blood pressure increases or decreases as you gauge how he is responding. You may want to gently caress his phallus manually while you are bathing his balls with your tongue and spittle. Remember, the balls are extremely sensitive to pain and he will lose his erection if you stimulate them incorrectly."

Someone was using a reflex hammer on Marlon's balls. He yelped with every tap on his loose-hanging sac. Stroker had one guy virtually chewing on his scrotum, and winced with pain and pleasure.

Two students were chewing on Vincent's foreskin and ball sac. The professor discussed him: "Over here at 96, you notice the foreskin being stimulated. The known functions are: (a) to cover the glans for mucosal development, and (b) to protect the glans from bacteria, feces, and urine, and (c) to minimize everyday friction such as rubbing against undergarments, and (d) to keep the area moist with the oils of the body so the nerve endings will be ripe for sexual pleasure."

I so wished I had foreskin as I watched them play with Vincent's olive protrusion. He looked so much bigger than me with that extra flap of lovely skin.

"Notice how 69's widened urinary tract shows a bigger meatus—or slit—as he gets more swollen. He is a fine example of coronal swelling. Note the purple coloration."

I'd not yet become comfortable with the professor describing my intimate erection for the class, whether it was a notable thing or not.

"On 69, droplets of pre-ejaculatory fluid are seen in the urinary meatus, indicating the prostate and Cowper's glands are ready for orgasmic contractions."

I was hoping for a full-on blow job, but we were only getting our balls licked this time around. Back at the showers in Steve's office, Vincent tried to lead us all in a circle jerk. I was only too willing to join in, but the others just watched.

"You guys are always trying to recruit," Marlon scowled, as he turned away and soaped up his cock. "I told you I'm straight."

"Straight and narrow," Vincent shot back. "And how 'bout you, aren't you just ready to shoot after getting your balls licked for an hour? Come on, asexual boy."

Stroker *did* have a hard-on in the shower, a far more impressive one than I had ever seen in class.

"You ever been fucked, Stroker?" Vincent asked. Stroker shook his head, and Vincent said, "Neither have I. I'm just waiting for the right guy before I let someone have my butt. You know anyone who'd like my butt, Mickey?"

I walked out, a bit embarrassed, and got dressed with Marlon. But out of the corner of my eye I watched Stroker and Vincent come simultaneously in the shower.

I went back home to my dorm and jacked off as I told Joey about it.

The semester was winding down, and the Penile Biology

class was gearing up for its final climax, so to speak. Joey was so jealous that I got to be naked with the handsome Vincent. But I was jealous of the guys in my class who got to touch him. I was tired of having to observe him from afar.

But today was different. Today was the biology class's Anal Stimulation Day.

"It is a particularly sensitive area, and one that can absorb fluids through a thin membrane," droned the prof as the students poked our opened buttholes with pencil erasers, feathers, and other soft prods.

"Now we're going to have anal-penile stimulation, with 69 topping 96, and 27 doing 55. OK, move your subjects to the bench and sheathe the proper penises."

I was a bit dazzled, but delighted. Did I just hear right? Was Stroker really going to fuck Marlon? Was I really going to get a crack at Vincent's crack?

Marlon protested, and the professor shushed him.

"It's not a big deal—certainly not from 27. Just lie back and enjoy it. Now mount the subjects, guys."

I looked down at Vincent, who was a bit red-faced and uncomfortable about the whole thing. Meanwhile, Marlon had his body bent over a table, face down in desperation as Stroker walked toward his skinny behind with a hard-on.

Vincent wanted to face me, and I looked down at him as his legs nimbly went up on either side of my shoulders. My hard-on strained and I gently pushed the very lubed stiffy into the hole in front of me.

"Now get where you can observe these virgin bungholes being entered. See if you can observe any puckering, bleeding, or swelling."

I heard Marlon squeal as Stroker's fat, smaller cock invaded his virgin territory. I smiled at the thought of having this frat boy hypocrite finally getting his butt poked after doing it to me during my frat initiation.

Vincent looked into my eyes and welcomed me with a

smile. His eyes told me to take it slow, so I did. I read his silent cues as I slipped deeper, and a little deeper, until I saw him wince and felt his butt muscles tighten around my member. Soon, I felt him relax and welcome me even deeper.

He looked into my eyes and gave me an angelic smile. That's when I started pounding.

"See if you can observe the sensations going on around the insertion points, and don't forget to measure the heart rates and tumescence of each partner."

I never heard another word from the prof that day. I was lost in the insertion of my cock and the smiles on Vincent's face. I was drowning in ecstasy as I built up my stride. I couldn't care less that my heart was being monitored and that plenty of eyes were focused in on my cock and Vince's anus. To me, it felt like just the two of us.

Vincent's smile beckoned me closer, and I took the plunge and placed my lips onto his. My tongue entered his mouth and flicked over his tongue. We kept our mouths open and he allowed me to linger there as my penis drove its full length into his virgin ass and slipped almost all the way out before plunging back inside.

I pulled out when I couldn't stand it any longer. Frantic hands ripped off my condom and Vincent and I both shot without touching ourselves, our loads spewing all over, splattering a few lucky onlookers.

The students were gaping and the professor started clapping. Then the students joined in the applause, as did Marlon and Stroker, who were already spent on the other table.

Vincent smiled again at me and gave me another kiss.

"Guess we graduated," he beamed.

ONCE BITTEN

Already in the right month of my diaries, I remembered a story told to me on Halloween and flipped to that page:

I saw Big Red at the urinal, and I couldn't help but stare again at his cock, which was more than a foot long and almost as long limp too. He had those two great freckles right on the tip of his cock.

He noticed me staring, and he showed his cock a bit more as he pissed into the urinal trough.

"Didn't you say there was a story about those marks on your cock head, those freckles?" I asked as I walked with him back to the lounge area.

"Yeah, that's how I learned I was gay," Red said. "I had a fiancée for the longest time, and then I was bitten once and for all."

In the lounge, Jason and Johnny were being simultaneously serviced by Joey's oral expertise, while Marlon, Jake, Stroker, and a few others lay around naked, watching the football game. Soon we would all be heading out to the Halloween parties. A few of us launched into talking about our sexuality.

Sandy talked about how he knew he was straight, Marlon talked about how he always dreamed about pussy and tits, and Stroker discussed how he always dreamed about cocks and believed everyone should have one.

Then Big Red talked about being once bitten.

"Not this story again," said Marlon. "Not during the game!"

"Oh, come on," said Jake. "Mickey hasn't heard it."

"It is a great story," said Johnny, as he shot a load. "Especially on Halloween."

"Score! They scored!" Marlon high-fived Sandy. They hugged.

Here's how Red told it....

Last Halloween, I went to a costume party with my fiancée Donna. It was in the nice house of the frat Marlon belongs to, the Phi Kumma Lotta house, a big antebellum with gardens out back. It looked like one of the country estates that Donna's rich-bitch friends own.

It was there that I was bitten, and I've never recovered.

Donna was dressed as a princess with a long, flowing gown. I was her handsome prince in a ruffled, royal-blue shirt and white satin tights. I wore a black mask over my eyes and my curly red hair poked out from under my royal crown. The satin tights were tight enough to cause a few gasps at the party.

Donna liked showing off my big dick; she liked her friends knowing what she was being poked with every night.

I liked the way the muscles of my arms gave an erotic shape to the blue satin, and I especially liked the way my thighs strained against my white tights. I was a little self-conscious over how frilly my costume appeared, but I realized my six-foot-four stature and swimmer's build—along with my fiancée at my side—would dispel any questions about my masculinity.

The instant we walked in, I saw him. He was standing across the room, halfway up a flight of stairs, and staring straight back at me. He had penetrating deep-brown eyes. His long, slender body was clad in a dark cape. My heart pounded; he was the most captivating vampire I had ever seen.

I broke my stare, then glanced back at him for a moment.

The sleek dark-haired stranger with the flawless face was still watching me. I walked away but continued to steal glances at him. Those wicked, haunting eyes were always staring back. They sent chills down my spine, but they weren't chills of fear. I was breaking out in a sweat, unable to concentrate on any conversation with my fiancée or any of the frat boys there.

My fiancée noticed something was wrong. She suggested I get some fresh air, so I stepped out onto the terrace. I was perplexed as to why the stranger's stare unnerved me so much.

Beyond the stone-surfaced terrace was a landscape of gardens, and I stood there, looking out, holding my drink with both hands. I watched the leaves of the trees shimmer in the light of the full moon.

Suddenly I sensed someone behind me. "Good evenink," he said, with such a thick Romanian accent I couldn't tell if he was putting me on.

I turned and was taken aback by the sensuous sight of the dark stranger up close. His velvet black cape flapped in the wind, revealing a blood-red satin lining. Under his cape he wore a tuxedo so form-fitting I could see the muscles of his shapely stomach rippling through his shirt. His shiny black pants were snug across his sexy buns.

A lump grew in my throat as I noticed one growing in his pants.

"You have a great costume," I managed to say.

"You should be carrrrreful out here," he said rolling his *r*'s dramatically. "You are verrrry likely to become a victim of the crrrrreatures of the night."

I laughed nervously. I figured he must be an actor.

"You've got a super accent; it almost sounds authentic," I said. "Hi, I'm Red—they call me Big Red."

I extended my bare arm, thick with red hair. He extended his white-gloved hand and gripped me with a tough, iron-like handshake. His cool smile intimidated me.

He stood there, staring at me through his dark, mysterious

eyes that penetrated my baby blues. I felt exposed and transfixed, and I trembled—but not from fear.

After what seemed an eternity, I broke the stare-down. "I'm going for a walk. I need to be alone," I said irritably.

I couldn't figure out what I was feeling, or what he was doing. I wasn't interested. I walked in to find my girlfriend.

"Suit yourself," said the dark stranger, remaining very much in character. "But again, I varn you, don't become prrrey to the crrrreatures of the night."

Frustrated by what had been left unsaid between us, and unable to find Donna, I quickly walked out into the soft green garden. I was furious that he didn't tell me his name. Suddenly I wanted to know everything about him.

I wondered if this was some traditional way for homosexuals to hit upon one another. I figured this was their style: no talk, no introduction, only sex.

I was disgusted and kept walking angrily. As I walked farther away into the garden, past stone gargoyles illuminated by the brightness of the moon, I realized that I had become lost in a labyrinth of bushes towering above my head. Lost in thought and anger, I had walked so far that I had lost sight and sound of the party. I was completely alone.

If only I had invited him out there, maybe then I could have talked to him and broken him from that fake accent.

Instantly, he was there, right in front of me. And his dark eyes bore straight through to my very soul. Even though I wanted to run from him, I felt drawn, hypnotized. He called my name and I slowly moved toward him. Then he said the words I needed desperately to hear.

"I vant to suck your cock."

He removed his gloves, revealing strong, masculine hands tapering to long, black fingernails.

"Show me your lance, Sir Lancelot."

He smiled and I saw white, shiny, thick fangs glistening in his spit-slicked mouth.

He ripped a hole right through the front of my satin tights, revealing my swollen cock, which sprang out ready for him to take. I looked up and watched him spread open his cape, and underneath he was now completely naked. What I saw was a beautifully muscular body and a raging hard-on pointing at me. He then leapt on top of me, enveloping both of us under the smooth, red satin of his cape.

His mouth smothered mine, and our tongues entwined. I licked the sharp fangs in his mouth and I thought for an instant that they might not be false. But at that point I didn't care.

He tore my clothes off my body with his hands and began licking down along my torso with his serpentine tongue. He slurped and sucked my belly button and then slowly worked his way down to the area that needed him most. He grabbed my cock, holding my balls with one hand, gripping my bare ass from underneath and hoisting my dick up to his face with tremendous strength. His sucking was exquisite. Every stroke of his tongue sent shivers through my muscles and one of his long fingers began to probe my asshole, causing me to writhe with pleasure.

"My hunky Prrrince Valiant, now you arrre mine," he said in his deep voice, obviously pleased with himself for being able to deep-throat a cock that had choked many expert female mouths.

His thick cock hovered over my naked body, and as he ravaged my dick with his mouth I could feel his sharp fangs on either side of my cock. I had never been so close to another man's cock before, but now I wanted his, I wanted to taste it.

As if he read my mind, he stood up in front of me, and I knelt before his commanding cock. I could see the blood throbbing through the thick veins of his long, slender tool. It was a beautiful piece of meat and much bigger than I imagined, but somehow I managed to swallow every inch of that monster. His curly brown pubic hair tickled the inside of my nostrils as I breathed in the delicious, musky, ageless scent of his crotch.

Slowly, I circled his demanding cock head with the tip of my tongue and gradually worked my way down to its sensitive base. Then again I engulfed his entire hard-on, feeling it slide down along the back of my throat as my own throbbing cock was being caressed by his toes.

Then he shoved my head off his nearly erupting cock in order to save his load. As he turned me over, my immediate response was to resist, but I badly needed what he was about to do to me. He had me in his command. He knelt behind me and spread my legs apart. I knew what was coming and despite the fear, gave myself completely to him. He raised my ass close to him. Fondling my raging hard-on, which stood stiff against my belly, he positioned himself to penetrate me.

I howled out in pain as he entered my ass. It hurt so good. He slid in all the way and then waited until I caught my breath. When he felt I was ready, he began to hump me, faster and faster, until it felt as if his cock was driving right through me, pushing into my own cock from the inside. I howled with pleasure. Sensing just how desperately I needed his cock, he plowed into me more violently, sucking on my neck and squeezing my dick. I was completely consumed by his sexual power.

With perfect timing, he exploded inside of me, releasing his grip on my cock, which shot its load high in the air. He tossed away his come-filled condom, which I had never even seen him slip on, and he looked down at me with a big smile.

Once I recovered from the sexual turmoil, I looked behind me and saw that my vampire was gone, nowhere to be seen. The rest of the night is a blur.

I made up some excuse for my fiancée as to why I had been gone so long and why my clothes were in tatters. I looked everywhere in the frat house for that dark stranger and asked a lot of people at the costume party if they knew him. He was gone. I was sad.

The next morning, when I woke up and saw my fiancée lying in her usual place next to me, I began to vomit. I rushed to the bathroom and threw up all over the full-length mirror and her makeup kit. I continued to vomit as Donna rushed in to see what was happening.

I stood bent over the sink, and as Donna came near me I became even more nauseous. She looked in the mirror and screamed.

"Oh, gosh, what happened to you?"

I looked in the full-length mirror and realized what had shocked her. I grabbed my cock and Donna went screaming out of the bathroom and out of my life.

On the head of my cock appeared two red marks. It was apparent that someone had bitten it.

And ever since then, I've never been the same.

THE SEXUAL OLYMPICS
MAY 12, 1991

It wasn't something you'd think one could rehearse for, or condition for, or practice for, but there certainly were a lot my students boning up for the Sexual Olympics. And it brought me back to the days when I helped participate in the games.

This is a contest F.U. has championed for years with pride. I went to my diaries to flip to the year we were in close running with the University of Florida Studs and the UCLA Dudes.

It was warm that spring day, and the guys on campus were randier than ever, so it was perfect timing for the judges to come to campus.

It's time for the Sexual Olympics.

Our college hasn't lost its place in this marathon of male sexual proclivities since 1909, when the first recorded Sexual Olympics took place among fraternities throughout the world. First conducted as a scientific experiment, it has since become a matter of professional pride among the bastions of higher education and phallic fraternity.

We thought we'd have the Longest Cock competition wrapped up with Big Red, but there was a college basketball player in Utah who measured 12½ inches soft and literally hung down past his knees. The only thing we could hope for was that Mormon guilt would shrivel up the Utah player when it came time to pull out his measuring stick.

We watched as Big Red strained for a full stiffy, pumping

that long garden hose of his but never achieving a good, full rod. He broke out in a sweat. The judges measured him at 13.1, but we knew he could eke out a better number if he had a second go at it. It was rather a disappointing start for our Olympics, and talent scouts for the porn world gave up on signing Big Red. He obviously buckled under pressure, and that's not something they want from a porn star, particularly a potential big one like that. It's OK, Red was always self-conscious about those red marks on the side of his cock head anyway.

Next the judges would grade us on Sperm Shooting, and we had two world-class shooters: Paul Morton and Spike, both members of my fraternity. Paul and Spike would later join the adult industry part-time, to help put themselves through school.

The guys lined up in the gymnasium, standing with their erect penises in their hands, and when the judges blew their whistles they wanked and pounded on their cocks with full, voracious effort.

Paul is a straight guy with blond hair and a rather short, stout body with a thick round cock. He stroked it like he was milking a cow, caressing the sides as he squeezed tightly, with his hands following through at the base of the cock.

Spike is a Tenor who uses both his hands and eases his cock skin down to the base so that the shaft is very tight when his hands hit around his balls as he strokes. That way, he says, his spunk shoots further.

As the judges stood about 12 feet away (the record was Paul's 12.7-foot shot from last year), guys along both sides of the masturbators were egging them on.

A few of the guys on the sidelines pulled their puds out and joined in the jack-off session as they watched Paul pleasure himself. Cocky Paul didn't seem to notice, tossing his head and enjoying the feel of his own hand as he worked himself up into a frenzy.

Paul's head snapped backward as he let a shining white

spew gush from his red cock head. His cock arched high into the air as the splooge spurted out. One of the judges had to step back a bit as it plopped well past the 12.7 record-marker.

We roared, and two guys on the sidelines splooged in their hands as they watched Paul break his record and hit 13.1 feet for his come-shot. It was quite impressive.

Then Spike pulled his pud to climax. This time even more guys were jacking themselves off on the sidelines as Spike worked both his hands up and down his shaft. Spike's cock is bigger, and he's more known around campus for sharing his cock with the crowds. That's why they were all for him today.

"Oh, man, I'm commmming," exploded Spike.

We all gasped simultaneously as we watched a wad of semen spew forth from Spike's red cock head and arch over our heads toward the referees. It seemed magical as the splooge flew through the air with globby grace. It far exceeded Paul's wet spot.

"15.3!" shouted the referee.

Oh, my God, Spike had outdone Paul Morton's past distance record and set a new world record for the Long Distance Come-Shot.

When Spike regained his breath, we high-fived him, then let the referees shake his rather sticky hand. The guys carried the skinny, naked Spike on their shoulders, and at least one head was between his legs already, slurping up the spent cock and getting him ready for another round.

Fastest Erection Revival was a lock, with my roommate, Joey Dillus. He could come and get it back up in 11 seconds. I'd seen him do it when we were jacking off together while telling sex stories across the room from each other in our beds. He's amazingly able to get a boner up and ready in a moment's notice.

But today Joey looked nervous as he stood naked in front of about 40 guys who were pinning their college hopes and reputation on him. A rather stiff-looking referee read him the rules: "You must have enough ejaculate to at least fill the test tube to this line."

"On your mark, get set, go!" sounded the referee.

"Go! Go! Go!" came the cry from the sidelines.

The stopwatch started as soon as one referee nodded that enough semen had filled the cup to qualify as a complete come-shot. Now Joey was to replenish the cup after reviving his hard-on and coming again.

His cock was limp, but his expert hands made his piece of meat spring to attention again quickly, and he masturbated and pulled and tugged on his cock until he came again in a mere few seconds.

"12.10!" shouted the referee.

Drats! I had seen Joey hit it in 11 seconds and come again with a full load in Naked Dorm, and I wondered how we could re-create that mood here in the gym. When I first saw him come again so quickly, I didn't believe it, and so a few times I timed him myself. He shot an even bigger load the second and third times. But today he was a bit off. He was nervous.

"Come on, Joey," I encouraged him loudly. He nodded over and smiled.

"I need some assistance, guys. Let me see some dick!" he bellowed.

Immediately, a dozen guys unleashed their hard-ons. Joey worked on massaging his cock with the lube given to him by one of the referees. Joey watched the guys with their cocks out around him, and he came—fast and furious.

"It's a new world record—11.7 seconds!" the referee shouted.

But no, that wasn't enough. Joey nodded for the referee to plunk down another empty tube and focused his eyes on three fraternity brothers who were mesmerized as they unzipped their zippers and held their fat beefy dicks in their hands, stroking themselves raw.

The frat boys were staring not at each other but at Joey's twitching, dribbling cock, and Joey was focusing on them.

The stopwatch started, and Joey blasted a huge load that filled up well past the marker in the tube. The three guys stroked harder.

"Ten seconds exactly. We have a new record!"

Joey smiled as we all roared around him. The three frat lads pulled their puds back into their pants, and Joey tried making his way through the crowd toward them, but they were gone.

"Rats," he said, "and they're probably going to jack off to me tonight alone in their bunk beds."

I gave Joey a big hug, and we went outside to where the Continuous Orgasm Contest was continuing. Outside, the three frat guys were standing against the wall, and Joey stopped to smile.

"Um, there's some unfinished business," one of them said, grabbing his still-hard crotch stretching in his jeans.

"I'll catch you later, Mickey," Joey smiled as he slipped away with the frat guys. "Meet you at the Continuous Orgasm Contest in just a sec."

Now this is a bizarre contest. And a tricky one too. It usually goes the full length of the Sexual Olympics but that's only three days, and this time our statistics experts hoped our school would make it a little longer.

See, this is about having one continuous orgasm from guy to guy to guy. The trick is that the come-shot and the orgasm has to overlap with the guy who is just having one, and then the next orgasm has to be timed just perfectly so there's a continuous stream of semen going into a big metallic vat in the middle of the courtyard.

If the momentum of come is broken, the school's team is disqualified; there's no second chance. It's got to be one continuous orgasm. Our dark-studded leader, Vincent Lamaz, had kicked us off the day before with a powerful orgasm, followed by the long-haired Science Boys, Wilbert and Bob, who expertly came one after the other into a large vat in the center of the quad as the school rooted them on.

I wandered over to the continuing orgasm vat, where the guys were lined up, when a smiling Joey joined me.

"You signed up for a time?" asked Sandy, the lanky surfer dude. Sandy doesn't get excited about much, but he was determined to help out with this particular contest. He had already spilled his load twice in the continuing orgasm, and he wanted to make sure there was always someone on standby. "I have you down for 3:30, Mickey, you want to sign up again?"

I already thought it was going to be awkward to time my orgasm, much less do it in front of a massive crowd, but twice in a day would be just too much pressure. We were watching Jason and Johnny, the two astronaut wanna-bes about to have their blasts into space and school history.

Jason wasn't completely naked—he's a bit shy. His jeans and white boxers were down at his ankles as he worked on his boner and waited for his come-shot. Next to him was his roommate, the cute, sandy-haired Johnny, watching intently for the cue with a raging hard-on in his hands and standing completely naked, with his hair slicked back neatly as if he were heading for a job interview.

About five or six guys ahead were having their orgasms, shooting into the vat as the referees counted off, "768, 769, 770." The numbered guys had their come-shots consecutively. A serious blond-haired stud was next, and he released his load on cue, gushing as he pointed his cock down so that the precious drops fell into the metal vat. But his load was small and didn't dribble very long, so it caught Jason off guard.

"It's here, I'm coming," Jason said as he squeezed his cock and the referee bent down to look closely. Jason spewed his wad, screaming, "AAAH, ooh, that's good, aaah."

But as Jason came, Johnny was watching rather than

paying attention, and he almost broke the momentum. Recovering from his own orgasm, Jason took his thumb and jabbed it into Johnny's butthole, and the sandy-haired stud gasped as he shot a load across the metal vat.

"Good going, Johnny!" we hollered from the sidelines.

The next guy popped his load quickly at that exciting sight, and the memory kept the line going consecutively for quite a while.

"Wanna stick that thumb up my butt for my come-shot too?" asked Stroker Palmer from the sidelines, wriggling his fat, hairy ass at the svelte cadet. Jason smiled and kissed Johnny as they put their clothes back on and new guys joined in to continue the ongoing orgasm.

I was half hoping the line would be broken by the time my turn rolled around at 3:30, but after getting all hot and bothered watching them measure the biggest testicles and the longest hard-on, I was ready to orgasm on command.

I had quite a rager by the time I came back, and I saw Sandy wanking his long, skinny cock again as kind of a stand-by stunt cock in case someone wasn't ready to blow. Dean Richie was looking in on the orgasm line, and it seemed like some of the guys were shy about doing it in front of him. Others were doing it just to spite him. I was glad he left before I had to pull mine out.

About five minutes before my orgasm, I saw a line of handsome men in front of me all beating themselves off to a near climax and holding off until just the right time. I pulled my pants down, but I suddenly went limp as the pressure of the school record was suddenly upon me. Hundreds of eyes rested on my flaccid state.

Yikes. I looked down the line and there was Shane Coley, the handsome blond swimmer, just stroking away at his cock much like he did as I spied on him in his private corner in the library. I looked over at him enjoying his rubbing all to himself; when Sandy cued him he shot a load with perfect grace and timing.

That helped me spring to attention. He was my dream man.

I was handed lube, and then Marshall O Boy and his friend Allan were on either side of me, stroking themselves too. Marshall came first, in long streams of jism, and Allan followed, then they both immediately grabbed my cock. Allan squeezed under my head and Marshall grabbed at the base, near my balls. The two had expert hands.

"Go, Mickey," cued Sandy.

I had a back-snapping orgasm and I heard an "oooh" erupt from the crowd as I shot my load and the perpetual orgasm continued.

Sandy shouted: "Numbers 1484, 1485, 1485—line up and whip it out!"

I went off to the side and thanked Marshall, who kissed me square on the lips, and then Allan and I went off to watch the Fattest Cock Measurements.

Allan and I walked over to the main auditorium in the SPARTACUS building, which is where the Sculpture, Portrait And Religious Tableaus, Artifacts, and Crafts Undergrad Studies are going on. In the center was a bunch of the fattest, ugliest cocks I'd ever seen on any human being.

Three of the guys had cocks almost as big around as they were long. Square dicks, if you will.

"They're LUMPWUGs all right," said Allan, who was so disgusted he had to step out for a smoke.

Charlie, from the Naked Dorm, was definitely a Large Unwieldy Massive Penis on a Weird Ugly Guy. He was 300 pounds of fat and could barely reach around to stroke his flabs of fat cock down under his belly.

There was Jason again, big boxy cock and all, ready to be measured, but it was already obvious that a few of the guys had him beat, particularly our Hawaiian friend Kam Likikime, who sported a beer can–sized cock that seemed fatter than my fist.

"Hey, Mickey, Victor Nichols is about to set a new record, c'mon!" Allan said, rushing in as someone in the room was measuring a 13¼-inch around cock.

We rushed into the SPARTACUS auditorium, where Victor was sitting at a table smirking while a very muscular, dark-haired referee seemed a bit perturbed as he said, "That's right. That's the 38th correct estimate."

The audience applauded, and Victor waved to Allan and I as we raised our fists and whooped. Victor has always had a knack for estimating cock sizes, both soft and hard. His was a gift, and it was finally paying off, in the Best Cock Estimator competition.

Five more men from competing schools walked out in their underwear, all white cotton briefs. I knew from experience that Victor could estimate cocks through baggy pants, corduroys—even thick overalls—and get to within a half-inch of a guy's hard-on. Guessing through underwear was easy.

The first guy hung left; he had a bit of a boner as the crowd whistled at him. He looked shy as Victor guessed "5⅜ inches."

The guy then stripped his underwear off, stood in a corner, and got hard as the ref measured the cock from the top, and said, "5⅜. This is number 39."

Victor winked at the ref, who looked even more disgusted.

"Is he flirting with the ref?" I asked.

"You know Victor. Do you have to ask?" Allan said. "The world record is 40. If he gets the next one right, we've won this competition."

The next man in underwear stood in front of Victor. He was bunched under, kind of hidden. Victor paused, then said, "6¼."

The guy pulled out his cock and worked it up. The ref laid his stick on the dick and barked out "6¼ inches. We have a new world record!"

The crowd erupted in applause. Allan and I hugged as we cheered for Victor. He smiled, took a pad of yellow Post-It notes, walked over to the remaining three guys standing in their underwear, and said, "This guy is 4⅝, he's 5½, this one is 5⅛." As he spoke, he scribbled and posted the measurements on each guy's chest.

Then Victor took the last Post-It note and slapped it right on the zipper of the ref's black pants, and said, "You, sir, are 7¾ inches, and this has my dorm room number on it."

The crowd erupted into thunderous roars of laughter and whoops as the ref turned beet-red.

Victor walked out as the commotion continued. We found out later that Victor's final score was in fact 44 perfect predictions. But his real score was with the referee, who did find Victor back in his dorm.

Allan decided he was going to enter the Most Cocks in One Mouth contest, and since I had suggestible gag reflexes I didn't think I should go to watch.

I wandered over to the SPARTACUS courtyard to watch the cock-fencing matches, where guys jousted with only their nimble hard-ons. It was a weird sort of cockfight, with cocks straight up at 2 o'clock high striking each other like drawn swords. The trick was to push a buzzer set just on the underside of the shaft of each guy's penis.

A handsome blond secretary, Barney, who worked at the Cryolab, where he observed guys masturbating into plastic jars, seemed particularly good at that joust. He stood there with his curved-up cock, and I watched him bring down two handsome frat studs by poking their buttons.

Then long-schlonged Eddie, who'd already won a gold medal in the Pubic Shaved Art contest, went at it with the Brazilian stud Toro. Toro had a thicker cock, but this was a game of courage and skill. Eddie won that bout, then beat out Barney. Finally, it was John Rex against Eddie for the gold.

John came out with a proud hard-on pointing upward. It wasn't as big as Eddie's, but it was strong, and he held it out gallantly. They crossed swords and then went at it, with Eddie jabbing wildly as John dodged elegantly.

I sighed and wondered if John would ever pay any attention to me. We were never in the same classes, because he was always in the hard classes like Ball Stretching, Business in the Sex Market, Healing Qualities of Urine, and Sodomy Laws 450. Anyway, he was amazing as he jabbed and dodged then plugged Eddie's buzzer with skill and grace, winning the competition.

Outside, the Perpetual Pissing contest eked on. The judges were measuring the guy with the longest uninterrupted piss. Our big drinking friend Jimmy was off to the side chugging whole pitchers of beer as he got his gut ready to let go. He drank five pitchers just while I was standing there, and I cheered him on.

When it was finally his turn, Jimmy opened up his pants, pulled out his Stubbie-sized pud, and let his kidneys rip. He went a full 3½ minutes, and we cheered him the whole way. After a momentary break, he peed another full two minutes, but the judges considered the lull a stop in continuous flow. Anyway, watching Jimmy arch his pee into the air for a full three minutes was something that gave me newfound respect for our obese friend.

When it got dark, torches were lined all around campus, leading to the vat in the quad, which was now ankle-deep with come. The judges noted that we were nearing the three-day mark for the continuous orgasm, and they wearily watching young man after young man line up and come into the vat.

Obviously, the men of COCK College and F.U. were very talented in the ways of their penises. We had mastered great control. That's what we wanted the world to know.

I actually added one more squirt into the vat because we were running out of available, viable cocks. Sandy was frantic and all spent out too, and we were nearing the end of the line.

Dean Richie came out to watch the final throes of the orgasm, and we knew we were only a few guys away from at least tying the record. I knew that Dean Richie's presence could only hamper our chances, and I tried diverting him, but he pushed his way to the front of the crowd.

There, Stroker Palmer and Marlon Brandeis were about to come when Stroker shriveled to a tiny Butch-sized cock and Marlon came on cue. Uh-oh—the momentum was lost. No one was ready to keep the coming going.

We were sure to come to an abrupt orgasmic halt when Dean Richie unzipped his pants and sprung out at full attention. He began a prolonged, dribbling orgasm that kept us qualified. The judges nodded with approval as Dean Richie shouted a high-pitched squeal of a come-shot that resounded off the buildings on campus. The few dozen or so of us out there erupted into cheers. Dean Richie suddenly became a sort of good guy—at least for a minute.

Our school actually captured 50 more orgasms after Dean Richie's big-O save, and we broke the Longest Continuous Orgasm record by almost two hours, capturing the Golden Dickie, which still sits in the trophy case of the Board of Trustees and Terms of Management (BOTTOMs) building.

As it turned out, that record would take almost a decade to break again; and we did it, of course, when I came back to school as a professor.

THE SPERMARIUM AND CUMM MUSEUM
NOVEMBER 11, 2000

Yep, I taught my boys well. They beat our old record for the Longest Continuous Orgasm by 100 extra shoots, and I must say that this professor also added to the vat, as did Dean Richie and his son Connor, along with Lance at their sides. What a nice father-son event that turned out to be.

My first semester back at school was going by so fast, I hadn't even had a chance to look up some old friends who were still on campus. My old professors from Oral Stimulation 2000 and Advanced Anal Probing were still teaching their popular classes.

There were also some new classes in the curriculum that I wanted to find out more about, such as Berdache and Balinese Sex Rituals (something I've had firsthand experience with), Spontaneous Sperming (orgasming secretly in public places), Male Undergarment Fashions (bulge-enhancing clothes and cockring fashion), and Building Your Own Erection Set (creating a machine that stimulates your erection).

Then there was the whole new section of F.U. that had to do with plants. I had to look up my old pal Nikko Nadooley because I knew he was involved. Nikko and I were once stranded in the desert for a few weeks with a tribe of nomads determined to milk us for all the come we could dish out. But that's another story....

When I was a student, Nikko was the assistant chief

nutritionist for the agriculture department, and in the decade I was away he achieved notoriety and fame studying Penoponics—the dietary value of semen.

Although he's still interested in these environmental studies, he was promoted to the position of curator of the Collection of Ultimate Male Memorabilia (or CUMM Museum) in the Library of Information on Carnal Knowledge (LICK).

He was a bit balder than I remembered, but we greeted each other with the traditional genital rub of Nikko's homeland.

"I see you are hanging strong and well. That is good," Nikko told me. "Come, I will show you around this place. We have amazing exhibits from all over the world. We have statues of Balinese gods that have both male and female genitals, papers of Ancient Grease and the Roaming Empire, and letters from Suck-Raw Testes and other great philosophers."

We passed a water fountain whose spout was a squirting penis. I took a sip.

"We have items sent to us by Setset and Lik-Lik from the tribe in Borneo you once visited, and they have provided us with photos of their male insemination ritual, which you documented so well in your past book. No foreigner has ever been allowed to participate in their secret ritual as fully as…uh…you did."

"Ah, how is Lik-Lik? I still have his photo on my desk," I said with a smile, leaving out that the handsome native is sporting a huge brown boner that diverts me from my work.

"Good, good, he remembers you fondly too," Nikko said, slapping me on my butt.

He escorted me past sketches of Michelangelo nudes, erotic writings of Oscar Wilde, Foucault's pendulum (which was originally used as a dildo), a collection of male nude paintings Napoleon used to keep in his bedroom, and the first nude photographer Baron Wilhelm von Gloeden's collection of young Italian boys in the late 1890s.

I stopped to marvel at the naked youths with hairless hard-ons.

"And down here is the part of the exhibit I'm most proud of: the World's Largest Collection of Dismembered Penises."

I stopped in my tracks and looked into the rows of cases down a dimly lit corridor as about a half-dozen visitors pressed their noses up against the glass. There were jars and cases filled with penises of all shapes and sizes along the wall.

There was the famous penis of the gangster John Dillinger, measuring out at 20 inches. It was for real! In one case was a double-headed penis with two mushrooms poking out of one long shaft. That was the penis of the famed Siamese Twins from the early 1920s, Ling-Ling and Sing-Sing. There was also a penis with a shaft that split in two for about 6 inches, providing essentially two cocks that could both shoot semen.

Then there was the collection of boy penises cut off by a stalker who attacked youths in the bathrooms of Coney Island in the early 1960s, and the collection of male hustler cocks that Jeffrey Dahmer kept in lieu of devouring the rest of their bodies. In one corner was a collection from the mass penis massacre that happened in Dag Hammerdijk, the nastiest go-go club in Amsterdam. I had heard of that cock crime and wrote about it in great detail as a journalist.

"That's the one where the club had a wall of cocks, like one huge glory hole wall. And you could fondle them on the way in, it was such a nice idea," Nikko sighed. "And then some psycho came in and chopped them all off with a buzz saw. What a nightmare."

An elderly woman with red hair and a shawl stood up from where she was sitting on the bench in front of the Dag Hammerdijk massacre window. There were pictures of some of the victims and glass jars containing some of the dismembered cocks. She looked at me and said, "Thank you," then handed me a card.

"She's a weird one, comes here once a month and sits in

front of that case," Nikko said, as I looked at her card, which read SAMMY LEFILLE.

"You know who that is? That's Sammy LeFille, who worked at the go-go club and was one of the victims of that massacre," I said, remembering the story I wrote about so long ago. "She was one of the survivors of the massacre, and became a woman after that. She must be coming back to visit—oh."

Nikko and I looked at the case where a long, fairly nice penis sat preserved in a jar.

"Her penis. She's visiting her penis," Nikko said unnecessarily.

What Nikko really wanted to show me was behind the Male Museum, and that was his Spermarium, a glass hothouse filled with the most beautiful orchids, bright flowers, and colorful hummingbirds imaginable. Entering the Spermarium was like walking into an animated color cartoon—only different. You had to check all your clothes and shoes in at the door and you walked along these tufts of fluffy grass that oozed between your toes. And everywhere you looked, behind the bushes, under the trees, among the roses, there were guys fucking and sucking each other, or just masturbating on the plants.

Sure, it was like walking into a cartoon, but this one was triple-X.

"The average total of sperm a man ejaculates in a lifetime is 14 gallons, and I estimate that nearly 100 gallons of precious semen is flushed down our campus toilets every day, so I've turned this into a place where men can have sex freely with one another, under the condition that they spill their seed only on the garden and not into one another."

Down deeper into the Spermarium was a steamy waterfall where guys washed the come off their arms, legs, and crotches.

"A teaspoon of semen contains seven calories of nutrition that is great for plant life and foliage, and the scents of lavender, licorice, chocolate, and pumpkin stimulate sperm in the testicles," Nikko said excitedly, as I recognized a few of my students jacking off on the edge of the waterfall. They waved to me.

"I've found that the larger penises tend to have the largest volume of sperm and that gay men have the larger penises—after personally measuring 5,172 students," Nikko continued, reaching over to a green-eyed guy who was getting his balls sucked by Yuri, my Russian exchange student.

"This is Zeke. You're hanging nice, my friend," Nikko said.

"And I know Yuri," I said as the guys turned to smile; they didn't seem to mind the interruption.

Nikko continued talking about them as Yuri kept sucking on Zeke's matted hair around his balls. Zeke had his head down watching the Russian work his tongue and mouth around his testicles expertly. We watched how with a flick of his tongue, Yuri slid each testicle between his lips as he sucked on them gently and popped each one in and out of his mouth like gumdrops.

"Zeke hangs 9 inches and may be an exception to the long-cock rule since he's a heterosexual," Nikko noted.

My back arched quizzically as my cock twitched hard from watching.

Yuri stopped his ball-licking for a second and said, "After I hear about this boy in our class, I find him out and see if I can turn him not so phobic about homo sex."

Yuri went back to proving his oral skills on the German-Asian, who was feasting his green eyes on the mouth that engulfed his balls.

"Is it working?" I asked sarcastically.

Just then, Zeke erupted in a shot that squirted over Yuri's shoulder and into a purple orchid. The remaining drops dribbled onto a few monster-sized cucumbers in the fuzzy grass.

We continued on into the greenhouse, and I marveled at Nikko's incredible setup.

"This is the best bathhouse I've ever seen," I said.

Justifiably, Nikko had the gayest guys on campus coming to his green, steamy bathhouse and jerking off as much as they could so he could feed his garden. But what a garden! The tomatoes were plumper, the roses richer, the plumerias more aromatic.

"My, how your garden does grow," I laughed.

"With silver streams and cocks-and-balls and pretty boys all in a row," laughed Nikko. "You ain't seen nothing yet."

He was right. I wasn't quite ready to see what was around the next grassy knoll.

Around the bend from the stream and the falls was a garden of fuzzy, rather large plants with soft, purplish orifices—flowers. Guys were shoving their cocks into the plants' flowers. As soon as a stiff cock entered the furry, purple opening, the flower snapped shut. And the guys seemed to enjoy it.

"My Apollo Mantrap is a version of the Venus Flytrap. I've been developing it ever since I last saw you." Nikko cackled like a mad scientist. I shivered and covered my crotch with my hands. "I've developed this plant to be attracted to a blood-engorged specimen, and what better than a penis?" Nikko smiled excitedly. "If I can develop this right, then a guy just has to have a plant like this to give him the best blow job in the world."

I shuddered. "Do you know what that means?" I asked. "Are you aware of the implications?"

Nikko rubbed his hands together. "Yes—the world as we know it will cease to exist!"

I watched as a cute red-haired student stood in ecstasy before one of the fuzzy plants. It seemed to be milking him dry. I recognized him as one of my best students, Aaron Rymer.

"Well, how does that feel, Mr. Rymer?" I said, standing next to him as he fucked the flower.

"Oh, Professor Skee, it's really nice," Aaron answered. He bucked his hips delicately forward and the flower seemed to suck down harder on his red crotch. "Oooh, ah, oh, my God, I'm coming!"

As Aaron shot his load, he pulled away from the flower, and it broke off its stem and fell to the ground. Aaron kept spewing semen.

"Oh, I'm sorry Professor Nadooley. I wasn't careful again." Aaron squeezed out the remaining spasms of come from his cock.

"It's alright, laddie," Nikko said. "We're developing a stronger plant. That's the problem, the guys are too rough. They want to fuck the plant while they're being sucked off."

I watched as an incredibly hung kid let his semihard cock be engulfed by another flower. I couldn't believe how the plant took the whole thing without even a gag or hesitation.

"That's Tripod, the big-dicked kid in the dorm they've been talking about in class," whispered Aaron before splashing off into the warm waterfall to clean off.

I watched Tripod's huge appendage get bigger as he stiffened, and he moaned with pleasure. "This is the best, man, I can't get anyone, boy, girl, nothing to feel as good as this," Tripod testified to no one in particular.

Nikko looked over to my own raging hard-on. (Watching this inter-plant sex had given me a stiffy in spite of myself.) "Mickey, it does feel good—you want to try?"

I did want to try, but it was just a bit too weird.

I went up to Tripod and asked what it felt like.

"It's like some velvet lips are spitting warm lube over your cock and sucking it with tiny slurps from every pore on your dick...it's really wonderful," the kid told me.

I knew that someday when I got up the nerve, I'd have to come back. For right now, though, it was best to just watch.

Meanwhile, since I was naked and getting hard anyway, I decided to stay and play awhile. Nikko joined in, and since I hadn't tasted his uncut foreskin in such a long time, it was a welcome change. I went down on Nikko and chewed on his ample foreskin, letting my tongue explore the inside of his hood and his big cock head.

Within a few minutes, young guys from all over were joining us, taking turns popping our dicks in their mouths.

"Why, dear Nikko, would I want a fuzzy plant, when I can have one of these?" I asked my friend as I pulled the ears of a 20-year-old closer to my crotch.

"Why indeed?" he shrugged as he pulled another closer to his.

BLAST OFF INTO A BLACK HOLE
NOVEMBER 13, 2000

After a few hours of great sex in the Spermarium, Nikko told me to come by his office a couple of days later to read this incredible document he found. So, two days later, I went by his office in the Collection of Ultimate Male Memorabilia. I put my jacket on a whale-penis coatrack he had in his dark office of the CUMM Museum, then I sat down in front of a typed message with dots and dashes above the typed letters.

"As a journalist and sociologist, I knew you'd be intrigued by this. It came to me from a local observatory that has translated this story from a series of blips and beams that seem to be a form of Morse Code," explained Nikko. "We thought it was simply a prank of some sort, because it was of such a strange nature, in content and vernacular. But we traced the names mentioned in the text and found that they are from a missing persons report of nearly 20 years ago in Vitalia, just north of here."

I was intrigued, indeed. "But what does it say?" I asked.

"Read it," Nikko said. "Just read it…"

I was just walking down the street, minding my own business just like I always do. That's all I was doing, I swear it.

T'was just another day in boring ol' Vitalia, that ol' swampbottom town I knew I was destined to stay in all my livelong days, just farming Uncle Joe's bean field and boffing the same ol' gals I've seen since they were pimply-faced kids without any tits.

I was looking for love, some real down-home, feel-good, chills-down-your-back loving. Not just sex, although the sex was good. Sheesh, I tell you, ya get tired of the same old tits on those same few eligible gals in Vitalia.

I bought me a box of condoms from ol' Mr. Jensen at the drugstore while I was getting some tools for Uncle Joe. I knew Mr. Jensen and my Uncle Joe were old pals, and as a kid I saw them wanking together in the bean fields when they were young men, nothing gay or anything, just hanging their wangers out and playing with 'em.

And ol' Mr. Jensen knew right then and there that I was going to be seeing Miss Sunny Mae Pricktooth that night and she was going to make me whoop and holler in the hayloft. Seems like ol' Mr. Jensen knew just about what everyone had their business into, and my business was itching to be inside Sunny Mae that night.

"You be careful out there, 'cause ol' Mr. Pricktooth said he saw something funny in the woods the other night," Mr. Jensen said.

"Aw, Mr. Pricktooth's been licking the still a bit too early," I said.

"Sure 'nough, he saw bright lights and whirring and swears it on his mother's hide," Mr. Jensen warned. "Something funny's going on these-abouts, it's the third such story we've heard in two weeks."

"Mass hysterectomies," I said, funning.

"You just be careful with Sunny Mae," Mr. Jensen said.

Sunny Mae's a great girl, but you don't want to be kissing her because she gets all sloppy and wet and she has this sharp tooth like a vampire's that cuts the shit out of your lip when she's in the heat of passion. Anyway, it'd been awhile since we'd done it, so I knew she'd be horny. And I prided myself on being a scarce commodity. Keep 'em hanging, y'know.

See, the only other nonattached dude in Vitalia was my friend at the auto shop, Fred Mayferd. We'd hang out by the swimming pond and sneak up when the Bustaboli twins'd go skinny dipping and sun their nipples in the meadow, and sometimes the boy twins in town, Tim and Tom, would come along and pork 'em and we'd watch. Or sometimes I'd just be hanging out with him at the auto shop and we'd sniff the seat where Bambi Wankershift sat in her '67 Mustang convertible, because we knew she didn't wear any panties—at least Fred was pretty sure of it.

Anyway, Fred and I would take turns picking the girl we'd be givin' the benefit of our meat that night, and we'd make sure we weren't going to get attached to any of 'em, so that there'd be enough of a variety for each of us to go around. Vitalia is a small town. There were six chicks, so we'd make sure they were might horny before we'd take our pick, and the next week we'd switch. The girls didn't mind.

With my sack of tools and box of condoms, I dropped by the auto shop to see Fred. He was standing spread-eagled over an engine, revving it up.

"So's you're boffing Sunny Mae tonight? It's Vinnia Suckley for me tonight, and I want that girl to chew me up till the cows moo."

I winced at Fred. It pained me to hear him talk personal about his private parts and intimate moments like that, even though we were the best of friends. But I just didn't want to have to imagine that redheaded filly slobbering away on Fred's weiner. 'Course I've seen him nekkid before, 'specially when we were skinny dipping together as kids all the time, but I just couldn't possibly think of my best buddy with a stiffy. It just wasn't within my realm of imagination.

'Course we hadn't been nekkid together in a long time, not since we'd growed up and got bigger. He didn't want to go skinny dipping last summer, and he's been putting it off this summer too. In fact, just the weekend before when we were downing sixes of Blue Ribbon and whizzing off Jaquinoff Hill I noticed him turning his back to me so I wouldn't look. It was the first time in a whole lifetime of communal peeing that I noticed him shying away from me. I was almost a little hurt about it.

"Yep, I've got Sunny Mae in the hayloft tonight, and I've got my extra large rubber-band protectors right here," I smiled.

I took a look at my buddy, with his straight brown hair hanging over his hazel-brown eyes. His hair was almost down past his neck in the back, and he looked good with it that long, although some of the older folks whispered he looked like a girl behind his back. The girls knew better, though—he was quite a lover. I've heard them screech clear across Balzack Woods. He was looking for love too. We didn't think we could find it in Vitalia, but everyone knew he was a catch, darn tootin'.

His hands were greasy and his overalls hung loose. I knew he didn't wear nothing underneath them, 'specially in this heat. I knew those sweat dribbles pouring off his forehead and down his chest went plopping right down to his private area, and that if he looked down his overalls right at that moment, he could see his pube hairs poking out, and unlike most of the fat slobs in town he could look down and see his limp wanker hanging down without being obscured by a pot-belly. For the first time, I noticed Fred's got a fair share of tight stomach muscles, beefy biceps, and chest muscles. I shivered, I think in irritation.

"Where'd you get them muscles?" I asked, as he looked me up and down my rail-skinny blond body. I straightened up a might bit, and thrust my hips out.

"I been working out, getting off some o' that steam," Fred said, flexing one arm a little so it bulged. I copped a feel.

"That's right, the heat sure does make you horny," I said.

"Gotta do somethin' about it," Fred winked.

I looked away and turned beet-red. I couldn't even believe that Fred was talking to me about jacking his meat. Jeez! I mean, I remember many times when we were talking like kids do when we were still in school and we were out camping almost every Friday night and we'd each be in our sleeping bags.

I just knowed he was jerking himself off like a dying jackrabbit 'cause I could see his hand pumpin' underneath the sleeping bag—the Boy Scout bag with uniformed guys all over it saying "Be prepared" and "Do a good turn daily." It was like he wanted me to say something about that bouncing, but I didn't.

At least when I was going at it in my own sleeping bag I wasn't as obvious, and I enjoyed it more because I was slower and savoring the feeling. It gave me lots of hidden smiles to know my buddy and I were getting stiffies at the same time, and most times our conversations ended abruptly at about the same time, knowing that our juices were filling up our hands and we'd be wiping it off on a nearby sock.

"Y'know, y'should take some of this oil with you, it's real slick for sex," Fred said. He smeared some on his exposed leg hairs and massaged it around. His hand went up his leg slowly, coolly, then he pulled it away.

"What? You gotta be crazy!" I retorted. "No lady's gonna put that in her hole!"

"No, no, silly, you put it on your wanker."

"What! I wouldn't put that goop on my wanker, no way."

"Aw, it ain't so bad—here." Fred took a gob of oil and smacked it in my hand, and it slipped and slid through my fingers in long globs.

"You total buttface!" I shouted.

"Hey, I was just—"

I stormed off. I wasn't really mad at him. I just had to get away because when he gets in a horny mood there's no telling what he'll say. Anyway, I went home and the sun was going down and after I washed the supper plates I walked back down to the barn and looked up at the two bright stars I saw in the twilight.

Wait a minute! There's usually only one bright star up there. Tonight there was two, just blinking away. It sure looked pretty.

I got in the barn and sat in the hay and waited, and waited, and waited. My horse Elsie's raw horsey smell was starting to make my loins rustle. I kept looking at my watch—Sunny Mae was half an hour late. My dick was just too hard.

That did it—I unzipped my Levi's and let my hard-on catch a little air. I spit in my palm and rubbed the round, smooth top of it that was just poking out of my pants, straining against the teeth of my zipper.

"So let her come late, I don't care if I pop off. It'll serve her right," I said. I stood up a little and massaged the length of my rubbery shaft as it grew straight out. I started riding myself, wailing on it hard. I felt my juices boiling up in my balls.

Suddenly, the barn door started shaking. I thought Sunny Mae was at the door. But it was more than the door, the whole barn started shaking, and shaking up a storm. Then a blinding white light beamed down like it came from right through the roof of the barn. I felt my feet leave the hay, and suddenly I landed flat down on hard, cool metal. All my clothes were gone, even my underwear. There were blinking white lights all around me and strange noises, like a hoot owl in heat.

"What the fuck is going on? Where's my clothes? Who are you?"

I saw a horrifying big-faced green man, with a head the size of a watermelon, pointy Mr. Spock ears, and bug-eyes bigger than Sunny Mae's. He spoke in a gurgly voice, like when Uncle Joe's teeth got loose.

"Did we get two of them?"

Another monster in a white jumpsuit nodded. "They're both in the primary mating state. It's a good match. We've succeeded."

I stood up and cupped my hanging testicles with one hand.

"What the fuck do you think you're doing? You can't get away with this!" I shouted.

On the other side of the roundish room, I saw a crumpled figure, unconscious and naked. It was Fred!

"Fred Mayferd, what the fuck is going on here, is this some kind of joke? Are these your buddies from FSC?"

Fred wasn't laughing. He was dazed. He was very, very naked. He had grease all over his body, rubbed on him from head to foot.

"Man, who's the dudes with the Halloween masks?" he asked.

"Don't know, don't know."

We watched the two monsters looking at a screen of the map of the United States—but it wasn't a map, it was the real thing. Then quickly, quickly, quickly, we saw the whole entire Earth, just like in the movies, and then it became a speck as we got farther and farther away.

"They should be put in their habitats now, so we can observe them before it's too late," a monster said.

"Hey, hey, get your claws off me," Fred said as we were shuffled into a smooth room with leaves and grass, pillows, beer, and potato chips. The door shut behind us and a panel opened up overhead and we could see the four bug-eyes of our two captors staring down at us.

Fred and I huddled in a corner together, shaking and silent.

"The psychological trauma may have desensitized them."

"That didn't happen with the Frickerbeests. However, the gestation of the Noowamples did slow because of the shock. Don't you think this is a coupling about to take place?"

I moved over to Fred. He crouched in his nakedness.

"What's happening? Are we being kidnapped?" I whispered.

"I think so," Fred said gravely. "And I'm not sure anyone's going to ever be able to help us."

We were in that room for a long time, and they kept feeding us and watching us. It was so weird. We'd just stand there butt-naked and they'd watch and write down notes in some weird handwriting. We found out they were Oonnomatts from the planet Onasia. One was named Thuk. And the greener one was Pith. We tried asking them what they wanted with us, but that ended the observation period and the panel slammed shut. Otherwise, they seemed friendly 'nough.

I spent a lot of time naked with Fred, and I immediately noticed why my best buddy became so shy of late. His body was tremendously handsome. In one summer, he had grown hair all over his thick, muscular chest, and his dick was so long I wondered if he'd just stretched it out of joint too much by playing with it. It was longer than his hand, even when it was soft. I couldn't believe it.

One night—I think it was night, anyway—Thuk opened the portal where they were observing us and he stripped out of his jumpsuit. We both let our jaws drop to the ground when we saw him pull up a long, green, garden-hose-like weiner, about two feet long with thick, blue veins and large, bright- pink balls.

"We are built not unlike you," Thuk said.

His green cock lengthened in one long, quick jolt, like a carnival balloon, then he twisted it around behind him. Thuk turned around. On the other side, between his olive-green cheeks, there was a perfect little unshaven pussy! The lips were just oozing out goo. I couldn't believe it. Thuk popped his long rod right into that pussy hole and squealed. He pulled it in and out for a long time in front of us, massaging his long green rod, which snaked stiffly underneath him.

"He's fucking hisself!" I said.

I looked over at Fred and he had his hand over his dick— but one hand can't hide a boner. I couldn't help but stare at it. Parts of his hard-on down by the base that was as thick as my wrist. I hid mine. We both got darn hard watching the out-of-this-world fuck scene, and I was a might bit embarrassed.

"That's wild!" Fred said dreamily. I saw his fingers wiggle

in that soft area between his balls. He looked over at me, at my crotch.

"We want to observe your mating customs, so we are demonstrating our procedures. It's only fair," Thuk said. "We know enough about your culture to know you are not sole replicants like we are. We bear our own young and don't need intimacy with another party."

Fred and I didn't quite understand.

"You see, we picked two earthlings who were priming up sexually at that moment for their reproductive process. We chose a remote but typical area of your planet, and we picked you two."

I turned to Fred. "Hey, Fred, why were you covered in oil and grease that night we got zapped into this spaceship?"

"Well, I was jacking off in the shop with my oil, and then I was here," Fred said. "I got stood up by Vinnia and I was hornier than a toad. All the dads in town stopped letting the girls out 'cause of all the mysterious sightings in the sky. Guess it was these dudes. Guess it was all true."

"So you were jacking off with all that oily grease all over your body?" I said accusingly, bothered by his kinkiness. "You smeared that all over yourself?"

"Well, yeah, what were you up to?"

I suddenly realized. "Why, I was jacking off too! Oh, my gosh! You don't think they got us because we were the only two in all of Vitalia who were hornier than jackals, and they honed in on us to snatch us away?"

Fred and I started howling with laughter. We were hysterical.

"And they think we're gonna show them how to fuck!" Fred laughed hysterically. "They think we can have sex with each other!"

Suddenly we stopped. We needed to explain the error.

"Um, Thuk, y'see, you've made a big mistake, you gotta drop us off or get us a pair of girls. You see, we can't have sex, 'cause one of us ain't a girl. There's boys and girls on

Earth, and, you see, we're made differently and there's something that we do to each other that feels good, and so, you see, we'd be glad to demonstrate if you zapped up the Bustaboli twins—"

I was exasperated. Thuk's wide eyes certainly didn't grasp the concept of the birds and the bees. Pith came in, scratching his bug-eyes. We lost our hard-ons.

"I think they are not yet in the mood," Pith mused.

"Um, sir, or m'am, or whatever," said Fred, trying not to giggle. "Y'see, we're never gonna get in no mood, 'cause we're guys. We're buddies! We don't do stuff like that, you perverts. Take us back to Earth immediately!"

"We're not authorized to make a return trip," Pith said. "We will observe you until you incubate an earthling."

Well, that dilemma certainly provided us with some laughter for a few days. But then we realized they were serious and weren't taking us back. We weren't going home, and they didn't believe we couldn't make babies.

After a few more days they gave us freer reign of the ship, but they still wouldn't give us our clothes back because they figured that as soon as one of us would spring to attention then the other of us would want to mate. We tried to explain about privacy and intimacy to them, but it didn't seem to work. We watched them use some of their amazing equipment.

"We are coming to Coxis Seven," said Pith.

"Goody, we will nab a pair of Penipusses," Thuk said. "Set the Orgometer. Scan the area."

No one had to explain—these weirdos were preparing another hapless kidnapping on two unsuspecting people. A whirring little orgasmic triangle spun around wildly, trying to find the best creatures to bring up.

Suddenly a bright flash appeared and two 10-foot tall, purple-skinned creatures howled at us. They were up on their hind legs and had awfully long scales on their backs and heads, but when they turned their crotch area had two incredibly long penises, snaking through the air like arms. They were limp but floating like they were probing for something.

"OK, now for a little cross-breeding test," said Pith. "You won't do it amongst yourselves, so here's something just for you."

We were locked up with the two large purple monsters, and we were scared. The purplish men-monsters stood up and sniffed us. One of them held me down while the other snorted and sniffed me all over, breathing its sweet grassy breath over my chest and armpits and lingering at my crotch. Its mouth opened over it. I screamed.

Fred rushed over. Immediately, the other creature pinned him down and did the same body exploration.

The creatures grabbed our crotches roughly and yanked them toward their own. I squeezed my eyes tight as our dicks tangled in among their long, purple duo-dicks. It was scary. Their dicks felt warm as a drool of honey in a live oak. It sent prickles up and down my spine.

The one that grabbed mine did so gently. His hands were clammy and my dick sunk into them like clay. It was a nice feeling. Fred was being yanked too and seemed to enjoy it. These scaly creatures were so soft in the front, and they seemed gentle.

Then each of them shoved one of his long purple shafts into his own belly button, and they seemed to moan with pleasure. The appendages went in and out independently, without any of the necessary hip action I had gotten so good at with Sunny Mae. They were like oil drills, pumping and grinding on their own. Then one of their clay soft fingers reached into my butthole like an icy-cool thermometer. I shouted and pulled away, but the creature got rough with me. Suddenly I was pushed over and the other whirling purple dickhead was shoved inside of me.

My butt was burning with pain, searing as the purple drill pumped deeper and deeper still, all inside my butt. I felt like it was drilling to the other side.

Fred was down on his face too, looking desperate.

"Just don't move, don't say anything, and maybe they'll stop," said Fred. "Don't cry out in pain, but oh, shit this, uh—oooh, it hurts."

As the pumping reached farther and farther, deeper and deeper, I could see Fred wasn't wincing anymore, and he seemed to relax into it and smile. I looked at him and smiled too. It was starting to feel good, but I'd never admit it. I reached up over my head and squeezed Fred's hand.

The creatures were rubbing our dicks raw. Even in their soft hands, without anything slick it hurt. They stroked too roughly, too harsh for me.

Then this reptilian creature on my back arched his back to me and shot an icy vein of liquid inside of me, causing me to squeal. It felt like icy piss filling me up. Fred got his a few minutes later. The four bug eyes were staring down at us, and I was angry. They took the beasts away from our room, and I looked at Fred, still splayed out on the floor, and I saw white come dripping from his dick. He laughed at the experience.

"You had an orgasm in all that?" I was hurt and betrayed that he had actually enjoyed that violation. He rubbed his aching butt, and his dick flopped—still a bit stiff. I squatted in a corner and rubbed the ooze off me.

"It was pretty incredible, wasn't it?" he said.

"I guess, but I wouldn't want it to happen again."

He reached over and squeezed my arm. I nuzzled with him, rubbing the chest hairs that hadn't been pulled out of his chest during the rough session. I felt very close to Fred. I guess I'd felt it before, but not like this. I was trembling. We no longer cared about being nekkid.

"My dick is so raw," I said.

Fred gathered some spit up in his mouth, leaned over into my lap, and gently licked my dick. I was shocked, I couldn't believe it. My best buddy was sucking on me! But it was soothing, and cool, and nice. He bent me over a might bit, and I found my face next to his own crotch, and I thought, *What the hell?*

I smelled his musky crotch and the hairs tickled my nostrils. I popped the head into my mouth whole and licked lightly. He moaned and took me deeper into his wet mouth. I could feel myself growing inside of his mouth, and I could feel with my tongue how his veins were pumping more blood into his thick, red, perfectly shaped dickhead. His dick tasted so slick, so salty. I licked down the shaft and took his balls in my lips.

We had a wonderful sucking session, taking slow strokes. It tasted better than I'd ever imagined—nice, salty, and clean. I was sad we'd never done it before. This was the kind of great sex you read about in *Forum,* but the parts were all wrong. It shouldn't feel this great with a guy, but it did.

Then Fred turned me over with his muscular arms, and he guided his newly stiff rod into my backside, which had already been opened beyond proportions. I groaned, but this time it was definitely for pleasure. It felt hot and good. He eased inside, then built up to a slow pumping.

We both erupted, but this time it was special. It was real, it seemed. We hugged after, and then he kissed me—a long, deep kiss. His tongue probed between my lips, with his hand squeezing on my still-spasming cock.

"That was lovely," Pith said from above. "Just lovely."

"Can you do it again?" asked Thuk.

We didn't say anything.

"When are you taking us home?" Fred asked.

"We have a mission. We're going there," Pith said pointing at a screen. It was a deep, dark black hole, shaped like a giant butt out in the middle of space.

"We're blasting off into a black hole?" said Fred.

"We may never get home!" I wailed.

Thuk turned to us and said, "But don't you love each other?"

Fred and I looked at each other. I looked down, but I could

see that he nodded. I stood close enough to him so that my dick brushed against his hairy thigh. I nodded too. I reached down and slid my fingers between his butt cheeks.

After that, the Oonomatts seemed to let us alone for the most part. We're going from place to place, exploring the planets in the new dimension of the black hole. The Oonomatts, though quite intelligent, still don't understand that we aren't going to be reproducing any time soon. They gave us this opportunity to beam our story down to someone back home, but even if you can translate it I don't know how you could help us, really. They still want us to reproduce.

"Well, maybe there's something a little wrong with us," I said to Thuk.

Thuk's big ol' ugly eyes looked at us, sad and confused.

Fred smiled at me, and conspired. I could see his loins twitch a little.

"But hey, listen. We'll just keep on trying," he said, winking.

"Yeah," I added. "We'll try till we get it right, OK?"

JERKING OFF 2069 A.D.: FORBIDDEN FRUITS IN THE SEXUAL NUCLEAR WINTER

DECEMBER 15, 2000

Scott, my favorite student, came into my office wearing overalls, and I knew he had nothing on underneath. He leaned over my desk and plopped another big, juicy red apple on it.

"You know you got an A in the class. You aced the exam," I said.

It was a few days after the last final of the semester. Most of my students had already gone home for Christmas break. I knew Scott wanted something, but it was more than just another sexual tryst this time.

"Um, Professor Skee, um, Mickey, I know you're a writer too, and we didn't get a chance to talk much about that in your class, but I love your erotica," Scott stammered. "I love your writing. I mean, I get off on it, even though I'm straight and such."

I was flattered. I got off on him too, even though he's straight and such, and was tempted to tell him that I'd no doubt be writing about him in future books.

"Well, I was wondering if you'd read this story I wrote myself. It was something that came to me in a dream—kind of like a nightmare—and I wrote it down. Would you read it?" Scott asked.

I was flattered and delighted. And surprised, actually,

because it was good. I read it, out loud, with him sitting there. By the end, we both had our hands down his overalls, and my desk got a bit messy.

Here's Scott's nightmare, and my dream....

My fingers probed the forbidden bulge straining between my legs. I looked around for the Street Probes and couldn't find one pointing its intrusive cyclopean eye at me, spying my very horniness. I turned down a concrete walkway that throbbed with people who were all covered up, their noses buried in wraps so they wouldn't breathe in the cloudy, piss-colored sky, their faces protected from the A-rays of the deteriorating zone.

My blood boiled and my boner surged with every slow and sensuous step, creating a very obvious protrusion down the length of my right pant leg. My recyclable disposable fiber clothes weren't holding up very well, and I could feel the moisture of my protrusion steaming through the cloth. I saw a drain tube along the concrete walk and bent down to uncover the person-hole and curl up inside it. My face bent forward to see the delightful smiling outline of my cock head through the fiber pants. I released my cock and as it flopped onto my bare, hairy chest I nervously looked around and began to stroke the underside roughly.

Stuffed into that dark drain tube, I squeezed my fist into the joint just above my balls and pushed and turned. I then worked my way up, up the length of the thick shaft to that smiling little piss slit, being careful not to ooze too quickly.

My knees were almost over my head as I sat there executing my forbidden jerk-off. It had been a full two months since my allowed sex-release period, and although the government allows us four releases a year, the backlog usually means delays of many weeks. I couldn't wait another two months, so I jerked. I jerked my cock blue, even knowing the consequences, even under penalty of Gender Control.

As I ground my fist more and more into my extended, stiffening tool, I squeezed my deadly testicles until I felt pain. I grasped each of those tender grapes between my fingers and plucked at them as if milking out their poisonous wine directly from the ball-sac. I heaved my chest as my pulse quickened, but I couldn't groan, I couldn't scream, I couldn't utter a single orgasmic sound lest I be caught. You see, I was ID'd.

As I felt the build-up deep within the hairy root of my crotch, I fished around for a receptacle in the dark, dank drain hole that I was sitting in and found a discarded metal recyclable cover. I placed it between my raging red rooster and my hairy chest, and as I drove my fist deeper into my shaft, I felt the numb, hard top of my knob press against the cool cover. The first ooze poked through the lips of the smiling face of my penis, and I had to be quick to spit on it to dilute it so I could rub it around the rest of the shaft. I knew I had to do it quickly, or suffer the burns and scars of my lust. I had to get that ecstatic, erotic release, or else I'd go crazy. And I had to do it fast, or it could very well be my last.

I exploded. The white jism shot out. I moved my head to avoid a particularly noteworthy spurt. The rest of the gush poured into the metal plate covering my chest. Almost immediately, the sizzling began on the metal cover. The acidic jism scorched its way through the metal, and I rolled away quickly. As I slipped out I slid on my recyclable pants; the ooze had eaten all the way through the metal and was burrowing into the concrete, sending up a little rise of bluish steam as it crackled.

It's a bleak age—the age of the Sexual Nuclear Winter. It's the age of dreams coming true, but those dreams are your nightmares, your worst, most feared nightmares.

It started off slowly, 'round the turn of the New Millennium. The skies grew lightly gray in all the cities; now they're a murky yellow. The mass of swirling, squirming, writhing humanity on the streets is always passing, always destined for somewhere, or nowhere, but never touching. No way, man. Don't touch, don't jostle, don't even nudge. No contact at all.

It's the age of fucking diseases, man. The sun rays are synonymous with cancer, and only the lower classes have red cheeks or a bronze complexion. Folks are afraid to come out of their cubicles, even for a monthly air cleaning, 'cause of all the Z-strains traveling through the air. And then there's TAZ, the 13th and most deadly derivative of the sex virus. It's still only transmitted through sex, or blood, or some kind of internal ingestion, but this one's quicker and creates a toxic jism. It gets you ID'd and quarantined pretty quickly. Once you're ID'd, that's serious.

I don't remember what TAZ stands for anymore. I don't think anyone does, except the Sexperts and those in Gender Control. But now it seems more of the government's energy is expended on keeping us separate from the Normies than on finding out how to cure it. It's beginning to piss some of us off.

Until recently, I've avoided the roving, marauding, raping gangs of my quadrant. I've stayed in my cubicle, pretty much to myself, sticking to my regularly scheduled five minutes of potty privileges, staying within my allotted nutrition packets and keeping to my sexual-release periods. But when the telemessage came over the Street Probe about the newest recyclable, I just lost it. That was the last straw. OK, it was bad enough when they made us reuse condoms—pre-TAZ for me, of course—and it was pretty intolerable when we first were limited to potty privileges due to sewage overflows (funny, how quickly your body adjusts to a specific release time), but the toothbrush recycling was beyond any reasonable limit, and I just couldn't take it anymore. Having to share my toothbrush with seven other people in my quadrant—people I didn't even know—was just beyond personal limits. It's bad enough that the Street Probes are turned on even in our very own bedrooms to monitor our sex habits and control our bodily functions, but this was going too far. I joined the TAZ Mania Devils, a deadly gang.

The Devils were the worst of the fringe protesters, run by a lawless tall blond ruffian named Rolf who packed one of the largest cocks in the entire ID'd quarantine sector. The first time I was blindfolded and escorted into the devil's lair, my eyes were unveiled right in front of Rolf's hairless, powerful chest. With one hand, he gripped my neck and lifted me up as he ripped my pants off with the other hand and measured my limp, quivering member. But the feeling, the groping, the fondling of my loins caused me to stir. In an instant it was up, despite my uncomfortable position, and he grunted with seeming pleasure at my response.

Then he rolled down his own fiber pants and I gasped at his gargantuan protrusion. It was as big around as my wrist, and his fat cock head was the size of my fist. Initiation into the gang was to get that monster inside of me, and I knew it would be my death. I couldn't back out now, but I'd had no idea it was so huge. Not only would it rip right through my crack, but Rolf's TAZ-tainted come would sear my kidneys and I'd die of internal bleeding. I tried to squirm away, and to hide my raging hard-on, but he forced me onto the gritty ground face first as the rest of the gang pulled out their own protrusions and watched the heartless rape. Tears welled up in my eyes as he gripped both sides of my ass cheeks and positioned them in front of his third arm, sticking erect and hard. Two Devils slapped some motor oil over his throbber. It took four hands, and they used meta-latexed gloves on their fingers to coat my hole, which was already puckering in horrific anticipation. I hadn't had anything inserted into my butt since I was ID'd more than four years ago, and I was hungry for it—even though I knew it was suicide. I cared no more. My dick reached its full 10½ and was almost vertical in front of me, causing a gasp from some of the Devils. I closed my eyes as my death-fuck approached.

But Rolf was gentler than I'd expected. I could feel his thick, sinewy arms press against my shoulders as he eased my backside onto his rod. He wriggled the crabapple-size blue bulge into my dripping butt. My sphincter seared for what seemed like an eternity and then the shaft eased in slowly as he bumped and drove it like a very controlled power drill or oil rig. Eventually, he built up speed. The Devils around us were breaking the law unmercifully by pumping their own meat, some fondling one another as they watched. I felt like I was being pummeled by a jackhammer as he churned faster inside of me, and his golf ball–size balls slapped against my flanks like a harsh spanking.

Expertly and proficiently, before even the first drip of pre-come could wreak havoc on my innards, Rolf pulled out. He didn't come. He didn't even gush. He contained his semen. What a pro. I, on the other hand—and most of the dudes watching—all put holes in the walls, floor, and furniture with our seething spermatozoa. A few of us have developed welts on the tips of our cock heads, and I noticed that some of the uncut dudes had huge holes burned into their foreskin by the toxic jism, but most of us have developed a thick layer of scar tissue around the end of our throbbing members to prevent any further burning as we ejaculate.

So that's how I was initiated into the gang. After that, I was allowed to go on secret night raids in our sector, to take revenge on the elitist politicos. We picked our victims with care: those who were forcing diversions by passing orders that would result in our extermination. Many politicos said they would rather exterminate those of us who were ID'd than find a TAZ cure. Of course, I felt that way too, when I was a Normie.

My first excursion was for a Senator Cockswell of the 457th Quadrant, who was living with an elitist young man named Swain, the son of a factory baron. Cockswell pushed through an order that would allow the Gender Control Patrol to take those of us who were ID'd out of our restricted quadrants and turn us all into eunuchs. It was the greatest nightmare of all. My best pal in the Devils, Spandy, had a marvelous piece of meat that I often found between my lips, until one day he was caught masturbating along the brick alleys after curfew. The Gender Control did the cock cauterization right there on the spot, without a hearing. They hung his glorious, huge, decapitated penis and balls on the door of his cubicle for a week until it smelled and rotted. He nursed what was left of his singed hole for four weeks before ever coming out. It was so unfair—until he figured out how to fight back.

Spandy now is an Oral Master in the Devils, and he still gets his pleasure chewing our meat. But with our enemies, he has learned to do his own form of cock cauterization, with his sharpened teeth. His victims bleed to death.

Spandy, Rolf, and I, along with three other big-dicked Devils, approached the senator's cubicle and first gave him the ultimatum to rescind his proposed order, but he refused. His lover, Swain, begged us not to hurt the two of them, and he cowered in a corner with his smooth white skin—all naked and hunched, his long, flowing black mane rolling past his shoulders. We had apparently interrupted them in a legal sexual-release period. Swain was like a kept pet in the senator's cubicle, only serving the pleasure of the powerful hypocrite, who refused to acknowledge he was a queer himself. Even though it didn't seem to matter to anyone in the world as we knew it, the senator kept it his own private affair, choosing to abuse the factory baron's son.

I watched as Rolf gave a nod and let the three Devils ravage the senator, while Swain wailed from his crumpled position in the corner, shivering like a cold puppy. The senator had a 10-incher shoved into his butthole, while another 10-incher was straddling his face and the smallest-dicked Devil, at 8½, was prodding the senator's ear with his weenie.

I smiled as I noticed that the senator's fat, tiny dingy was growing into a grotesquely bent hardness as he was being ravaged, and Spandy quickly got on his knees and did some lapping. But Rolf ordered Spandy not to bite off this one. The senator liked it.

"I never, I never," the senator kept repeating as his harmless white come squirted out all over us. Swain was still bawling in a corner, his limp dick hanging almost to his kneecaps. I wondered if Rolf would let us ravage Swain. That's who I was waiting for.

The Devils came. The first gush hit the ear and surged into the senator's head, boring a hole right into his eyes. The senator howled in pain, and suddenly we saw the Street Probe in his room whir into action and point in our direction. None of us really cared. We knew we'd be out of there before Gender Control could get to this outlying cubicle. A glob of steaming jism filled the senator's mouth and his cheeks melted away, showing only his pearly teeth as it ate through his skin like water soaks into a sponge. The senator fell into death spasms as the third Devil let the dying man's quivering butthole milk him of his remaining jism.

Swain was bawling like a beautiful, white, hairy baby as he watched his fat, slobbering lover fall into a melted heap. We turned our stiffening cocks to him, and I felt sorry for the loss of this beautiful body, with is cock as long as a horse's. (At least that's what I had heard about horses. They were all gone.)

Rolf ordered me to pry the young man's mouth open, so I did, with my cock hanging out of its leather harness. I pushed myself deep into Swain's warm, gaping, wet lips. He deep-throated quickly, quite an expert. Swain's eyes bulged right out of their sockets as Rolf took the rear. I knew the pain and the pleasure, and wondered why Rolf would allow such a treat for this enemy.

My dick slid in and out of Swain's lips, and he looked up at me, pleading for me not to sear his throat and stomach with my lava-burning semen. I rubbed my fingers through his long brown mane and squeezed the cheeks of his face as he gagged on my ever-thickening rod. I was facing Rolf, and he winked his big blue eyes at my thin white body. Rolf leaned over and stuck his tongue down my throat, which sent a tingle all the way to the tip of my cock head, which was pounding Swain's tonsils.

Then Rolf whispered to me, "Don't come in his mouth."

I suddenly exercised the greatest restraint—as my gush was ready to pump into this angelic white face, I exited the lips and heard a pop as the sucking stopped. My orgasm was near and a few drops of precome started out of me. Rolf grabbed a golden goblet from the senator's shelf behind him and spit in it. Then he took the back end of my penis and shook some of the precome into the goblet and it immediately started fizzing. He spit a few more times into the goblet and drove his dick further into Swain's ass. The pain made Swain buck forward and open his mouth in a pained yell, and Rolf poured the searing, steaming concoction into Swain's open mouth. He tried to cough it out, his tongue burning, his throat gagging. A very diluted bit of my precome entered his throat, but it didn't burn through it, from what we could tell.

Swain shook in pain and anguish as Rolf's cock plopped out of his ass. Rolf again didn't come, and I admired his control. Swain cowered away from us.

"Go ahead, kill me now! Fill me with it, get it over," Swain cried.

Rolf walked over, yanked Swain's head up, and said, "We have no gripe with you, only people like him and your father. I'm giving you a choice. Come with us, or stay here."

Swain looked at us, with our long dicks hanging in front of him, and then he looked up at the camera of the Street Probe, wondering when they would arrive.

"They all know I'm infected now, I can't stay here anyway," he said. "I'll join you."

I was delighted to see Rolf's kindness and glad that someone as handsome as Swain had joined our ranks. I knew it would provide hours of enjoyment as we took turns poking the new boy, much like they all did me when I first joined. I planned to be the first to practice on him.

As months went by, Swain and I became coupled, and we often went on excursions together, infecting any Normie Rolf ordered us to, sometimes going a bit too far because of our horniness. Swain really enjoyed his new work. He cut his hair short and went on the Street Probe throughout the whole sector denouncing his father, and the politico Normies in his father's pocket. It had a great effect on public opinion of the TAZ Mania Devil cause. We were having a great time, but we were concerned about our leader, Rolf.

We always talked about wanting to allow Rolf to "get off" because I continuously noticed how his self control, which I had at first admired so much, was now becoming a source of distress and irritation. Rolf was allowing himself no fun.

Once while he slept, Swain and I each took a side of his protrusion and licked it stiff. I then held it up with two hands and coaxed Spandy the eunuch to mouth the head of the cock in order to give Rolf pleasure, but then he awoke. He shook us off like flies and scolded us.

"I just wanted to see you come, Rolf. I wanted you to enjoy it," I said.

"I enjoy working with the gang. That's my pleasure," he said, not allowing even a drop to fall.

On one ambush, Swain and I found a deadbeat scientist who was vivisecting ID'd guys to discover how their testicles churned up such potent jism. We cornered him at a brick walkway in the ancient quadrant, near a pile of recyclable containers. As Swain beat him with a club, I checked his identification card to see that we had the right victim. We did. The old guy almost allowed himself to be infected willingly, sticking his butt up in the air. But instead, I shot my wad all over Swain's club, and he in turn shoved his down the good doctor's throat.

"No, not me, not me," the scientist said, trying to spit up. "I don't want to die. Oh, I don't want to be ID'd."

"Neither do we," I said.

"Go back, and do us some good," Swain ordered. He booted the scientist in the bottom and sent him scurrying back to his lab cubicle.

Rolf laughed when he heard of the doctor's reaction, and he rewarded our successful excursion by inserting his dick inside us. First he did Swain until Swain popped off and burned a hole through a door. Then he entered my hindquarters, as Swain licked Rolf's butthole with his tongue. I had practiced super control with my ass muscles and I held Rolf's penis inside of me to the point that he had trouble pulling out. Swain and I had conspired to take this risk, so Swain kept tonguing his ass and keeping Rolf from being able to pull out. Swain's body pinned Rolf and I together and my tight ass-grip kept Rolf inside, much to his continuing distress. Rolf tried hoisting Swain off his backside, and then tried lifting me off his dick, but just as he had nearly succeeded Spandy scooted between us and lapped up the wet shaft of the underside of Rolf's dick—all of it that was not totally inside of my asshole, that is. We went at it, over and over, and suddenly we felt that Rolf was losing control.

"NO! NO! Let me loose!" Rolf barked. I knew I was most in danger of getting burned, but figured it was worth it. I tightened my butthole grip as he screamed. "NoooooOOOOO!"

He erupted in waves of torrents. A white gob shot so deep into my ass that I shot off of his rod and was thrown against a wall. Milky-white cream hit Spandy right between the eyes and my lovely, pure-faced Swain got hit right in the mouth as the whole room was doused in Rolf's semen. I waited for the burning in my ass to melt into my kidneys and out the other side, since I could feel the sticky stuff far up in my abdomen. Likewise, as quickly as Spandy and Swain tried wiping the come off their faces, they expected the burning to start, and perhaps kill them. Nothing happened.

We looked at one another. No one burned, no one even singed. The handful of come in Spandy's palm wasn't burning, so we all took a sniff and a look. Swain licked his lips.

"That tasted good," he said. He dove his tongue into Spandy's hand and lapped up some more as I looked on incredulously.

"You're a Normie, Rolf!" I said. "But why?"

Rolf's monster protrusion slumped off his muscular loins in limp spasms as he sheepishly explained, "I wanted to help you guys out here in the ID'd quadrant, but I didn't want you to know I was not one of you. I wanted to be accepted. There are lots of Normies fighting for your cause, you know. We believe in you. I just didn't think it was enough for me to get infected too."

Spandy handed me a come-covered finger and I sucked it off with a smile. It was warm, slippery, and tasty. I'd never licked it before, and I envied the Normies who could produce so delicious a substance.

"I guess I'll have to go back to my quadrant now," Rolf said. "I guess the jig is up."

"It doesn't have to be," said Swain, still licking his lips. "We could certainly keep your secret."

"But why? Why would you do that?" Rolf said. "You have nothing to lose."

"Ah, but we have everything to gain," Spandy said, picking up the shriveling limp dick hanging in front of our fearless leader.

I started to understand, and I nodded in approval.

"Great idea!" I said.

"W-what?" gulped Rolf.

"You let us suck you off once a week, and let us drink your jism, and we'll let you keep your secret and lead us," Swain said.

"No, I can't—"

"Why not?" I asked. "You may begin to enjoy sex again."

Rolf agreed to let us have a trial period. Because we all three couldn't suck him off at the same time, we had to visit him on separate occasions. Rolf was servicing us about two or three times a day.

So, we were kept very happy. Rolf is still our leader, and he's smiling a lot more now. It's our first breakthrough with the Normies, as we see it, and we know it won't be our last. Things are looking a little bit better for the future of the Sexual Nuclear Winter after all.

A HOT ROMAN HOLIDAY

JULY 28, 2001

It's a boring, hot summer. The campus is all but closed up, but they're shooting a movie with famed director George Cuckold, the offbeat, closeted director. My favorite TV stars, Mitch Kelles and Jay Churchly, are supposed to be in the film, so I begged my way into the cast, along with some of the other students and faculty who remained on campus for the summer. It turned out to be a star-studded experience.

Oh, yes, that is the same Jay Churchly who was in my frat for a while. He became a big super TV star, but somehow doesn't talk in interviews about how he likes a cock in his mouth.

I love living on campus. My friend John visits occasionally and I've introduced him to this generation of hot new meat. But this summer he's off again at some exotic place, and I'm supervising the dorms on campus and teaching an easy summer school class.

No one's paying attention to schoolwork, though. A TV movie's being shot on campus....

The tall man's sweaty hand grasped the shoulder of the bare-breasted warrior and steadied the fallen hulk in the battlefield. The dashing commander ripped off his blue velvet robe and stood there almost nude as he cradled the fleshy maleness of the youthful warrior in his own mighty grip and stroked the hairy chest of his fallen comrade. He let his fingers curl up into the hairs of the youth's chest. He massaged him tenderly, stroking his cheek with the back of his fingers. He was sobbing.

He then leaned over and planted a kiss on the youth's lips, softly, deeply. *Pause.*

"CUT!" The assistant director shouted it too loudly and broke the intense concentration of the actors and the audience watching on the sidelines, but immediately the rest of us broke into applause and the director smiled widely. Of course, we all had hard-ons too. The actors were still enmeshed in their embrace and broke their kiss as if they had just awakened.

One of them, Mitch Kelles—a burly actor whose wife is a TV news anchor—quickly stood up, and the rest of us could see that his formidable protrusion had not yet subsided under his robe. And the bulge under the loose-fitting robes of the young handsome lead actor Jay Churchly was even more pronounced, much to our delight.

Neither of them knew when they first signed on that their roles in the Roman period film being shot on campus would be quite as homoerotic as they'd turned out to be. No doubt it was all due to George Cuckold, the well-known director of very bizarre and cutting-edge films. Only he could have gotten these two household names into such an embrace and make it appear believable.

I was impressed with the idea, but I wondered how even a famous, powerful director like Cuckold could continue this level of blatant gender-crushing scenes in his mainstream, $60 million movie. Sure, the life of Cocklickula did have a hint of sensuality, and the history books housed right there on campus prove that a lot of sex went on between him and his men, but to bring it to the mainstream—that's a challenge.

Obviously, the sensuous nature of *Gladiator* sparked interest in big-studio copycats, but they wanted to do something different with Cuckold. In fact, the pitch line was: "It's *Queer as Folk* meets *Gladiator*"—and the studio chiefs frothed.

Cuckold convinced them at DreamJerks that the legends of Spermaticus are pure unadulterated history, and Cuckold seemed bent on reliving as much of it as he could get away with *and* avoiding an NC-17 rating.

"Can I show pee-pee? I want to show pee-pee, let's see if we can get pee-pee on TV," Cuckold kept telling his A.D. Those of us in-the-know were laughing because Jay Churchly's past costar on that teen show just showed his willy in a dramatic scene on the TV show *Ooze,* which takes place in a prison. Jay was jealous and immediately signed up for his full-frontal role in this project.

The costumes were all soft velvet with feathered hoods. The robes were draped so that hairy bare chests were evident; a few of them wore muscular breastplates and thick jockstraps that showed their bare hips. The cock-guards were large and protruding metal bulges, made as they were originally.

Hot, squat campus historian Nikko Nadooley was the consultant hired for the project, and he made everything as authentic as possible. Nikko's the curator of the Collection of Ultimate Male Memorabilia, or CUMM Museum, on campus, and he explained to the costume designers how the costumes should be made.

My favorite student, Scott, who graduated and became a well-known porn star for Hot House studios, got a role in the movie because Cuckold was a fan of his work. Nikko used Scott as a model for the costumes, and of course I peeked in to watch.

"So you see, there were feathers located on the inside of the cups in order to tickle the troops to erection at the time they were called to action," explained Nikko as he dressed Scott, whose muscles bulged from a recent workout. Scott smiled shyly as he apologized for sweating profusely in the heat.

Off to the side, in tight shorts, Sam, the A.D., was visibly moved by the costume of feathers and velvet. He particularly had his eye on Scott's codpiece. Sam was a film student at the school who had just graduated and lucked out getting a job on this big shoot. I always thought he'd be better directing porn because he was perpetually horny.

"I need to keep the costs down, Professor Nadooley. I don't understand why the feathers need to be inside when audiences can't see them anyway," Sam protested.

"Well, it's authentic, and this is the reason why," said Nikko, unbuckling the codpiece and revealing Scott's hard-on. Scott looked over at me standing in the doorway and came over to hug me, his boner pressed up against my left thigh.

"Scotty, you've grown!" I said, slipping down to my knees and quickly getting the length of Scott's smooth cock down my throat.

"Professor Skee, I've got a shoot tomorrow, I can't," Scott said, coyly pulling away.

"But I don't have a shoot tomorrow," smiled Sam, as I saw his dark red cock head poke out from his jeans. He approached me while I was still on my knees and in seconds I had his 10-inch Middle Eastern cock down my throat. Nikko approached as Scott stood by and stroked himself.

"You see, with the tickling going on inside the codpiece, these troops were obviously ready for anything," Nikko said, pulling out his own thick, hardened cock and waving it in my face. I took them both in my mouth.

"And it would make the guards stand stiff at attention at all times," explained Nikko as his cock slid against Sam's while in my mouth. Sam looked over to where Scott sat on a box with his boner stiff and upright. Scott didn't touch it, knowing he had to preserve his load for a porn shoot in the morning.

"I see what you mean, it's a good idea," Sam said. "But I need to only have one feather inside then, that's all I can afford."

"It's a deal," said Nikko as he squirted a load in my hair over my left shoulder. Sam came quickly after, on my right shoulder, and I rubbed the come in my shiny blond locks.

The cock-guards were held up on the warriors by a thin gold strand, and there was little else to the costumes so many of the actors showed their fine hairy asses and long sinewy thighs.

On the set, many of them also fell out of their cock-guards, some seemingly on purpose, revealing their true assets. Sometimes, the intensely sexy action on the set caused some of them to get hard-ons, which knocked their guards out of place. Then they needed the grips more than ever. I finally understood what grips did on the set. Scott made a point of falling out a few times during the scenes where the warriors stood at attention, and that assured him that the director would keep moving him closer and closer to the camera.

"I want more than just an extra role," Scott said, as he was moved to the front of the line after his cock had peeked out of its cover.

"You are more than an extra!" exclaimed Cuckold.

"I want more than a cameo," Scott said, a bit shyly.

"You will get a part before this is all over, my boy, a big part," the director promised. I rolled my eyes.

All the men in the cast and even the dozens of extras, mostly from campus, were carefully selected, handsome, buff bods, and in their prime—some of the top names in the movie industry and the adult industry had begged the director for cameo appearances in the much-talked-about film project.

The casting directors were specifically looking for long-haired blond guys, and that's where I came in. Along with a few surfer dudes who had no tan lines at all, and a few guys from the college swim team who grew their hair out for the summer, there was me—fresh from a summer of sunbathing naked. I thought I might have been too old, so Sam put in a good word for me. But the casting director wanted to see more.

I'm lucky, see, because the casting director immediately asked us to stand in front of him and pull down our pants, and I was ready for him. I was almost insulted and shocked enough to walk out, but I stayed because I wanted to see what else was going to happen, and I wanted to see what some of these surfers and swimmers were packing. I wasn't disappointed, and the whole bunch of us had at least a minor stiffy during this spot inspection.

"Can't have a tan line—you're out. Can't have too hairy a butt—you've gotta go," said Shaw, the white-haired talent scout as he went down the line militaristic-like, dismissing guys left and right. When he came to me, he cupped my cock in his hand and gave it a gentle nudge and cooed, "Oooh, it looks like this one's been out in the sun too long. If you need some suntan oil later, let me know and I'll help you rub it in."

My sincerest thanks go to Sam, who must've landed me the role after my bodacious blow job, and Shaw, who flirted unmercifully. I wouldn't have even minded putting out for Shaw, but luckily that never came up since he was always rubbing oil on the crotches of the younger members of the swim team.

I was lucky enough (perhaps horny enough) to be pulled out of the Longhaired Blond Extras troupe and land a five-line scene with Mitch Kelles and young, studly Jay Churchly. They both earned great careers as TV actors, but they're both trying to break into big-screen stuff. Of course these days the easiest way to make your mark is to play gay-themed roles in funky independent projects.

I was cast, no doubt, because I was a bit older than the college studs and could easily play the wise sage they needed. The actors were famous, but I wasn't impressed with them, really. Not yet, anyway.

Mitch is the one with the overly protective wife, and Jay always played the handsome leading man on TV and was plastered on the cover of every *Teen Beat Off* magazine on the stands. I'd always heard Internet rumors about Mitch's sexuality but never had any firsthand solid evidence of his proclivities—until now.

Not necessarily a size queen, I was impressed by the enormity of it all. The sets built around the campus quad were enormous. Large phallic pillars were erected, just like in a genuine city. Nikko helped authenticate the original architecture of the day as much as possible, placing long, skinny Ionic columns here and thick, bulging Doric columns there and flaring, fancy, jutting Corinthian columns in between. Much of it was incorporated into the phallic pillars of the historic buildings on campus.

Large, hot steam pools were built along the grassy hills near the Spermarium and slick slabs of granite and marble were placed all over campus for the soldiers to bask their naked bodies on, to get rid of the tan lines that Shaw hated so much.

The set was teeming with testosterone. Every morning Cuckold would take the men to the steps of one of the temples in the mini city he had built and tell them the story of the sex warrior Cocklickula and how much the historical, hysterical fag loved his men. He told us stories about the warriors and their orgies, and he added more explicit detail each time, to the point that I thought it was going to turn into a circle jerk every morning.

I was astounded by how intrigued Mitch Kelles was by the interaction of the men of the Roman Empire. He often raised his hand to asked questions like "And did they really have hard-ons when they went into battle?" or "Did they really have oral sex just after slaying someone with their swords?" He was an actor who was doing his research, all right, but he seemed to be enjoying it a bit too much.

I noticed one night, during a break while shooting a party scene, our very straight leading man, Mitch Kelles, was walking around the set, seemingly a bit agitated. He saw me and ordered me over. I was in nothing but my robe. He was in nothing but his codpiece, and quite a commanding one it was at that.

"Don't I know you from somewhere?" Mitch started. "I mean, somewhere other than this shoot?"

"Oh, no, I've never acted before, this is my big break, Mr. Kelles," I lied. Indeed, he'd have me thrown off the set if he knew of my porn-writing connection. Maybe he recognized me from cameos I'd had in a few of the porn movies he may have watched, but I didn't want to mention those. "I just teach here, and we're on break now."

"What are you playing in this?" he said, mildly ordering.

"A sort of wise slave," I swallowed. "I think we have a scene together."

"Sort of? You can't sort of be wise or sort of be a slave, you have to get into character," he said. "Let's rehearse."

I wasn't quite sure what he was up to until he softened his voice just a little bit and said, "I love your long flowing blond hair."

Aha, that was it? He wanted to fool around?

I was willing to play hard-to-get if he wanted to play that way, but I really wanted to be caught. Especially by him, the macho guy I watched on television for such a long time as a teen, hiding under the covers and working up my hard-on while using his face as my jack-off fantasy.

"Come here, peon, get on your knees and kneel to your god," he bellowed.

"Are you sure those are the lines?" I asked, already on my knees.

"SILENCE!" He looked down at me, wild-eyed and powerful. "For that insolence you will clean my feet."

I looked around for a basin, or a prop of any sort.

"With your tongue!" he snapped.

Without thinking, I was licking his feet, sticking my tongue between his toes and working my way up his ankle to his hairy brown legs.

"Enough! On your feet," he said, and I obeyed. "You're a good slave, you will be rewarded."

His handsome square jaw and grizzled face were inches away from my lips. He pressed them against his face, and kissed me. It soon became a free-for-all. We kissed and hugged and stroked each other. We splashed around in the pool and wrestled on the edge of the spongy grass. We stopped for just a brief second as we realized what we were doing, and that any of the cast or crew could have spotted us. Or even worse, the dean at the college or some of my students could have seen us.

Finally, we didn't care.

I found myself on top of him, looking again into his haunting green eyes. I wriggled a little and felt our crotches stirring as they pressed together. We were not naked, not yet, but had only thin layers of cloth keeping us from being nude together. He squirmed under me, and I wriggled some more as I could feel both of us getting hard. I felt the outline of his member. Our cocks intertwined as I pressed even more. Mitch smiled as he squirmed beneath me. I dominated him this time. He didn't like the feeling of helplessness, I could tell.

We kissed deeply, with my tongue delving into his tonsils and molars. Then I inched my way slowly down his body, tasting everything along the way: an earlobe, a nipple, his smooth chest, a belly button. Why not? I had already had his toes. He didn't have too much hair on his body near his chest (it must have been shaved, I figured), so licking was more fun there. And as I slid further and further down, he wriggled and moaned even more.

Then I caught sight of his massive pillar of a cock. It stood up hard, and as I held his uncut cock upright it surprised me to find that I could put my other hand on it too and still have plenty to swallow down my throat. Mitch closed his eyes and I circled my tongue around his head, peeled the skin back, and licked the throbbing underside of his cock. I tickled his balls ever so lightly and he moaned and gyrated.

We had a steamy series of sucking each other off and then we showered under the isolated waterfall built in a corner by the lake.

As we fondled each other's backsides, a tall, thin, stunning young man stood over us with an erect cock. He was another member of the cast, and we realized that a whole host of beefy extras were watching us, dicks erect. They began a fuckfest around us.

We joined the others. One of the Greek guys was playing with his tremendous protrusion as we rolled around some more. Some of the men were singing, some had their mouths full of food, some had their mouths full of cock. As everyone paired off and were heading separate ways, I urged Mitch to find some young guy, someone other than me who wasn't so spent. I pointed to where Scott watched the two of us while three buffed guards were licking his butt cheeks and cock.

"No, I want to be only with you," he said to me as he looked over at Scott.

I was flabbergasted, and I looked back at the bronze blond bods around us and said, "Sure, we can be together, but now we can be together with these guys!"

"No, I want you for myself," he said.

I couldn't believe my ears; I still wonder if he really meant it. I stayed with him, and we found his private trailer and made the most passionate love. The trailer rocked, and I knew some of the others had watched us go in and were hearing our grunts as they stood outside and listened.

He was the no-nonsense, rough and rugged type. Luckily, I was versatile, but he didn't quite ask me if I was. He rammed two fingers in my hungry butt, slipped a thin sheath over his hairy stalk, and wrangled it up my bulbous bottom. I squirmed more than he rammed, and he seemed to like that responsiveness.

"More than the wife gives me at home," he grumbled. I just heaved and wriggled my butt cheeks some more. It seemed we could go on all day. He was insatiable. We were recuperating and almost ready to go at it again when there was a knock on the door. It was Jay Churchly.

"Come on in, lad, I've got something to show you," said Mitch, wiping the come from the face shot I gave him just after he pulled out of my aching anus. Jay walked in before I could hide my dribbling, throbbing, waning wanker. I guess it really didn't matter.

I saw a smile come across Jay's face as he surveyed the scene, and I realized that he may have had some history already with Mitch in the recent past. History like I had with Jay's cock. He lifted up his robe and sported a huge cock—long, red, and erect.

Jay muttered shyly, "I never knew how to do any of this stuff properly, I never knew how it felt so good until I got this role." He smiled. "I guess when in Rome—"

Jay had a long skinny body and he immediately mounted the both of us. He wanted his long, thick 3-hander sliding up my squeezing butt and then sliding inside Mitch's hairy hole too. We tried a triad as Mitch recited some history about three-way fucking among Roman soldiers.

Jay matched my stroking beat and pumped into me with the same stride that I pumped into hairy-chested Mitch's ass. Sometimes I stayed steady and felt myself being pounded as I took long slow strokes inside my wriggling man-stud. I watched in the full-length trailer mirror as I dove into his dark-haired sweaty body and I watched Jay's brunet frame pound into my buttocks. I felt the warm stab of pain stretch my insides and at the same time my grunts grew stronger and more red-hot, deep inside Mitch's hips.

I rubbed the hairs around my belly button and then the ones on Mitch's bottom, then reached over and fondled his stiff erection as I pumped into him. I grabbed his cock with both hands and could feel the blood pulsate with each stroke as I accepted a long, probing cock from behind. I'd imagined what a middleman would be like, but never could have imagined it with two of the most famous mainstream stars in the world.

The pumping from Jay was becoming frenetic. It made

both of us breathless, and I was losing all consciousness except the will to be a part of this horny, steamy sandwich between two of the most handsome hunks that exist on TV.

In the mirror, I could see both sets of famous eyes roll in sexual euphoria.My spurts were drawing toward the tip of my head, and I knew my eyes would be rolling back into my skull too. I watched my dick pull out and then slosh back in to Mitch's aching ass as I massaged his hairy balls and squeezed them as they tightened into smooth and perfect fist-sized orbs. I looked back and saw Jay grunt as he held my back and shoved his uncut monster as far into me as he could.

We went on for what seemed like hours. I was exhausted, but with each breath I somehow got a harder and larger appendage between my legs. Yes, this was probably a day when I hit the 7-inch mark, no doubt. My dick was out of control. It seemed to be a different part of me, yet I knew it was the main source of my pleasure.

We didn't need to say it. It wasn't as if we planned it. We all shot off at the same time. We were so much in sync with one another anyway it was inevitable that the puddles of semen would all shoot out at the same time.

Just then, Jay leaned over to me and said, "I still read your reviews and columns and books all the time, Mickey."

I was flabbergasted and didn't know what to say. I tried to lie: "I don't write reviews," I stuttered. "I teach here on campus. I'm just an extra in this movie, I'm not writing about it."

The two actors looked at each other and gave me a pair of shit-eating grins.

"We're talking about those great gay porno reviews—I know you watch a lot of them, and you show up in a few of them too," Mitch chimed in. He reached behind the VCR in his trailer and pulled out a copy of my *Best of Gay Adult Video* book. Then he held out a pen and asked me to sign it, as my cock dribbled a drop of semen on the dedication page.

I grew a bit red-faced. I didn't think any closeted celebrity

MICKEY SKEE

could possibly know all that about me as a porno reviewer.

The next night, after we thought Cuckold was tucked away in his trailer on campus, the three of us were out by the pond again. Jay and Mitch had a novel idea. Mitch had a large dildo in his hands, and Jay was suddenly being very passive, shocked at the size of the dildo but afraid to object. Mitch slapped Jay until he knelt down, and Mitch mounted him at the edge of the pool as he screamed and sang for us. Some of the other guys in the cast gathered poolside to watch.

Mitch slid the dildo into Jay's hungry butt and joined in singing, as Jay was writhing like a virgin. Some of the other longhairs came closing in on us, and no one objected.

At my end, the hands around me in the pool were all reaching for hot spots between one another's legs. I had four dark paws groping my chest, thighs, and bottom, and within come-squirting distance was the infallible, smooth, hairless bronze body of Jay. I squirmed my way his direction as we watched Mitch glide the dildo in and out of the groaning mass of flesh at the edge of the pool. When Jay saw me coming near he pushed away the others who were feeling him off—and allowed me access to his bobbing cock.

What a sight to behold: All of closeted Hollywood came out of their trailers and joined us in a mutual romantic Roman pud-pull. They were all there: the burly TV detective with the curly hair, the hunky blond spiritual star who just finished a surfer film, the famous actress's son from Ibiza, and the conservative macho movie idol who was rumored to have been taken to a hospital recently with a vacuum hose stuck to his dick. Nikko, Sam, Scotty, and Shaw joined in too.

A rock star, the O Boys, and three other naked superstars groped their way into their own three-ways as Jay pulled himself up and sat at the edge of the pool with his smooth hairless legs dangling in the water and his thighs spread wide in my direction. Gee, someone could make a fortune with photos of this if they took them to *The Daily Sleaze* or *The*

National Inquisitor, I figured. I got out of the pool and looked around for any lingering photo equipment or spying photographers.

Jay's long, curving arrow between his legs poked a pink eye through a dark condomed sheath as he nodded for me to come near. I dove in the pool and let my slick watery body glide toward his very slowly. I waded over, with my head between his thighs and my nose practically touching his tight ball sac, dangling over the edge of the pool.

"How's the water?" Jay coaxed.

"Not as nice as the view," I complimented. I looked over to where director Cuckold was standing, watching me, winking. I breathed in the musky odor of the quivering cock above my nose and took the plunge. I lowered my mouth over the uncut cock of Jay, and he let out a low, growling, chant-like moan. I let the loose skin swirl around my tongue, tasting every inch inside that rubbery chasm while I delicately and expertly rolled his balls between my long fingers. My tongue probed into his slit and then bobbed up and down the bronze length of the aching shaft. Jay sat back far enough so I could slip my pinky into his ass and I let the little fishy wiggle him to a near orgasm.

Mitch joined in and we all heaved excitedly and erupted in spurts that shot clear out of the pool and onto the marble. As we pulled away from one another after some sloppy, soggy kisses, we noticed the applause and hoots from our audience, the entire cast and crew. Cuckold squatted next to us and said, "My delicious nasty sluts."

Jay heaved, exhausted, as did Mitch. Cuckold yelled "CUT!"

We gulped. Just in case I was ever tempted to write about it, Cuckold warned, there would be a recording of the incident.

"Don't try to blackmail us," Mitch warned the director.

"Yeah, I give Mickey my permission to write about it all," Jay said.

Well, by George, it's all here in black-and-white, I don't give a fuck, and I will show my personal version of the video to whoever wants to have their own private screening (and jack-off) with me. The guys didn't seem to mind, after all.

Mitch knew by then that I was an occasional lover with a former rock star years ago, and Jay was friends with the now-superstraight (ha ha) soap star Brian DeJanni, my former bicoastal boyfriend.

"We'll have to make another movie sometime," smiled Jay. "Maybe a movie Mickey can review!"

Mitch smiled, gave me squeeze, and grunted a "yeahhh-hh."

And I mumbled, "Let me know, guys, I'll always be up for that."

Then we continued with my favorite three-way sandwich. This time, Mitch got the middle, took me from behind, and plowed his sausage deep inside my buttocks.

Weeks later, I would discover, on the Pair of Mounts Studio Cafe menu, they would add a mysterious new dish, requested regularly by Mitch and Jay on the studio back lot. If it's not on the menu, don't worry, they still cook it up. You might just have to ask the most handsome waiters about it, and they'll give you a mouthful.

It's called the Mickey's Meat Sandwich, loaded with ham and sausage and a piece of cheese in between. Have a bite, on me!

THE MEAT SANDWICH

Recollecting the Mickey Meat Sandwich reminded me of another funny story. My dashing older pal Larry was visiting campus, and we poked our heads into a few of the classes. We checked out Penis Binding 101, Artful Back-Shaving 202, Creative Crotch-Shaving 303, and Length Enhancement 400. He sat in on my Advanced Masturbation class before we wandered into the How to Be Gay lecture series.

Larry was particularly interested in that class because he wanted to bring it to a college back east. The course description was simple. Larry read it out loud to me from F.U.'s course catalog: "Just because you happen to be a gay man doesn't mean that you don't have to learn how to become one. This course will examine cultural artifacts and activities that play a prominent role in learning how to be gay: Hollywood movies, grand opera, Broadway musicals, camp, diva worship, drag, muscle culture, style, fashion, and interior design."

"Hey, what about dildos, poppers, and porn?" I chimed in.

"Things have certainly changed since I went here," Larry said as we headed to Le Café Cock and Balls on campus. I looked at my friend, this handsome Bostonian with graying hair, and realized he was a good two decades older than I was. Still, it hadn't mattered 10 years ago—that summer just before I started school here—when we were lovers.

His cock was always hard—still is—and nice and long and white and smooth. I'll always remember how he slurped down my come so that "we could be one." Anyway, that was

175

a long time ago. Now we sat at the restaurant and giggled over the menu. There were Cock Dogs, Protein Shakes, Hairy Buns, Cock-a-Cola, Big Head Beer, Cream of Some Young Gay, and assorted Fruity Cock Tails.

"Let me tell you this story," Larry said. "It started here in this very restaurant, before it was the crass and low-scale place it is now. This was the Decadent Dining Hall back then, and the worst thing on the menu was Bull Balls—and those were real."

Our waiter came over, wearing no shirt and an apron that barely kept a flap over his crotch. He gave a flirty grin and let his cock slip out and wave a little "hi."

Larry giggled. "Yep, things sure have changed around here."

Then he told me his story....

It was his first day on campus. Larry was wearing a suit on his way to the Decadent Dining Hall after a long orientation session. His girlfriend Betty had driven out to help him unpack and was meeting him there to grab one last bite to eat before she drove back home to Boston. Larry arrived earlier than their scheduled meeting time, took a seat, and just about fell over as he looked up and saw his dashing, olive-skinned waiter.

The waiter wore a tux with tightly fitting black pants. His slicked, jet-black hair and deep-green eyes mesmerized Larry. This guy was just his type.

"Are we dining alone today?" asked the waiter, smiling hopefully.

"Yes, uh...no, she'll be right here," Larry stammered.

Sitting down at the table, Betty lost no time noticing that Larry could barely keep his eyes off the waiter. "What are you staring at?" she asked him.

"He reminds me of someone I know," Larry kept saying.

When the waiter went off to the bathroom, he nodded at Larry with a sideways glance. Larry excused himself, then walked into the bathroom and up next to the waiter at his urinal.

"So you're new to campus," the pissing waiter said, looking at Larry. "First time and all?"

"Uh, yeah," said Larry. He'd never felt this way about a man before, and he really wanted to gawk at this guy's penis. Even limp, it was rather big, hanging out—with a thick, spurting yellow stream. The waiter didn't try to hide his dick. In fact, he was rather wagging it at Larry as he shook it off. Larry suddenly got uptight. "Yes, sir, I'm going STRAIGHT back to my fiancée at my table, and I expect you'll be washing your hands before you serve us."

The waiter zipped up and laughed. "Oh, sure. I've got me a girl who lives off campus too. I'd live with her and boff her every day if I could afford to, but I can't."

Larry felt disappointed. He wondered if he'd ever see this handsome stud around campus again. He introduced himself anyway, and the guy held out his washed and wet hand.

"I'm Dirk Bartley, your new roommate."

Larry was beside himself all through the lunch. And as each plate was served, he eyed Dirk's crotch through the tight black pants. He didn't tell Betty that this waiter would be his new roommate, just hurried her off so she could catch her flight back.

That night, Dirk Bartley came in with his girlfriend. They said hello to Larry then proceeded to neck on the sofa in front of him. "Can't go into his bedroom because girls aren't allowed to," she said. Larry figured that if they were going to neck they might as well do it without an audience, so he went into his bedroom and listened outside the door to their grunts and moans. Larry felt turned on by the heavy petting sounds coming from the next room. He rubbed his long, skinny cock through his pants and white underwear, but was too nervous to pull it all the way out.

When Larry came out of the bedroom a short while later,

she was gone and Dirk was sitting on the couch with a very obvious stiffy poking his tux pants skyward.

"I'm so glad we got each other for roommates. You know, both of us being straight and all," Larry said nervously. "I mean, there's so many *alternative* types here. And you know what those guys want to do all the time."

"You're darn right about that," Dirk said, spreading his arms and legs apart to show off even more of his protrusion.

"You know, Larry, my best friend and I, well, we grew up together and kind of helped each other mature sexually. Neither of us was gay or anything. We never did any queer stuff, but gosh, when we got all hot and bothered we did something pretty fun."

Larry listened intently to this handsome stud who'd been left horny and hard by his inconsiderate girlfriend. *What were the girls thinking by not putting out? A guy had to get off somehow, so why not go all the way?* he thought. Larry never understood that. "I mean, I guess you don't want to develop blue balls or anything," he said.

"Damn right," said Dirk, looking suddenly pained. "Anyway, you know, my friend and I used to do this thing called a Meat Sandwich."

"A Meat Sandwich? What's that?" asked Larry.

"Well, we sort of rubbed our bodies together and got all aroused and stuff," Dirk said shyly. He stood up and walked to about 6 inches away from Larry, and Larry stepped back. "I mean, it wasn't a homo thing or anything...." He put his arm around Larry's back and gently nudged up against Larry's pin-striped pants. Dirk's bulge rubbed against Larry's thigh. Only a few thin pieces of material separated their cocks.

"You know, the girls always get us so hot and bothered and leave us with an erection, and it's just mean, I think." Dirk was rubbing a bit more erratically. "What do you think of this?"

"Seems innocent enough," Larry said. "It's nice."

"We used to do it in our clothes at first, but that would just stain them, so most of the time we did it in the altogether," Dirk said. "I mean, you know, it was just something to do with the guys, just to get friendly together and stuff. I wouldn't want us to get our nice suits all sticky. I've got to wear mine to work tomorrow anyway. I don't know if you're up for it, but it's just a friendly getting-to-know you thing that they teach in the Kama Sutra 12 class. It's not a gay thing."

Oh, sure, of course not, thought Larry. In seconds both of their nice suits were thrown across the couch where Dirk had just necked with his girlfriend, and the two of them were on the couch doing the Meat Sandwich. Dirk stretched out on his back with his hard cock flopping up against him, and Larry dove on top.

"You want to put your sausage there between my legs and I'll squeeze them together real tight to feel just like a pussy," Dirk said. "I'll spit down there and you'll see how good that feels."

Larry placed his cock between the thighs of his new roommate and loved the feeling. It didn't feel just like a pussy, but never mind. He ejaculated quickly between Dirk's thighs, then quickly jumped up and washed himself off in the bathroom. Larry was going to get dressed when Dirk came out and said he wanted to do the same Meat Sandwich thing to Larry, so Larry turned facedown on his stomach and let Dirk go between his thighs from behind.

"It feels real nice this way," Dirk said. "I don't think I ever tried this position with my friend."

During their first semester, Dirk and Larry tried many variations of the Meat Sandwich in their dorm room—usually after Dirk came home from a date with his girl. Sometimes when Larry's girl was in town, they double-dated, and afterward the men would come home and have their Meat Sandwich. Dirk would even rub his sausage right between

Larry's buns, and even pour real mustard or mayo there to make it slicker.

They teased the girls about the secret "Meat Sandwich" they were going to share without them. "Silly boys," the girls would say.

Meat Sandwiches got to be a daily routine, sometimes three, four, or five times a day. Larry's girl finally broke up with him, because of the long-distance relationship. But Larry didn't seem to mind, and Dirk comforted him that night with a Meat Sandwich.

When Dirk married his girlfriend, Larry was the best man at the wedding. As a special wedding gift, he gave Dirk a Meat Sandwich right after the bride and groom got hitched. During the reception they were drinking heavily, and the two of them found a room in the church rectory and went at it. That was their last one though, and the guys lost touch with each other after a decade or so.

"But I'll always remember that Meat Sandwich," Larry said.

"What a great story," I said, still perusing the menu. "And look, Larry, it's funny but there's a Meat Sandwich right here, listed as a main course. Look, it reads, 'With our own Special Sauce, dedicated to a lost friend.' I guess you guys weren't the only ones—"

I looked over at Larry, and he was turning pale. He called the waiter over and asked about it.

"I don't know, sir, but maybe our manager does," the waiter said, summoning over the handsome man in a tux who stood in a doorway to the kitchen.

"Oh, my gosh, you've returned," the manager said. "Larry, you're back!"

"Dirk, what are you doing here?" Larry asked.

The two men hugged, then kissed, then spoke softly with each other, catching up, and comparing notes. Divorced? Yes.

F.U.

Ever married? No. They exchanged numbers and hugs.

We ordered, and at one point I noticed Dirk motioning for Larry to follow him to the bathroom. Larry wiped his mouth and followed.

I was done with my Weiner Delight before Larry came back from the toilet. Guess he had his Meat Sandwich in there.

THE SEXPERIMENTS

I had never really explored the campus much since returning as a professor. But after more than a year on the faculty, I decided to look into the more seedy parts of campus that have cropped up since I left. I already knew about the Spermarium, and Le Cock and Balls Café, but I wanted to find out more about the Sexperiments. The mood on the campus—and everywhere—was a bit low and we were all looking for new distractions.

Dean Richie wouldn't give me a permission slip to go because I am a writer, and he didn't want any of the university's secret experiments to get out to the world. Then one day I noticed one of the professors, Putzman Borelli, looked very much like one of the guys in the pictures the dean kept on his desk.

The dean will always regret telling me about his days of fooling around with his friends.

"Is Professor Borelli your old friend Putzi with the long cock?" I exclaimed loudly. "How convenient! How incestuous! How cozy and quaint!"

I wasn't really going to bribe him or out him or anything, but the dean put up his hands and said, "All right, all right, I'll have Putzi show you around. Just shut up, and don't write about it."

Yeah, right...

It was a part of campus I had always heard about but

never visited. Back in my student days, the Sexperiments Labs were where the perverted professors experimented with the guys on financial aid. The profs just used these classes as an excuse to touch the horny young bodies while they were jacking off. You'd hear stories of profs forcing guys to try all kinds of kinky things in the name of research.

Professor Putzi Borelli, my colleague who teaches Blue Balls: Fact or Phallusy, Advanced Ball-Stretching, Testicle Torture, and every other Testicular Biology class, got me a pass into a brand-spanking-new building called the SPERMIES Lab (which stands for Secret Penis Experiments and Research with Mechanical Implements and Electronic Stimulus). All the sexperimentation on campus was moved to this building.

"You'd be amazed what we're doing in here. This is where they figured out how Viagra works, and where Caverject was started. This is where the first successful penile enlargements began," Borelli said in a Frankensteinian manner that shook me up as I followed him past the naked statue of our first president. "This is the lab where the penis is being perfected!"

Two large metal doors swung open as Borelli waved a card over a scanner at the SPERMIES Lab, and we walked down two hallways before entering a cavernous room. The deep room stretched three or four stories down and was like a cock factory.

Strapped into beds, naked young lads had big hard-ons attached to tubes. Other naked guys were walking around with their cocks strapped to measuring devices. Some naked youths took breaks, or were sleeping on cots. But they all sported hard dicks. In one corner guys lined up with large hard-ons, waiting to insert themselves into slick holes. The ones pressed up against the holes were shaking with pleasure.

"We're perfecting the perfect fucking machine," Putzi said. "These guys are trying out some incredible synthetics and state-of-the-art lube machines that can be adjusted to feel like a wet pussy or a scratchy ass—whatever texture you like."

I watched a burly, hairy jock lean his hips forward and insert a squat, stocky cock into one of the holes. He pushed into it and smiled. His eyes rolled back in his head as two guys with notebooks and lab coats recorded his reactions.

"It feels like someone's sucking my cock. But it's too warm...no, wait. Oh, man, it's delicious. Ooh, oh, I'm shooting...I'm coming!"

The scientists shook their heads. "Failed again. Next."

"That didn't seem like a failure," I said, watching the jock pull his cock from the hole. It twitched in the final stages of orgasm. "That seemed like quite a success!"

"Too fast, he came too fast," Putzi said. "Remember, we're seeking perfection here."

Another young man poked his erection into the hole as the lab coats adjusted the machine.

"Some of these devices keep the guys hard for a whole day, and there has been some danger in that," Putzi said. "However, we have found that a certain degree of lengthening goes on when the cock is engorged for greater periods of time. It's helped us develop natural penis-enhancing techniques. The more you jack off, the larger you get. Gosh, we don't want that to get out into the real world, do we?"

We went into another glass room, where a scrawny kid sat in a chair with a large vacuum-like suction pump working on his cock. His legs were spread apart, and he smiled as we walked in. I recognized the kid as Don, one of my first students, the one who worked at a hospital.

"So you know Don, eh?" Putzi said. "Don came to us with a slight problem." Putzi picked up a nearby file and tossed it to me. "You probably didn't know about this."

I opened the file and saw a photo of Don with a hard-on as big as my pinky. Then I looked at the vacuum covering the cock. Don pressed a button, the pump came off, and there was a solid throbbing Choker of at least 9½ inches standing straight up in front of me. I looked back down at the photo.

"In less than two years, we pumped that penis up almost a full 7 additional inches in length, and now it's almost 6 inches around too," Putzi said. "He's our greatest success story."

"Go ahead, touch it, professor," Don said proudly, waving his red, swelling cock in my direction. This is the shy kid who got straight A's in my Advanced Masturbation class. I went over and felt the smooth, young, veiny meat, and it sizzled in my hand like a hot dog on a spit. A perfect, round, long cock.

"I'm going for a perfect 10," Don said proudly.

"Let's not overdo it now," Putzi said as Don turned the vacuum back on.

As I continued to marvel, and my mind was spinning with the possibilities, Putzi waved his hand and said, "Don't even think about it. It takes an inordinate amount of time and effort to get what he has. Don dropped out of school and he's been pumping on that thing for 10 to 12 hours a day. It's become an obsession. Once a shy, withdrawn lad and a straight-A student, he lost his job, his friends, even his will to go into penile medicine."

"He was such a good student," I said. "What happened?"

"He's obsessed with his big dick. He lost his job at the hospital because he was showing it to all the patients," Putzi said. "Now he pulls his cock out in the supermarket to show people how it compares with the cucumbers. He's been arrested twice for indecent exposure. He's addicted to vacuum pumps. But we're going to slowly wean him off—once he reaches his 10 inches."

We walked into a dimly lit corridor and could see some naked guys sleeping behind the glass with electrodes attached to their shaved skulls. Above them, screens projected images of penises and female tits.

"Now in this room the guys are sleeping, but you can see how we're monitoring their dreams. Every time a penis, a vagina, or a set of tits is in one of their dreams, this TV screen interprets and projects that image, and we then measure the hardness of the guy's cock."

The young studs were in various angles of repose on the comfortable cots. One of the guys had his screen flashing alternately from cock to pussy, and his cock went up and down accordingly. It stayed hard when a pair of breasts remained on the screen. One kid with curly red hair had a vagina up on the screen, then suddenly it flashed to a cock and the measuring device around his hard-on went high into the red zone. I knew him as Aaron Rymer, who had pulled out his big red bush and uncut cock more than once in my class

"We're finding that guys dream about sex about 90 percent of their REM—or rapid erection movement—state, and that the strongest erections occur during the times they're dreaming about a penis. That is across the board: straight-identified, gay, or bisexual. Now, the question is, are they thinking about their own penises or others? That's what we're trying to figure out."

Aaron spurted a big load of white jism all over himself as a big cock appeared on the screen above him. A wet dream.

"In this next room we're developing a spray that will help spies," said Borelli in a rather hushed tone. "This section of the lab is cosponsored by the federal government and partially subsidized by them. The spray is made out of semen that will leave different DNA strains and fingerprints on materials touched by spies. It could render DNA tests invalid."

We poked our heads through a window into a room where nude and seminude men with dark sunglasses were being sprayed with spritzer bottles.

"This Orgazmometer instigates prolonged orgasms and can maintain the spasms for more than an hour," Borelli continued, holding a door open for me. I got a whiff of sticky semen smell.

Strapped to a wall, three guys were in various stages of orgasm as white-coats watched and wrote in notepads. One guy screamed as if in pain, "I'm still coming! I'm still coming! Oh, jeez, stop it!" The second guy had a more peaceful look on his face and his cock seemed to be squirting continuously for the dozen minutes we stood and watched. The third guy was simply in the middle of heavy breathing, heaving his chest up and down, rubbing his hands over his chest as his prick kept ejaculating.

"They'll go on for hours with these things if we let them," Borelli giggled.

I whistled in awe as I felt my own cock itching to try some of these devices. I wondered if they'd even offer.

"There's the Testosterone Increasing Room, where the guys are so horny they'll fuck anything: chairs, poles, bottles. We spray the straight guys with this spray, and they'll fuck an ass in a minute. We can make the gay guys fuck a pussy too. Over there is the Engorgement Control Center, and here's the Surgical Enlargement Lab, where we've given one man a functional cock that measures 17¾ inches."

We stopped at a bulletin board with some snapshots tacked to it, and saw in one photo a rather plain-looking, middle-aged businessman with his cock held erect in front of him. Two lab-coat types had to help him hold the appendage. It looked obscene.

"You must be crazy!" I shouted. "How could men of science give a guy such a freakish monster of a cock?"

"Well, because he's funding us," Putzi said, waving his hands around. "He's one of the richest men in the world, a computer geek. I think you've heard of him. I can't tell you who it is, though, because if you knew the gates would be open for any billionaire to get the world's biggest penis."

I looked again at the photographs and recognized the guy immediately.

"So the biggest dick in business is really the biggest dick after all?" I mused. "Well, at least he's putting his money to good use."

We walked past the Anus Enlargement Area, where a porn star I know got a surgery so he could put whole sofa arms up his ass. He was famous for taking an orange street cone all the way up his ass in one video, but his staple trick was inserting pineapples.

As we continued down the sterile corridors, I noticed that the signs on the doors of the labs were fascinating. One door's sign read "Bush Hair vs. Virility," and the one on the door across from it said "Blow Jobs to Offset Attention Deficit Disorder." Another room was for "Homo-Haters Tumescence Research," and I knew this was where they proved that the most violent fag-bashers were actually very horny and hard when they talked about how much they hated gay guys, and in fact were embarrassed about their attractions to men.

I felt like Charlie in the Chocolate Factory, wanting to open every door and explore every corner. But Putzi ushered me into one room that looked like a gym locker and said, "This is the one I wanted to take you to. Take your clothes off."

"Huh?" I said. He was already out of his white smock, though, and I was astonished to see a nicely formed hairy torso underneath, plus a finely curved, half-hard cock. Dean Richie's stories about Putzi's long dick had not been exaggerated.

"Come on, man, off with it. You're going to enjoy this," he urged.

I hesitatingly stripped and partially covered my crotch with my hands as I followed him, naked, to the end of the room, where he told me to shower up. I looked across the tiled showers to see Putzi Borelli get hard, and I followed him into another area full of steam.

I couldn't see much, but I followed his voice as I stepped down into a pool that I could tell right away wasn't water. Instead, it was like a soft, warm gel. I followed him in, and the warmth around my whole body felt great.

I was enveloped like a glove, like I was in the womb, with sticky, subtle goo all the way up to my chin.

"Isn't it great? It's a sensation you'll rarely get to enjoy," he said. And of course, anticipating my question as to what and how, he pointed upward to the roof.

There, around a glass ceiling, were about a dozen or so guys jacking themselves off above us, shooting down long streams of come.

"It's a come bath. Isn't it just divine?" Putzi leaned his head back into the liquid.

I couldn't believe it, but it really was. I didn't think I would have dove into it so willingly if I had known, but I looked up and saw the handsome men spilling their seed over us one by one and I felt like royalty.

"Cleopatra was known for using come baths to keep her skin young, and there are some other qualities of that sort we've been able to document here," Putzi explained. "Semen is great for baldness, acne, depression. And in addition to its curative qualities, it just feels so good."

I heard another guy orgasm overhead and as I felt his precious droplets mix with the warm splooge all over me, I wanted to reach up 10 feet to feel his quivering crotch. Instead, I felt my own crotch quiver as I felt something brush against my raging boner. It was Putzi's foot. I leaned back and pressed my crotch harder against the foot that was expertly massaging my shaft.

I'd never had a foot job before. But Putzi knew how to work the balls of his feet and his heels, grasping my whole shaft between his arches and toes and working me up.

"I was in one of the early experiments here in the old days when they were a bit more cruel to us," Putzi said, almost sadly. "They pumped me up with testosterone and other hormones that made us horny and then tied our hands behind our backs. We were such horndogs that we learned how to jack ourselves off with our feet. We jacked each other off for days on end. I think I was one of the best."

His toes scrunched around my mushroom head and pulled me off to climax. My jism mixed in with the pool of countless hundreds or thousands of other men who had masturbated into this sticky mess. It was great to feel a part of so many orgasms and come-shots. I looked above and saw a couple of guys jacking each other off. They smiled down and nodded as they watched both of us add to the collective pool.

"And now the best part, " said Putzi as he beckoned me to follow him to yet another room. I looked around and saw no towel, no shower.

"I guess we're going to shower off?" I gulped, not knowing what I could possibly expect that would be stranger than what I had just seen and felt.

"Shower, no. In this room they'll clean us off, though."

As we walked in, I saw come-covered gents lying spread out on tile and stone perches while other guys bent to lap the sticky liquid from their bodies. Tongues explored every crevice, every orifice, and the guys on the slabs looked like they very much enjoyed it.

"You ready to come again?" Putzi asked, hopping onto one of the stone slabs.

"Oh, yeah," I smiled, as at least four tongues started on my toes.

THE SCIENCE BOYS

After dealing with all those experiments and science guys with lab coats at the Sexperiments building, I flashed back on two of my friends from my school days. I missed them a great deal.

After flipping through to the day I finally "conquered" the Science Boys, I decided to look them up again. And yes, they're still together.

First, though, I wanted to remember them as they were back in school. Here's the entry....

I became unnaturally obsessed by two guys who were in a few of my classes. I think I was attracted to their brains as much as their looks. They had sexy brains.

They both had long hair, Wilbert with straight hair that almost hit his buttocks, Bob with curly dark hair that fell past his shoulders. They were both brilliant. I dubbed Bob and Wilbert "the Science Boys."

Wilbert, the quiet one with the long straight hair and the strong cleft chin, was in my Cockitecture class, where we studied phallic structures throughout the world.

Bob, the guy who talked a lot and had the curly hair and glasses, was in my Geographic Cockology class, in which we studied penis length in different parts of the world and different cultures. But just after my Study of Underarms class on Tuesdays and Thursdays, I had both of them in the Penises in my Animal Kingdom course. That's where we got to know one another better.

They were a quiet couple, and so brilliant. I know, because while in school Wilbert developed an implantable microchip that can cause erections for impotent men (which would have made him a billionaire it weren't for Viagra), and Bob discovered two new planets in the Erotic Astrology course—and named them after himself and his lover. He made national news for that. Sure, it was overly sweet and geeky, but they were both very sexy nevertheless. I had no idea how I could ever get close to them.

For a long time, I admired them from afar, too shy to talk to them. I wondered what they were like in bed together, and I fantasized about being between them.

I sat behind them in the Animal Kingdom lab and got horny as the prof talked about measuring girth at midshaft when the penis is erect, and how the mosquito's penis is $\frac{1}{100}$ of an inch long, while a cat's is ¾ of an inch, a stallion's comes in at 2½ feet, and the blue whale is the biggest of the animal kingdom at more than 10 feet long. I wondered how my Science Boys ranked.

"Moby Dick!" I exclaimed, trying to impress.

"Gee, I guess they never heard that before in this class," grunted Bob. I wasn't sure if he liked me, but he was definitely unimpressed.

They were my lab partners as we dissected penises.

Our professor, Putzman Borelli, droned on: "Note the sponge-like vascularized tissue that fills with blood to create an erection. Blood is pumped into the penis under enormous pressure, and a series of valves lock it in to maintain the erection. Note the glans on this species. Compare the veins on that species."

We looked at the bony penises of manta rays and the fat round penises of gorillas. Just before our midterm, our team agreed to study together and pull an all-nighter. I couldn't wait.

I knew they were lovers and lived in the same dorm room. One night, they invited me over to their place, because I was too shy to invite them to the Naked Dorm, too shy to be naked in front of them just yet. They had already cracked opened their books when I arrived.

"Asari reports that Michelangelo believed the male form was divine, so do you really think it's a surprise he was gay?" I heard Bob argue as I approached from outside the door. "And Baron Golden's photographs in 1890 of his Italian boys reflected that fascination, in particular prepubescent youths."

"Your point is?" Wilbert asked quietly.

"Mankind was fascinated with cock, young cock, always, far before Foucault invented the word 'homosexual,' and so I think our textbook is wrong! I think there's an error that needs to be corrected."

"Hi, guys," I interrupted. "What's up?"

Wilbert was strewn out on the bed with books all around him, and he seemed like he was up indeed. Bob was pacing in front of him. They both hugged me hello. I never knew if they had an open relationship, but according to my roommate, Joey, they both spoke at great lengths about monogamy in their History of the Chastity Belt class last quarter. I knew I had to break them of that mindset.

Intellectual stimulation seemed to get Bob hard, so I tried seducing him with my brain cells.

"In my Historic Men with Large Dicks class we talked about how Caesar, Napoleon, and Hitler were so hell-bent on world domination. Do you think their small dicks made them such megalomaniacs?" I asked. "What's your take on that?"

Bob contemplated the question and said, "You know, in Perpetual Orgasm Studies, I found out that men with bigger cocks are more passive for the most part. They don't have to prove themselves."

We both looked over at the silent Wilbert. He just smiled and moved the eraser of his pencil down to his white shorts where I could definitely see the outline of a bulge—a mighty big one.

"I suppose that's true," continued Bob. "Last year in the Penile Lengths and Economic Surges class, I did a paper on the extreme cock sizes during the financial boom in New Orleans from 1870 to the 1910s. I found that the men with the bigger cocks had the most money and said the least about their wealth."

Never mind how he ever figured that out, or even studied it. I was feeling grungy and tired, but ultimately horny for these two overly easygoing longhairs. I didn't want to study. I knew my animal anatomy; I was more interested in my animal urges.

"There's also the theory that Native Americans were massacred mainly because of jealousy over their big cocks," I pushed. "Aren't you part Indian, Wilbert?"

"Native American," he smiled.

"So, if that's true, you must have the biggest dick in the room."

"I think that's right," Wilbert shot back.

"But how do you know? You've not seen mine!" I teased.

"Oh, we do our research," Bob said. "But we have to find out firsthand."

It was a challenge. Bob found his Big Daddy Ferguson's Penis tape measure and said, "Let's hit the showers."

So we all marched down the hall to the showers and stripped quickly as the water turned hot and began steaming up the place. I started lathering up and watched Wilbert point the nozzle away so he could soap up his crotch all slick, and Bob yanked his growing meat with one hand while rubbing his tit with the other.

"You're from Polish and Dutch extraction, which means that your cock size is in the largest of the European categories," Bob said. "You're a Grower, I imagine."

"I show too," I said, revealing that my limp cock was

rather sizable. "And you're Canadian, French, and uncut, which makes you at least in the upper 25% range."

I could tell that even limp, Wilbert would win this bet. I didn't want to seem too eager (i.e., desperate), so I prayed my erection would subside a slight bit.

"Irish and Indian, what a combo," I breathed heavily. "You've got us beat!"

Wilbert turned and sported the best hard-on, with thick oozing juice slowly dripping from it. Even in the shower, it dripped down his thighs in smooth, silky globs.

Wilbert's deep brown eyes had a lust-filled look as he slowly pumped his precome from his bulging rod. I walked over and gently grabbed the base of his cock, getting near his smooth body as Bob nuzzled in between us. We turned the water off and the three of us kissed hard and wet, letting our tongues mingle with one another's.

"We talked about this, and I approve of our commingling with you sexually," Bob said. "I think it would be a splendid mix of our culturally hybridized sexual identities."

Wilbert put a tongue in Bob's mouth to shut him up. I held my tongue out as a mix of their hot spit joined the three of us and I let the dribble slowly follow me down to my knees as it dripped off their chin and rolled down both of their bodies. I was on my knees on the hard tile floor and they both thrust their pelvises forward.

Bob tried to speak again, and Wilbert deep-kissed him.

I could smell their masculine crotches, and it almost made me shoot right there. I slipped both of their cocks between my lips, Wilbert's long, curved cock and Bob's nice, skinny one.

Both pieces of meat pulsated in my throat. I almost couldn't take it; my eyes welled up as I nearly gagged. I wanted to drink in the smell of their crotches, so I tried taking them as close to the hilt as I could, my mouth expanding and dripping with spittle.

Both of them bucked as my tongue then went for each of

the four balls displayed in front of me. Salty, hairy, not bad. I got to practice a bit of my Testicle Torture Techniques as I chewed gently on the balls, and I noticed that Bob seemed to enjoy it the most. If I had sucked and chewed on his sacs even harder, he would have been perfectly happy.

"I learned a lot about ball play in the S/M Masculine Erotica class, but I heard there's more in the advanced classes," Bob said. "Mickey, do you think I should sign up next semester for Anal Sex with Fruit or Anal Sex with Vegetables?"

I bit on Bob's balls. He yelped, and Wilbert stuck a few fingers in his mouth. Then I felt their four hands around my head, playing with my hair. We were near the end of our shower sex. I held both of their shafts on either side of my head and let them spew sticky sperm all over my hair.

"That's the kind of hair conditioning we like to use too," Bob said. "Learned that in Advanced Alternative Uses for Spermatozoa. It's the best ingredient for shampoo—three companies already use it in their products."

Shut up, I wanted to say.

We all aced our Animal exam without much studying, and they invited me to "study" more and more over at their dorm room. Even during the day, when Wilbert was out on the porch sunbathing, I would be asked over, always with the two of them there but sometimes with only one of them participating while the other one watched.

Wilbert liked it when I worshipped his cock. He was quiet and horny. I always wanted to go over there without Bob watching, but he wouldn't do it.

Bob liked sex rough and pushy, and liked to be dominated. One of the best times I had with them happened in their dorm room in the middle of the night. It was all right, since I had been in bed masturbating to the thought of them anyway.

We were in the last stage of our final exams. It was so hot

on campus it didn't even get below 90 degrees at night. I knew that even the shy Science Boys were probably walking around naked. They were particularly randy that evening.

As soon as I walked over to Wilbert to kiss him hello, I felt Bob's sweaty body behind me, with a strong, thick finger exploring my ass. I rubbed my hand along Wilbert's slight chest hair and Bob reached around to tweak my nipple, making my balls clench. I rubbed my fingers along Wilbert's tanned torso through the lines of perspiration forming on his chest.

Wilbert had a ponytail, and Bob's curls on that hot night were even bouncier as I saw how his chest dove in a V-shape and his rounded pecs seemed even more pronounced as he pumped his rigid cock in front of me.

Wilbert reached for a nearby pitcher of lemonade and I took it from him and splashed it over my heated body. It splattered them, and they laughed.

"Now lick it off," I ordered as they both slurped on either side of my cock. Their tongues felt warm as they each went for a testicle. Bob sucked my ball too hard and I pulled away, but he made up for it by allowing me to shove my cock all the way down his throat, rubbing my thighs against his face. I then pulled out and shared a white stream of jism between their mouths. Seconds later, they both shot intense loads and we used the rest of the lemonade to wash it off our steaming bodies.

That night was a first, because I curled up and slept between the two of them, forming a C with their moist bodies. It was comfortable and sticky.

The next morning we went to the hill to sunbathe. We didn't want to get too toasty—or burn our balls—so we kept a check on one another.

When it was time to turn Bob over, Wilbert spread out face-up in his lawn chair, sporting a big erection. Without a word, I knew it was time to do some summer relieving, and the other guys on the hill were ready to watch us three long-hairs get it on.

I waited until Wilbert lubed himself up and covered his big cock with a red condom, then I wriggled my way down onto it. Bob watched, but I slapped his butt and turned his cock and his heavy-hanging balls away from me. I spun him around and parted his thighs all the way to his muscled crack.

As my ass was stuffed with Wilbert's pork sausage, I licked and tongued his lover's asshole while we all twisted and moaned in unison. I wasn't sure I could take Wilbert all the way.

I felt the curve of Wilbert's prodigious cock inside me as I squatted up and down while sticking my tongue into the hairy hole of Bob. Then I shoved first two, then three fingers up Bob's crack while Wilbert bucked into me from that shaky lawn chair. Bob's hips rocked against my face and his boyfriend's huge cock got deeper than I thought was possible.

At the top of the hill, guys from the Naked Dorm were jerking off to our performance, but I ignored them as we continued.

Just then I felt the flared head of Wilbert's uncut cock swell and he shot a hot load into the condom. I could feel it right through the rubber. As he pulled out, I promptly peeled away the rubber, wrung out the precious liquid, and smeared it into my blond hair. It was now shoulder-length. I wanted to grow it out as long as I could, just for them.

Jeez, I wanted us to be the perfect threesome. I could be the Farrah of the *Charlie's Angels* team. I wanted it to go on forever.

Bob shot his load in my hair and rubbed his quivering cock through it.

Three months later, my hair had grown out even longer and we *were* the perfect threesome. We looked great together, and we looked even better when we were naked. When we recreated our first shower scene, the other guys peeked in to watch us. One guy said we were so hot we could've charged admission.

Sometimes I enjoyed just watching the two of them go at

it. I'd stay back and pull out my raging hard-on as I'd watch them fuck. Wilbert would fuck Bob, his ass moving front and back, his balls banging up against Bob, and I'd get pretty turned-on.

Bob has a very nice cock. The head is a little more bulbous than my own, and makes a popping sound when it comes out of Wilbert's mouth.

I always knew just the right moment to join in, and they never seemed to mind. They would come over to the Naked Dorm and we'd have sex in the hot tub, or I'd go over to their dorm and we'd wake up their neighbors with our pounding and grunting. I rarely slept overnight there, but I definitely became part of their regular sexual routine.

But gradually it seemed more and more often that Bob would get jealous of me being alone with Wilbert. He became less interested in joining in, and even less interested in watching. Things were turning sour.

One of the last times we were together was a hot summer night, when I went down on Bob and my own prick was so hard it could have cut glass. I pressed the knob of his cock head against the roof of my mouth and licked the underside as Wilbert got on his knees next to me with his obedient, open mouth.

Bob popped his cock out of my mouth and then into his boyfriend's, alternating his cock into each of our mouths. Thrust, thrust, thrust, and switch. Thrust, thrust, thrust, and switch again. His cock made popping noises each time it left our mouths. We'd gasp for air, then go back for more.

Bob got wilder, knocking our heads together, thrusting hard before switching mouths. He reached down and grabbed his throbbing cock and whacked our faces with it. This semester's Domination and Bondage class was bringing out a new side of him.

I squeezed his balls, hard. He didn't shout, but he squirmed. When he began to talk, Wilbert and I gagged him with a few of my large ugly neckties. Over the weeks, we'd learned to keep him quiet with either a cock or a tie across his face.

But keeping me quiet was another thing. I told everyone about my sexploits with the Science Boys. Call it sour grapes, but I wanted more in the relationship. The problem with being the third wheel is you tend to not get equal footing.

I enjoyed my time with them, and still do in my adult years—but I've long ago given up on being a part of them.

The Science Boys were an atom you didn't want to split.

THE RUBBER MAN AT THE FREAK SHOW
AUGUST 10, 1991

I flipped through my journal for the summer of 1991 and realized I was a bit melancholy during that period. Almost exactly a decade later, I was feeling some of the same sadness, but I certainly wasn't lonely with all those young guys around.

Back then I was sad because my roommate and friend Joey Dillus was finally moving out after graduating. It was a lonely summer, but the guys in the dorm kept me company—and kept me satiated. I had no idea who my next roommate would be, and I had some anxiety about it.

I needed some distraction, so the guys dragged me off to this campus carnival. After that I was never the same, because it was the kinkiest sex I ever had in my life.

I always hated to go to those sideshows in carnivals or the little freak shows that traveled through the South and came up through Mexico. They were scary, and they seemed so sleazy and sordid. But this one caught my eye.

The frat boys were putting on some fund-raiser, and they invited this band of carnival performers to set up a tent and some rides on the football practice field. There was the Twister, the Spinner, the Flopper, and in a dark corner there was the Freak Show.

I looked at the larger-than-life paintings out front: the Wild Man from Borneo, the baldheaded Strongest Man in the World, the Caterpillar Man, the Human Pincushion, the Snake Man, and the most Rubbery Man in the World.

The last painting had me rather transfixed: A guy with long Doug Henning hair and a thin moustache had deep green eyes with long, seductive lashes and he was bent up like a pretzel, standing on one leg. What was most remarkable about the painting was that he sported a huge bulge in his pants that looked like a third leg. Whoever painted it may have known that many of us on this campus would notice and be intrigued by that bulge, whether it was real or not.

I was fascinated.

I begged my roomies to go out to the Freak Show with me. Joey, who was packing up to move up north, Kam, and Sandy seemed slightly interested, but they were more excited about the rides. They came along to the carnival but sent me off to the Freak Show by myself. My oddball friend Victor was in the carny crowd, and he joined me because he too was curious about the truth of the painting. Plus, he couldn't resist another chance to show off crotch-predicting skills.

On the podium outside the freak show, a nearly 7-foot man was hawking the crowd, sucking more and more guys into the tent.

"The Snake Man, fellas, has a snake tattooed all across his body. He lived with snakes all his life. Rumor has it one of them crawled down his throat one day and the next day he had the tattoo. You fellas know what it's like to have a snake go down your throat?"

The double entendre was too much. Victor plunked down his five bucks and said, "We're going in."

We were herded into an area where a handsome blond man sat in a pit with a mammoth python wrapped around his waist. A boa constrictor slithered around his arm, and a bright green snake I couldn't identify was coiled around his neck.

I stood there totally intrigued, totally enthralled. Some of the other guys around us were equally engrossed. The Snake Man was practically nude. He had only a handkerchief-size jockstrap on, so we could follow the tattoo that wound from his left ankle

F.U.

all the way up around his torso to his right shoulder.

"It's the snake in his pants that I want to see," Victor said. "Look at that bulge just straining to get out."

I looked and almost jumped out of my skin because I could swear I saw a snake squirming in the Snake Man's crotch, like a little snake head flickered out the corner of the pouch and then slipped back in. Victor didn't see it.

The Snake Man caught Victor's eye, and Victor grinned and shouted, "Hey, I like your snake!"

Suddenly, the tall barker motioned us to a center stage. There we were treated to the Strongest Man in the World, who broke bricks with his fist and picked up two guys in their chairs then held them over his head.

"Next year, he's going to Japan to try to break the world record by pulling a 747 loaded with passengers—all with his mighty penis!" the barker announced.

Victor and I burst out laughing. Some of the more serious guys around us shushed us up. Then a guy who looked like a wolf came out. He was black-skinned and had tufts of brown hair shooting from his cheeks, his chest, all over.

"The Wild Man from Borneo was captured only a few years ago, and we're still trying to quell his voracious appetite—for both food and sex." The barker smiled. "It's a tough job, but somebody has to do it."

"Oh, really?" asked Victor. "We could do that."

"He has to hump something at least a dozen times a day," the barker explained to the crowd as the hint of a boner popped out of the wild man's thong.

Then the Human Pincushion came out and stuck nails and pins in his cheeks, arms, and legs. He squirted a bit of blood out into the audience, and we shrieked. Then the Caterpillar Man wriggled out in a giant bodysuit and showed us the nifty things he could do with his tongue, including type, roll a cigarette, light a match, and comb his hair.

"He's even driven some of the cars we have here—he has

a very talented tongue," the barker explained. "You wouldn't believe what he can do with it."

"I'll bet," I said, nudging Victor. "Shouldn't we all have a Caterpillar?"

Next was the man who'd most intrigued me, the Rubber Man. Tall, sweet, with milky-white skin and bushy long locks, he amazed the audience by bending his arms back and throwing his legs over his head. He got into a contraption that looked like a maze; for an extra $2 we could go up to see him spread out in the box.

Victor and I were first in line. It looked like this handsome hunk had had his body parts rearranged like a Mr. Potato Head. His heel touched his head, his stomach was touching a knee, and I noticed that his very thin and skintight jockstrap could barely hold what it was packing.

"You're right, Mickey, he is big," Victor said a bit loudly. "Maybe an 11, maybe more."

The Rubber Man cricked his neck toward us, looked up from his confinement, and smiled. "There are a lot of things I can do, gents, you'd be surprised," he said with a seductive lilt that sent shivers through me. "Stick around."

I wouldn't leave the box. Victor finally had to drag me away, and we were among the last in the tent when the tall hawker from out front approached us.

"You know, lads, there's a private show that goes on in the very back tent that you can see for an extra $20. Our sideshow freaks will show you some talents we can't show to the general public."

"Yeah, this is where they gouge us for even more money," Victor scowled. "Come on, Mickey, let's leave. Joey and the other guys are waiting."

"Will the Rubber Man be there?" I asked. When he nodded yes, I begged, "Come on, let's go back. I'm not going without you."

"And the Snake Man is waiting for you too, Victor," the

hawker said. Neither of us recalled ever saying Victor's name, but this guy seemed to read people pretty well and acted as if he knew a lot more about us than we knew ourselves. We each handed our 20 bucks to him.

"We've been out on the road quite a bit, guys, and it's nice to have a friendly audience like you here. We've been waiting to be relieved with a group like this," he said. "Now, come on back."

He ushered us past another curtain and back there, in an open-air area surrounded by fabric, with a fire going in the middle, were all the sideshow acts, totally naked, some of them stroking themselves in front of the fire.

"Gosh, look, he can suck himself," Victor said, pointing to the Rubber Man, who was bent in over himself on a bale of hay. It was amazing how that guy worked his hard-on with his own lips. He stopped slurping, looked up at us, and waved us over with his foot.

The Wild Man had nothing on, and deep inside the matted hair we could see a monstrous, hairy cock, at least a 3-hander, and he was jacking it like a rope.

The Human Pincushion was driving long, thick needles into his penis shaft and uncut cock head on a tree stump table, and asked if we wanted to be pierced anywhere. "No thanks, man!" I gaped, as he seemed to get off with each injection into his shaft with the metal prods. But when he started taking the safety pins to his scrotum, that's when I squealed and moved on.

"Wow, look at this, you did see a snake down there," Victor said. He pointed to the Snake Man, who still had a python wrapped around him, and he was stroking his cock, which was tattooed like a big blue snake—head, eyes, and all. His massive purplish mushroom was a perfect snake head, and it looked as if his testicles were snake eggs roosting at the end in a nest.

I felt some hairy arms around my jacket as the Wild Man came up behind me, gave me a bear hug, and grunted, "Make yourselves at home, boys." I saw the Snake Man unzipping Victor's pants and I felt my clothes being tugged off by the Wild Man and the 7-foot hawker, who already had his clothes off—and a hard-on that rose halfway up his chest.

I almost resisted and ran away, until I turned and saw the dreamy-eyed Rubber Man poke his head up between my legs and smile. He had a hypnotic stare, and all I could do was smile back.

The Strong Man had the Caterpillar Man sucking on his massive fat cock. He stood up and the Caterpillar Man's mouth was still impaled on it: He was hanging from the cock. "One-two, one-two," the Strong Man bellowed as the Caterpillar Man was lifted up by the engorged cock and then down again. Those were amazing push-ups.

The Snake Man was doing a very sexy dance as he stripped away Victor's clothes. One of the snakes went around Victor's neck. My friend looked over at me, and I knew he was terrified of snakes before, but not anymore.

"C'mon dudes," said the barker. "Whip 'em out."

I reached for my zipper and yanked out my throbber. The Snake Man nodded in approval. "Lovely, lovely, lovely," he said as his ever-shaking, ever-pulsating form writhed in front of Victor, flicking a forked tongue over his face. "Now, which one of my snakes will get in first," he coaxed. "I want my every orifice filled with snake."

Victor dove in, fucking the Snake Man standing up as the Wild Man took Victor from behind, squeezing his big hairy cock into Victor's ass cheeks. The Snake Man motioned for the barker to stand on a nearby stepladder, so he could get his large cock into his mouth while being filled by Victor. Even with a full mouth, the Snake Man managed to give orders.

"Harder, more, faster, stronger," he bellowed. They complied as we watched, and the rest of us began a sideshow of our own.

The Rubber Man waved his long, thin cock toward my

mouth, and I took it between my lips. He then easily bent over and licked his own shaft with me, our tongues intermingling. Then I felt something squirming between my legs as the Caterpillar Man took my cock in his expert mouth and sucked me like a gentle vacuum cleaner, making my hips buck up and down. It felt so good, that warm soft tongue rubbing over me as I swallowed this Rubber Man's sword.

Just then I felt a fat, sheathed object skewer my bucking butthole, as the Strong Man's supercock sank slowly in. It felt like a rock dildo—strong, hard, and unyielding. He grunted as he lifted the Caterpillar Man and me on his cock, and I felt like I was on an elevator, going up and down gently. I enjoyed the ride.

A few times, to regain my balance, I grabbed around the Rubber Man's bendable frame and touched the naked torso of the man on the other side of my legs. I felt a shiver of anticipation and he smiled back at me between grunts as we simultaneously reached up and grabbed for the crotch of the Human Pincushion, who was getting his dick sucked by the Strong Man. He looked down at us with a nonthreatening smile.

We fucked endlessly, each of us taking turns, each of us coming and then finding a new position where we felt comfortable, whether it was in the velvety mouth of the Caterpillar Man, on the rigid pole of the Strong Man, or in the highly talented butt cheeks of the Snake Man.

When the Snake Man finally ejaculated, he did so in willowy hisses. Victor and I had crumpled into quivering heaps by then, each of us having come at least three times.

The Rubber Man gave me long, deep, unforgettable kisses and then disappeared back into the tent. Victor and I barely had time to regain from the sideshow stars we were all seeing when the barker came out to tell us to get our clothes on and be on our way.

As we left the carnival, we talked about the hairy cock of the Wild Man, the tough touch of the Strong Man, the pierced cock of the Human Pincushion, and all the rest. But Victor had his Snake Man fantasy all for his own and I had my Rubber Man to dream about for my own masturbation scenarios.

When we told Joey and the guys in the dorm, they laughed at us and refused to believe the story. Still, they loved to hear it in exquisite detail. (I happen to know that Joey, Kam, and Sandy held circle jerk late at night in the dorm after Victor and I told them about the experience.)

"Tell me how the Caterpillar Man felt again?" Sandy would ask. Then he'd run over and tell the other guys as they jacked off about it, imagining they were there.

One day, a few months later, Sandy came running into my room screaming about this new XXX video he just rented and pulled Victor and me over to sit in the front seats of the viewing room. All the other guys gathered around too.

"They've got a new tape in the kinky section of the video store," Sandy said, pointing to the monitor. "The Snake Man #19." Then he hit PLAY.

Victor gulped as we watched—sure enough, there we were, Victor and I, naked and fucking up a storm with the Snake Man, the Rubber Man, and the whole gang, in a poorly made, dark-lit video from some hidden cameras under the tent.

Our stunned expressions turned to chuckles and then full-out belly laughter. Victor and I actually looked pretty hot up there, and the guys in the dorm thought so too, and they cheered us on.

"Wow, look at Mickey with the Rubber Man, and look at the schlong on that tall barker," said Kam whipping out his cock while watching intently on the sofa.

"Check out that Caterpillar Man. I think even I could learn a few oral skills from him," said Joey.

"I never believed it was true, but seeing it is even better than imagining it," said Sandy as he slipped his hand down his pants.

All Victor and I could do was join in as the video progressed.

"I've got no regrets," Victor smiled, giving me a hug and giving my cock a tug. "Now we've got to catch up with them to branch off into our own series of sequels."

"We could start our own 'Road Freak Show' series," I said.

"I told you it was a scam of some sort," Victor said.

"Scam nothing," I smiled, looking at the Felliniesque porn video in front of us. "This is art."

SEDUCING MY STRAIGHT ROOMMATE

I pulled out one of the most painful chapters of my college days: the diary that chronicled my 21st birthday. I looked at the brown leather-bound book and saw smears on the pages. I seem to recall those as a mix of tears and semen.

It was the morning of my 21st birthday, and I was horny as a dog. My morning suck-off friend, Joey, was gone—graduated and moved away—and sorely missed, as any good blow job friend would be. I was in the mindset that I'd like to have a real boyfriend someday: someone regular to hold, to cuddle with, someone to spend a lifetime with. Or someone just to blow regularly.

I was 21, after all.

That morning, the guys woke me up with my hard-on at full staff, and they plopped a cake on my tummy with a big thick candle on it.

"Make a wish, dude," yelled Kam. "Make a good, big one."

I laughed and blew and they all saw the smile on my face.

"What was it?" asked Sandy the surfer.

"Can't tell you or it won't come true," I sighed. "But wishes like this never come true anyway."

When they left me with a slab of chocolate cake, I masturbated over it, thinking of the guy I wished would walk in my door and into my life.

Little did I know that within hours this wish would come true....

Flipping through my *Business in the Sex Market* textbook for my Hustling Accounting Class, I glanced out the window in time to catch a glimpse of one of the new naked freshmen streaking freely across campus. I let my hand slip down to my baggy shorts and let my fingers linger at the gaping pant leg where my increasingly building cock was barely hiding.

The door flew open; I didn't look up. It was one of the dorm rats bugging me to wish me a happy birthday again, I figured. I had already masturbated to the chocolate cake they left me this morning, and was already bored about being 21.

"G'day, I guess I'm your new bunkmate," came the deep, unfamiliar voice.

I looked up, adjusted myself, and stood up to see Shane Coley. I couldn't even speak.

This was the object of my wet dreams for the past three years: the swimmer with the slight Aussie accent whom I'd never met, never even talked to, but had followed around school ever since I first saw him on campus. I'd spied on him as he sat alone in the stacks of the library—in the same corner every time—reaching into his jeans and rubbing himself slowly.

"M'name's Shane Coley," he boomed, sticking out his strong, sinewy hand. "You're Mickey Skee? I'm looking forward to sharing your room."

I practically fainted and couldn't utter more than a squeak, but I shook his hand and squeezed it strongly as he walked past and I caught a whiff of his strong, masculine, gamy odor.

"Walked 'cross campus with this gear, gonna haf to wash up." He eyed me curiously as I stood there with my mouth half-open. "You all right? Have we met before?"

"I'm sure we've seen each other around, I mean it's a small campus and we've both been around for three years," I mumbled, trying to hide the wet spot at my crotch.

He peeled off his sweaty shirt and revealed his rippling waves of chest muscles and two well-defined pecs. I had watched him swim naked every once in a while at the pool.

"I've heard you're a good writer," Shane said, still stripping.

"You're the swimmer! You're the champion swimmer Shane Coley," I finally managed. "Gee, it's a pleasure. No, we haven't officially met, but I'm certainly honored to meet you, sir."

"Enough of the 'sir' already, kid," he smiled. He was slipping off his blue sweatpants now and he didn't have anything on underneath. I barely heard him speak. "I guess I'm taking this bunk here near the window. We're going to have to be equals here, sharing everything, so I don't want any of this star treatment or anything like that, eh? We're pals, mates!"

With that he turned to me stark-naked, walked over, and put my head in a friendly chokehold. My head was forced down to his belly button, and my eyes landed on the half-hard-on that glistened with his golden pubic hairs only inches from my lips. He held me there, and I saw his cock twitch upward.

"You a fly-boy, Mick? Don't matter if you are, just wondering."

"I rate Bi on the Klein Grid," I said, making my voice lower as I straightened up and tried not to look at his crotch. I didn't tell him I'm definitely on the gay side of Bi, however. "And you?"

"Got me my angel Angie in the outback, at home. She's my love," he smiled as he rubbed his hands over his smooth, hairless chest. One hand grasped hold of his penis. "And this piece of meat is for her alone—I just want to make that clear."

"Oh, perfectly," I stammered. "Oh, gosh, I certainly understand that. Heck, I had a roommate here for a while who would bug me every morning with one of those nasty blow jobs. He was always over at my bed sucking me off until I came. He said it was healthy for me. What nonsense."

Shane Coley's body was picturesque. The mounds of his

rosy butt cheeks were smooth and tender; his tall lanky frame was skinny yet meaty.

"Don't sound too bad, mate," Shane smiled as his cock twitched.

His cock was longer than I had imagined from the glimpses of it I caught in the library and the swimming pool. He didn't seem ashamed of his body; he seemed to love his body.

"I'll unpack when I get back," he smiled again with his icy sky-blue eyes and big, fat, red lips. The blond hair fell over his right eye just slightly enough to be perfect, and with just enough attitude to be cocky, but with an air of friendliness. He turned to whip me in the butt with his towel. I yelped a protest.

"Nice to be here, Mick!" He let his hand stroke his cock as he turned away.

As he left down the hall to the showers, I walked over to his sweatpants and shirt, cupped them in my hands, and breathed deeply into them as I exploded jism into my shorts.

"I absolutely can't believe it!" the supposedly straight frat boy Marlon Brandeis practically squealed. He tugged on his obvious hard-on while seated on my bed naked. "You got Shane Coley in the same room naked and you didn't dive on that cock?"

"I've seen him in the gym and wondered how big it got hard," mused my handsome dorm neighbor Johnny, who was spread out on my bed, also nude, with his stiffy flopping on his belly. "I'm staying here until I see."

"You are so lucky, man," said Kam, my big Hawaiian buddy, slapping my back hard as his chubby frame plopped down on my bed. "But we've got to measure him to put him in the Naked Dorm roster book."

The guys all turned to see a dripping wet Shane in the doorway, with the towel dabbing soggy parts of his body but not hiding his meat fully. The guys stared. He stopped and blushed, covering himself a bit more discreetly. I realized I was the only one in the room without my clothes completely off.

"This is Shane, my new roommate. Kam, Johnny, Marlon," I stammered. "They pop by every so often, you'll get used to it."

"Um, Mr. Coley, sir, we have a tradition at the Naked Dorm, and I'm the official recorder," Kam started saying. He had thought he'd enjoy inheriting Joey Dillus's job as the dorm historian, until now.

But Shane was OK with it.

"Oh, yeah, you need to measure this," he said, wagging his cock, which curved slightly as it got a bit harder. "Sure, go ahead. Hold on, let me work it up for you."

Marlon's hand immediately went to the long, skinny shaft, and Johnny pulled out the Daddy Ferguson Measuring Tape to get Shane's Dimensional Inch Count Knowledgeable Yardstick, or DICKY rating. Kam opened up the book and wrote Shane's name down.

Shane tugged a few times at his white monster meat and ignored the other naked guys in the room but looked directly at me and said, "So, what have you rated in the book, Mickey?"

I was a bit flabbergasted and said, "Well, they kind of caught me by surprise and were a bit rough on me when I first got here, but I ranked 6¾."

"He's a Score," Johnny said, looking over at me and licking his lips. I smiled knowing that my cock had been between Johnny's tender lips, but I was in no mood for sex at that moment. I was too nervous.

"Yeah, he's got a nice cock, but you do too," said Marlon. "Of course, I'm only talking from a clinical point of view. I'm studying to be a Doctor of Cockology, and I've looked at fine specimens in my Male Genitalia class, and this is a fine, classic cock."

"Why, thank you, Straight Man Marlon," Shane said

teasingly as he continued stroking his cock and looking at me. When his cock curved slightly upward and seemed to be at full staff, Johnny spread the measuring tape along the top of the cock, one end in the curly blond hairs of the root and another over the head to the piss slit.

"9¾," Johnny read from the tape.

Kam wrote it down the book. "You're a Choker. Only 3% of guys are within your size range. Congratulations."

"I'll bet you could be a Tenor if you had the right motivation," said Johnny, his lips salivating and his cock standing straight out in front of him.

"Well, we'll have to give it a whirl sometime, but not right now," Shane smiled gently as his stiffy subsided. He looked to me for help.

"OK, get out, all of you," I ordered. "Get out!"

My naked dorm pals scrambled toward the door.

"Hey, we're taking Mickey out on the town tonight. It's his 21st birthday, you gotta join us," Kam insisted. "Pick you both up at 11!"

They shut the door behind them and Shane let the towel drop freely once again. He turned to me, smiled, and got hard again.

"Boy, I felt like I was a piece of beef in front of a pack of hungry dingos," he laughed. "That Johnny's been eyeing me at the gym all summer. He's like a stalker."

I laughed nervously, thinking I must've been obvious—but not that obvious—while watching him on campus myself. "You must get that a lot, especially on this campus," I said. "I mean a lot of the guys would want...would like to...I mean, you're pretty good-looking around here."

"I feel pretty comfortable with you, Mick," he said, wiping himself completely dry. "You don't look at me the way they do. You're a decent bloke. A stand-up guy. I like that. Wouldn't want anything to jeopardize that."

With that he plopped back on his bed, letting his cock flop

up past his belly button. He made no move to put his clothes on and asked if he could call his girlfriend in Australia with my phone, putting it on his card of course.

"The guys got me all hard for their measurements and now I've gotten all hot and bothered for nothing, so I should call Angie," he smiled. "It's part of my Aussie animalistic nature, mate."

I nodded OK and pretended to get back to my book as he dialed. I eavesdropped on his sweet-nothings and "love you"s as he talked.

"Got this new roomie, he's a great chap, you'd like him," he said as he paced in front of me with his cock dangling like a bell. "No, not like that at all. A stand-up guy, he is."

Ugh, I couldn't concentrate on the business book, so I switched to the "Healing Qualities of Urine" chapter in my Biology class. I could hear his sentences getting shorter as it sounded like they were engaging in transworld phone sex.

"My wanker's waiting for you, love," he murmured as he finally plopped back on his bed again. He held the phone with his right shoulder and grabbed his cock with both hands. He turned toward me and asked, "Don't mind, do you?"

I shrugged my shoulders as if it were the most natural thing in the world to have the man you've lusted for jerking off in the bed next to you. I pretended to turn away and dive more into my book, but out of the corner of my eye I saw both his hands wrap around his thick, veiny cock capped with a round mushroom head that looked rosy as an apple.

As he got hard, his dick pulsated with a crisscross of veins both under and on top. His arms, thighs, and chest all twitched in perfect unison as his body surged with pleasure.

"I love your lips around my wanker, love. I want you to make me burst into massive love puddles," he whispered. I couldn't help but break into a smile. "I want you to take this all the way down your gullet, love. I know you don't like to, but try."

I giggled, and he looked over as he had both his hands pumping hard on his straining purplish pud, and he winked his beautiful blues at me.

Luckily, I was on my stomach, so my own hard-on wasn't obvious. He continued his phone sex a few more minutes until he was ready to spout off.

"Oh, yeah, love, that's the way, do it to yourself. Yeah, I'll wait for you, aaaah!"

He shot clear over his head and a plop landed in the middle of the room. I felt like cheering. He hung up the phone and heaved.

"Hey, Mick, pass me the towel, would ya?"

The towel was closer to him than me, it was near his bed where he dropped it, but I complied, and my stiff rod made my shorts pop out like a pistol was in my pocket. I acted nonchalant.

"Thanks, mate," he said, wiping up. "Looks like it's your turn."

He jumped up and headed back to the showers. After he left, I stuck my fingers in the goo on the floor between our beds and sniffed it. I came within seconds.

"How straight can he be if he's jacking off in front of you?" Marlon whispered later that night in the club.

"He's just being nice, that's all. He made it very clear that's all it would be," I said.

"Shh, he's coming back," said Kam.

Shane brought us all another round of Fallos Ale (brewed at the campus pub) as we celebrated my moment of legitimacy.

"So what do you want for your birthday, Mick? What's your dream?" Shane asked, looking at me-straight on as if he knew.

"It's the impossible dream. I just want someone to love me. As much as you love your Angie," I said.

"Let's drink to that!" Shane held his mug up, his muscle

poking out from his tank top. The guys all clanged their mugs.

We had round after round after round of beer, and all of us were a bit shitfaced as we stumbled back to the Naked Dorm.

"Time for a birthday circle jerk," screamed Marlon. "Come on, Shane. It's tradition."

He looked a bit shocked as the guys stood out in front of the dorm and started unzipping their flies. He staggered a bit as if he was actually considering unleashing his dick, then nodded to me and went upstairs.

"Go with him, he really loves you," Johnny said. "He's yours."

"Yes, he wants you," said Jason, Johnny's lover. "You haven't told Mickey our big secret yet?"

Johnny hit Jason, and I was too drunk to understand what was going on. Those two were always kidders anyway. Shane beckoned me to follow him upstairs. I staggered with him into our room.

"OK, get in bed and I'll give you a present," he said. "Hurry before I change my mind, because I'm a bit tipsy here."

I scrambled into bed as he shed every stitch of his clothes and turned out the lights so that only the outside street lamps bathed his naked body. He leaned against the white wall across the room from me.

"Are you naked, Mick?" he murmured. "I want you to follow me. It's time for a circle jerk, and I want you to match me stroke for stroke."

"Wow" was all I could muster as I saw his frame in the shadows. I followed, with my hands on my cock, just as I watched his own slide over his piece of meat. I matched him stroke for stroke.

We were beating ourselves into a frenzy when I got up and reached over to try to help him out. He turned his body away from me, stuck his face soberly into mine, and muttered, "No touching, Mick. You know the score."

He seemed to recognize the double entendre and said,

F.U.

"And a fine Score you have, but let's not start off on the wrong foot."

With that, we shot a load at the same time, wiped it up with his underwear, and went to sleep.

And so, here's how it went most of the semester. Shane Coley walked around the room naked most of the time, and about twice a week he called his girlfriend and jacked off in front of me. He seemed to disapprove whenever I walked around with a semistiffy, and we never jacked off together again after that night of my birthday, nor did we ever talk about it.

Finally, after hearing him talk again about his girlfriend sucking him off over the phone, I piped up as I pulled out my research for the Advanced Deep-Throating Techniques class that I was taking. "You know, I probably could help you teach her a few things. It's a skill," I tried coaxing him. He wouldn't hear of it. "It wouldn't be cheating on her, really, it would just be helping your relationship."

He said he'd never consider it, but when Angie next called he started describing her oral technique again in quite a bit of detail. He saw my ears perk up, and I watched his cock quiver to a massive near-10 inches. He nodded to my textbook and then with a turn of his neck beckoned me over between his legs as he spoke.

I pulled my pants down and landed between his legs, my eyes looking up at him for instructions. His cock waved in front of me and he lowered it down between my lips.

"I want you to start by sucking on my smooth balls," he murmured as he nodded to me while my tongue flicked his loose testicles. He groaned. "I want you to take each one in your mouth and roll it around on your tongue, gently, gently. Now take your tongue all the way up the underside of my wanker and chew on the tip. Gently, gently."

I followed every order as I could hear Angie on the other

end cooing as he spoke nasty to her. I became her cyber-tongue, her cyber-lips. His cyber-lover.

"Now can you get it all the way down your throat, love?" he asked. I cocked my jaw slightly back and allowed his veiny snake to slip down my throat, and I massaged the shaft with my slick lips on the way in and out, in and out. I took him down with ease and squished my nose into his golden pubes as he moaned with pleasure.

"Yes, you can do it, love, I know you can, I can feel you can," he muttered. She resisted doing what he asked, even over the phone. It didn't matter, he pulled out and shot all over my face. He smiled as he hung up.

"She says she wants to try something new with me next time," he said, smiling more wickedly than I ever remembered seeing. "I hope you'll be around."

That became our new routine. Whatever he described, or whatever she described, I acted out for him. Most of it was oral pleasure, and I was certainly willing to accommodate.

Then it was time for his birthday present. She called him and they talked a long time, and then it was her turn to do the stimulating. He repeated a lot of what she was saying, and he nodded for me to get undressed.

"Now what are you going to do with that thing?" he asked. "No, I don't want you to shove it up my butt. Well, start slow, just a little bit at first."

I was a bit astonished, but he distinctly pointed his finger at his butt as he rolled over and spread his cheeks for me. I slipped on a condom and he handed me some hand cream to put over it.

"Really, so you need to put something over the toys too, just to be clean and safe, eh, love? OK, be slow, just probe me a bit," he grunted. "Ease in it, love."

With that, he turned his beautiful butt to me and I rubbed my cock between the cheeks as if I couldn't believe it was truly there for me. I slowly slipped inside him. He was tight, but he wriggled a bit to welcome me inside of him.

I heard her tinny phone-voice say to him that she was amazed he was so open to this experience, even though it was over the phone. He merely grunted in agreement as she continued to explain how her dildo would be probing his butthole.

"This is amazing, fantastic," he swooned. He writhed and humped and lunged as I slipped deeper and deeper into his butt cheeks and pressed inside him. I gripped his chest as I wrapped my arms around him and I bit his shoulder lightly. He loved every minute of it, but not as much as I did.

We rode on. He dropped the phone. I could hear Angie shrieking on the other end as she heard our humping and the bed squeaking. Then I heard a click and dial tone, but Shane Coley didn't seem to notice. All he noticed was me inside of him. He wanted to face me.

I dismounted his big frame for a moment and once we were face-to-face my cock dove back into his willing bottom. His blue eyes pierced mine and his blond hair fell back out of his face and then he lunged his red lips over mine and his tongue invaded my throat so I could barely breathe. It was pure heaven. I felt a wash of warmth over my whole body as we both shook with powerful orgasms.

He quivered a few times, and I did too.

Then with our tongues still intertwined and our bodies still connected, his eyes opened and he stared at me in sheer and utter horror. It was as if he suddenly woke from a dream and found himself kissing a cocker spaniel.

He got up, pulled the spent condom from his butt, and rushed to the shower.

The next morning I got back from class and the dorm room was half-empty. All of Shane Coley's stuff, his posters, his books, and his clothes, were gone. I couldn't believe he moved out so soon!

I dove into my own bed, sad, and underneath my pillow found this handwritten note:

Dear Mick:

I knew you were the guy watching me in the stacks for the past few years. I put on that show just for you a few times. In fact, I did some research on you and followed you around campus for a while, I felt like a stalker. I still have the notebook you spewed off in and I take a whiff of it and think about you every day. I had to get to know you.

Then when I knew your roommate was graduating, I pulled a few strings so I could be in the same dorm room as you. I liked the way you sniffed my sweats when I left the room. I liked the way you admired me.

I was the one who planted Angie's idea for dildo play for my birthday, because I knew it would be the only way I could get you to fuck me. It was every bit as wonderful as I expected it would be.

What you don't know is that we had secret sex through a glory hole many years ago, and I saved this blue condom filled with your juices hoping that someday we could relive that experience. Jason and Johnny knew it, they saw me on the other end of the stall, but I asked them not to tell you.

What I wasn't ready for is that I would fall for you as hard as I have. I know that if I stayed, it would be impossible for me to marry my lifelong sweetheart, the only person I've ever known besides you.

I have to go back to her—now. I can't even say goodbye to your face. I'm afraid of my feelings. I'm going to finish my schooling back in Australia.

Forgive me for my obsession, but for the rest of my life, you will be my secret love....
—Shane

I looked down at the sticky, shriveled blue condom he left

under my pillow next to the note. I vaguely remembered the bathroom scene, when I watched Jason and Johnny fuck each other in the library bathroom while I had my first glory hole experience. I remember the blue condom disappearing, as well as the guy in the next stall.

I bunched up the letter into a tiny ball and cried—until I laughed.

ANOTHER PARTING SHOT

It's another New Year's Eve, and I'm itching for 2002. I've been asked to continue teaching. I'm not sure how long I will continue to do it, but as long as I can teach the students something of value, well, I'll be around.

It was nice flipping through the diaries I wrote as a young buck going to school in these hallowed halls. And I'm glad I could add to the stories as I returned.

I'm feeling older, but just as sexual, being a teacher among these young bucks. I'm still sporting my long blond hair, and I walk across campus with my two mini-sausage dogs Pepe and Rudi. Could any two dogs be more phallic?

They keep me company when my sweetheart, John Rex, is out of town. And whenever he's back, I'm always willing to share any of the "treats" I may have come across on campus.

Speaking of treats, threatening retirement after 10 years of jacking off together since we graduated, the O Boys said they would have a grand final orgy on campus for New Year's Eve.

It was an event I knew I had to join in....

He was licking my toes, making me squirm. I kicked him in the face.

"Oh, I'm sorry, Pepe." My mini red dachshund poked his head over the covers and blew his cheeks out angrily at me.

Rudi, the other mini dachshund, licked me in the face, as if to tell me to go ahead and go to the O Boys' New Year's

Reunion. I didn't really want to. John was out of town again, and I just wanted to sulk and ring in 2002 alone.

"But don't you see, Mickey, that 2002 is a very sexual year?" Allan had said, trying to coax me out earlier that night.

"A lot of your students will be there, and a lot of old friends," said Marshall, who was throwing the party not far from where I was staying on campus, in the Union room of Naked Dorm.

I heard that Kam, Sandy, Johnny, Marlon, and Jason from my old Naked Dorm crowd were going to be there, and also some of my favorite students.

My doorbell rang and I went over to answer it. The dogs barked as I was tackled off my feet, and I felt hands go for the zipper of my jeans. A familiar mouth tasted my limp dick.

"Joey Dillus! What the fuck are you doing here?" I said, not even needing to look down at the mouth on my now-erect cock.

"Came back to school for this reunion," he said between sucks. "Have you been shooting off three times a day, dude?"

I squirted in his face, then wiped my pants off. I made some coffee for us, since I knew it would be a long night, and told him that in fact I have tried to keep up with his three-times-a-day masturbation ritual, and it has seemed to do wonders for my health.

"You know who's coming back for this big O Boy Reunion, don't you? The world record–winners Spike, Paul, Charlie, all of them. And I want to get some of that action. I'm also excited about seeing Jason, Johnny, and Scott since they've become famous porn stars."

"Scotty is coming back?" I smiled. "I can't wait to see that great little body again, but isn't he married now?"

"Oh, sure he is, but he won't miss this," Joey teased. "And of course, there's my roommate replacement, Shane Coley, who's coming back from the outback."

"Shane's going to be here?" I gulped. "OK, I'll go."

Joey slapped me on the back and then went down on me

again as Pepe and Rudi growled at him.

Joey and I left for the orgy at about 11 P.M. and soon saw Jason and Johnny fucking in the bushes off the edge of our old quad. Right next to them was a younger version of that same "studly couple" prototype: Connor and Lance.

"Hey, Professor, we had a commitment ceremony last week on Maui," Connor said, getting fucked by Lance in the bushes. "My dad gave me away, thanks to you for getting him to accept us."

Lance waved, and I laughed because Joey and I had just a few years ago been to the commitment ceremony of Jason and Johnny, the astronaut cadets–turned–porn stars who were in the throes of passion just nearby.

As Joey and I passed the familiar 20-foot naked statue of one of the first university presidents, outside the main admin- istration BOTTOMs building, we saw a crowd of familiar faces. Nikko Nadooley greeted Joey and I with his familiar cockshake, and Marlon and Sandy were there too, watching Stroker Palmer up on the statue humping its huge hard-on.

"I always wanted to do this," Stroker said, splaying him- self on the statue, his butt pummeling the cast-iron cock.

"Get down from there, and you can have mine," said a familiar voice wandering up to the crowd. It was Big Red, naked as a jaybird, with his long cock and its two familiar red marks. "Stroker, you're such a nerd."

The group of us wandered into the building, where we had to check our clothes. Marshall handed me a baggie to stuff mine into and said, "You'll notice a lot of new couples around this joint tonight. We'll miss John, though."

Yeah, I would too. But I looked around the dark maze-like sex club and saw some familiar faces. There were the Science Boys, going at it in a hot 69 without even noticing me. Off in another corner, the now-out actor Mitch Kelles was coring his equally out actor boyfriend Jay Churchly in a corner while some of the young new students and wanna-be actors watched intently. Victor Nichols had located his dream lover, the Snake Man from the Freak Show, and was off introducing his serpentine cock to the crowd. Kam Likikime brought his young lover, my former student Aaron Rymer, to the orgy, and my old pal Larry teamed up with Dirk Bartley (they were making more than just meat sandwiches these days).

I saw Dean Richie with his boyhood lover Fratzi, the slick motorcycle stud. Their boyhood sex-partner, Putzi, was off in the corner with Shaw the talent scout.

"Hey, Professor, I heard you knew this guy I met on a porn shoot. He said he knew you," said Scotty, my sweet bird of youth. I turned to see the doe-eyed hunk arm and arm with the other fantasy man from my college days, Vincent. The two buff men looked postcard-perfect together, especially naked.

"I can't believe you two teamed up—it's a perfect match," I said, giving them both a hug and a tug.

Interestingly enough, my director pal Sam connected with my student Don, and the very hetero student Zeke went after the older transsexual Sammy, whom he met at the Collection of Ultimate Male Memorabilia, or CUMM Museum.

Just as I was going to drop to my knees and reacquaint myself with the familiar cock of my surfer friend Sandy, I saw my dream man enter from across the room. There was Shane Coley.

He looked older, as expected, and more haggard. But his blond hair and god-like body was still there and intact. When he saw me, his cock stiffened and he headed straight for me.

"Easy, Mickey, easy," said Sandy as he pulled his cock from my lips. "Don't go too crazy over him."

Shane gave me a big groping hug and then kissed me on the lips. I pulled away, not angrily but a bit unimpressed.

"I left Angie. I realized that I truly love you, that I'm gay, and that I've always hidden from the thought of it, mate," Shane said. "I'm yours if you want me."

I shook myself as if I was in a dream. This was a moment I had always thought I wanted, but for some reason I was totally repulsed by this god-of-a-hunk throwing himself at me.

Then I knew why.

Across the room, a tall, thin, blond-haired guy with cute blue eyes smiled at me. His naked frame came toward me and I smiled widely back. It was John Rex!

"I got back early. How could I miss a New Year's Eve orgy with you?" He gave me a big kiss.

I turned to Shane, whose cock was drooping sadly, and I introduced the two of them. Shane seemed a bit out of place.

I pointed across the room to where a hungry-mouthed Joey Dillus stood looking for a cock to service as Marshall and Allan were counting down the new year.

"Hey, Shane, see that guy Joey? He was my roommate just before you, and I know you two will hit it off well," I gave Shane a little push over in Joey's direction as I dove onto John's cock.

Sure enough, before anyone could shout "Happy Nude Year," Joey Dillus's talented mouth got Shane Coley off.